THE SURVIVORS

THE SURVIVORS

ANNE EDWARDS

*

HOLT, RINEHART AND WINSTON

NEW YORK   CHICAGO
SAN FRANCISCO

Published simultaneously in Canada by Holt, Rinehart and Winston of
Canada, Ltd.
Library of Congress Catalog Card Number: 68-11825

FIRST EDITION

8673303
Printed in the United States of America

For My Mother

THE SURVIVORS

LUANNE...

My reflection rode beside me in the train window. Ghostly. The thick black hair that is my one vanity, plasticized into a flat gray. There was only that guillotined head, severed from my breast, my hand, the foot that shifted restlessly. The eyes looked back at me expressionlessly. Irish had called them the eyes of a Tchaikovsky overture. It had upset me at the time. I did not want to think of myself as melancholy nor did I care for others to glimpse my inner sadness. They were small, narrow eyes as black as my hair, so black you could not see the pupils, heavy with lashes and brows, always in mourning. This one moment they were insensate in that guillotined head, holding no sadness.

"Good!" I thought, "No one wants a part of anyone else's sadness!" and I did not want to be faced with my own.

I passed my hand over the cold pane thinking I could wipe my ghost from its surface, but it remained. I turned to look across the aisle, but I was aware that it was there behind me— a face covered in black hair, waiting, the train window an open grave—and the trees beyond . . . the tall firs with outstretched arms . . . the mourners.

I took a cigarette from my purse and lighted it and smiled at the old lady and the little girl across from me. It was one of my best smiles. The kind I always managed for old ladies because I knew they needed such smiles. The little girl was round and red and sitting on the edge of the hard wood seat like a ball that would roll off at a touch. She looked at me with curiosity. I spoke English, though perhaps she did not know what language it was, just that it was not the Swiss-German she understood. The old lady leaned close to her and said something in a whisper and the little girl squirmed back on the seat and rested her head against her companion's great sagging breast, but the child's blue saucer eyes never left my face.

I took a chocolate bar from my pocket and offered it to her, holding my hand out very straight as I had done when I once had fed the deer in Richmond Park. The old lady cast a suspicious look, and stroked back the stray wisps of golden hair from the child's forehead. The child burrowed deeper into the warm lump of the old lady's breast and I sat back defeated. We would ride the rest of our journey in other worlds.

Why was I here? Why had I come so far? Soon, how long? Another week. It would be Christmas and wherever I would go houses would be warm with family. It had been ten years since we had all been together. I closed my eyes and I could feel the winter sun upon my eyelids.

Irish refused to sit at the head of the table even on Christmas Day. He was the eldest son and our father had been dead for nine years and rightfully the place was his. There was an unpleasant discussion about it every Sunday and holiday which grew more intense each year. Althea was next to Irish in age. There had always been war between the two, but to Althea's fury his offense was a smiling detached apathy for which she had yet to discover a counter-offense. We had all been seated when Althea entered. Irish had left the seat at the head of the table as usual to her.

"Anarchist!" she said with a slight sneer and a supercilious toss of her auburn hair. "And you needn't give me that underhanded smile—older brother! Rebel against authority but not against responsibility!" and with that Althea sat her narrow patrician self into the chair Irish would not occupy.

It would always end in our sitting in the same places as we always sat. Althea would be at the head flanked by our two younger brothers, Liam and Eugene. I would sit between Liam and Irish (whom Althea called by his Christian names, Ira Sean). Cousin Mary Agatha faced me and Uncle Stanley sat in his wheel chair at the foot of the table.

Uncle Stanley had been our mother's only brother and had come to live with us after Father died, bringing his daughter Mary Agatha (whom Liam immediately renamed Mary Agate). We knew nothing about Uncle Stanley's wife. It was a subject that was never mentioned. Our own mother had died when Eugene was born and Father never again spoke of any of her family. Liam was too young and Eugene just a baby so they could not have felt the change our mother's death brought to all our lives. There were no more summer holidays to Cornwall or excursions to Richmond Park. Except for outings in the Heath (which bordered our property) we remained in the great stone house that had belonged to our father's family, schooled by a succession of stiff-collared tutors, nursed by a maidenly Miss Pansy, and bullied by Althea (who at age eleven gave Miss Pansy the menu for each day). Father seldom spoke to us except at dinnertime and then we were not allowed to speak to him unless addressed first. Miss Pansy would often comment on how much he must have loved our mother to become such a solemn man, but I could not recall him otherwise even while our mother was alive.

It was I who discovered him the morning he died. He was sitting in his favorite chair, his newspaper (he always read the *Manchester Guardian*) still in his hand. I had been sent by Althea to ask for money to pay the milkman, but I knew he would not like to be interrupted while reading the *Guardian*. I turned to tiptoe out of the room but could not. There was an unnatural quiet where even my own breathing seemed an intrusion. I walked around to the front of the

3

great brown leather chair and touched his hand. It was the first and last time I thought to make him conscious of my presence. My touch caused his arm to fall loosely over the side of the chair and the *Manchester Guardian* slid from his lap to the floor.

We had never seen Uncle Stanley before our father's death. It had to do with money. Uncle Stanley had borrowed money and never returned it. That had not been our father's way. The next three years after Father's death were a happy time and I remembered it that way even when I looked down at the foot of the table where Uncle Stanley now sat silenced forever in his wheel chair, his speech gone, his left arm frozen to his side. If Mary Agate cut his food into small pieces he was able to eat by himself but Althea insisted he eat in his room except on holidays.

Uncle Stanley had been an artist and in those years before his stroke and after Father's death he had taught me about colors and paints and taken me on excursions to all the museums in London and once had given me paints and canvas for a birthday present. He looked much like our mother and spoke often about their early years in Ireland. I had not known that before we were born she had been an artist in her own right. None of her drawings remained in the great house though Uncle Stanley and I searched carefully for them.

Uncle Stanley's stroke returned Althea to authority. It also brought the war between Althea and Irish into the open. Irish began to stay away from the great house for days at a time. I was always frightened he might not come back, but then, there he would be, smelling of the outside, hair rumpled, clothes untidy. He would bury his head in my hair as he held me and then gently push me away and smile that beautifully crooked smile of his and kiss me on the forehead. "That was especially for you," he would say.

Irish was home even less after he began to write and had had a book published. The book had infuriated Althea so

4

that she had forbidden any copy of it to be brought into the house. Then she discovered that he was having an affair with Claudia Mitchell who was much older than Irish, and forbade her books brought into the house as well. I read them at the public library. I could not visualize the woman who wrote those books with my Irish. Her words were brilliant and sharp and cold like a large, polished, perfect diamond.

When he did come home, it was always late at night, and as Althea had taken his front door key from him, he would rap upon my window, because I was on the lower floor. He would step over the sill and into my room, kissing me on the forehead before even saying, "Hello." Then he would place his long bony fingers over his gentle mouth and we would both go quietly into the kitchen. He would eat standing up telling me stories in a hushed kiss of a voice. He never said where he had been or why he had come home. He never brought a suitcase with him and he never left our house with a suitcase. Somehow he had managed to create two lives for himself, one never touching the other.

I glanced around the Christmas table and with a small chill thought, "We shan't always be together like this." I must have murmured it without realizing it and Irish heard me.

"Life is only an illusion, Lululu. Even our being here now isn't real, so take that great throb out of your sad eyes," he whispered.

Mary Agate leaned across the table to us, "It's not an illusion when you're home, Irish," she said, having overheard the two of us. Then her ruddy face turned purple with splotches of embarrassment. Mary Agate smelled of mildew and sweat and boiled cabbage and I drew back instinctively whenever she came close to us. She returned nervously to her former stiff position in the dining room chair. Uncle Stanley had taken a piece of bread that was too large for him to chew and he spit it out.

"Do pay attention to your father, Mary Agate!" Althea called out hoarsely from the head of the table.

"Pay attention to your own duties, Althea," Irish said as he motioned to the roast goose Miss Pansy had just brought into the room and placed upon the sideboard.

Althea sucked in her breath and all of it seemed to go down to her small, beautifully firm breasts, both of which defied Irish silently as she remained seated.

"Are you going to carve the goose or not?" Eugene prodded, his sullen brown eyes hungry but not angry.

Althea considered it for a moment before rising ceremoniously and taking the few steps away from us to the sideboard.

Mary Agate did most of the cooking and Althea did the serving. Mary Agate loved to be in the kitchen rattling the pots and pans, slamming the oven and cupboard doors. She always made a terrible clatter. Doors invariably shrieked open and screamed shut, furniture shuddered whenever she passed and windows chattered. I could still remember our mother in the kitchen. There was the smell of nutmeg and spices then, and I used to sit on the kitchen counter where I could look into the bowls filled with ingredients that made our kitchen sage and thyme and rosemary and sweet basil and nutmeg and cinnamon and cloves. Now it was onions and cabbage and vinegar and wine.

There had been grapefruit first that day, warm and broiled and coated with sugar but tasting of too much wine. The sideboard held red cabbage and stuffed onions and roast goose with wild rice and currants. There was the traditional Christmas pudding that Miss Pansy brought us each year and endive salad and mince pie which Mary Agate always made a shade too tart. Liam had started a fire in the fireplace. The room smelled of burning logs and fresh pine. The silver tea service on the serving cart glistened from my polishing and the light of the fire. On the mantle our mother's portrait smiled down at us.

Irish kept a running commentary, smiling, amused at himself, from time to time his knee brushing mine under the table, letting a smile escape the side of his mouth so that he

6

could let me know we were confederates. His nearness brought me the same frightening pleasure it always had.

I looked down at the end of the table where Althea and Eugene sat next to one another. They looked the most alike and were incredibly like the portrait of our mother. Both had auburn hair and large brown eyes and were very beautiful. I was fond of beautiful things which was perhaps the reason I admired Althea more than I feared her. It was I who kept Mother's best china and silver shining and Father's leather-bound books dusted. I decorated the Christmas tree and arranged the flowers and took care of the garden. Of course, Miss Pansy came to us every day, just as she had done since Irish was born, but her eyes were not what they once were. She could never remember where things went, which figure on which shelf and at which angle. There were positions in which teapots and figurines and potted plants looked more graceful. Those were their rightful places and I tried to keep them that way. I would wait until Miss Pansy left each day and then go through the house and rearrange everything, removing specks of dust she invariably left behind.

Liam inherited our father's austerity and though he and Eugene were closer in age than the rest of us were, he seldom even spoke to Eugene. They shared a room, an arrangement made by Althea, and so never questioned by Eugene, but Irish felt the arrangement was not good for either of them and tried to get them to do something about it themselves. However, Liam didn't seem to care as he was perfectly capable of living in that room as though only he inhabited it and Eugene never was much of a fighter. He had been a laughing, beautiful child, but now he was a brooding (though still beautiful) young man inclined to great silences.

Althea played the piano after Christmas dinner and we all sang carols. Uncle Stanley fell asleep in his chair and Mary Agate wheeled him into his room. Althea continued at the piano for a time and then she insisted the boys go to their room and she went to hers, but Irish and I sat up by the

7

dying fire under our mother's portrait while Irish read aloud to me from my book of Keats.

They were only to be alive, all of them, Uncle Stanley and Mary Agate, and Eugene and Liam and beautiful Althea and my own most beloved Irish for two more days. Even Miss Pansy was to pass with them.

When I opened my eyes, the old lady and the little girl were gone. I thought I had imagined them but as I turned to look out the train window they were passing just below it. We had stopped at a place called Kublis. There were yellow and red potted geraniums in the window of the station house and the snow had been shoveled neatly away from the platform. The little girl and the old lady were met by a younger woman and the three of them made their way across the platform and around the station house. In a moment they were gone.

I leaned in close to the window and breathed tiny hot breaths of air on the pane. It clouded the glass. I could no longer see Kublis or the mountains beyond. Even my reflection was veiled from my eyes.

LUANNE...

I had chosen Klosters from the Swiss travel brochures the young chap at Cook's had sent to Laurel Groves. Mrs. Pritchett and I went over them together. The trip had not been my idea but, when Mrs. Pritchett suggested it, I rather liked the thought of going away. Laurel Groves was the nursing home where I had gone to stay shortly after the trial. I had remained there by my own choice for ten years, content to be out of touch with the world. And, perhaps, I would not have left had not Klosters looked so safe in the brochure photographs—the town covered in a soft downy blanket of snow, the mountains surrounding the village like a pair of comforting arms. There are times when a place is just right for what you are feeling. Klosters appeared to suit my mood. Cook's had sent along a brochure of the Weisshaus, too, and it had a warmth I knew I would like. Now that I was here doubt—no, fear—welled up inside me. The brochure had not deceived me. My courage had.

The platform was bustling with arrivals and departures but the porter from the Weisshaus found me straightaway. Perhaps Cook's sends out personal descriptions of all unaccompanied English ladies. It would have read, "Tall, slender, dark-haired—skittish with strange people."

Irish had called me a roan pony. He believed everyone looked like a member of the animal kingdom. Poor Mary Agate was a mole, Eugene a spaniel puppy, Liam a slick-coated beaver, Althea an apricot poodle and Uncle Stanley a kangaroo. In the days before Uncle Stanley was confined to his chair, he did rather walk in the manner of a kangaroo with great, loping steps, his short legs seeming to buckle beneath his long torso. And Irish—well, I told *him* he was rather like a cinnamon bear!

The porter took off his stiff cap with the "WEISSHAUS" printed across its band and smiled at me. He took my bags in his wide, well-used hands, their tanned skin lashed with straps of mountain sun, and as I saw him walk before me, leading the way, weighted down with my new cases, I was sorry that I had not remembered to give him one of my "thank-you-kindly" smiles.

9

It is difficult for me to forget the moment I entered the Weisshaus for it was then that I saw Hans for the first time. He stood in the high carved entrance, a tall oak of a man, his skis held against his shoulder as if they were his woman. He was surrounded with the wood-like scent of his burning pipe tobacco. He studied me with clear blue eyes as I made my way to the front desk. I felt awkward under his scrutiny and heard nothing the desk clerk was saying. I was presented with a key and the porter bowed to me and then, with my bags still under his arms, led the way up the narrow front staircase to a landing.

Hans was right behind me but I dared not turn for he was so close that had I paused we would have collided. But, in the moment when I opened the door to my room and waited for the porter to place my bags inside the doorway, I managed to glance toward him. He was going into the room directly opposite. The door closed behind him but the circles of smoke from his pipe lingered in the hallway and the traces of snow from his boots had not yet melted into the carpet.

My room was small and beamed and it smelled of aged wood and polishing wax, a sweet smell like dried flowers. It was to the rear of the hotel and its one slightly crooked window opened onto a small terrace that overlooked another terrace directly below. The bed was tucked into one side of the room, under an eave, and the bathroom ceiling was so low that I thought, "Cook's must have sent my dimensions as well!" One more inch and I could not have stood up before the washbowl.

Suddenly, I realized I was alone for the first time in many years. I sat down tentatively on the edge of the bed and looked around the room. Perhaps it was the sweet smell of the wood, or the room's size, the closeness of the walls or the white snow outside smoothed over the rooftops like clean laundered sheets, but I was once again in Hampstead, in the cedar wardrobe, with Miss Pansy's spotless linen stacked neatly on all the shelves that surrounded me.

The great house was silent now. Not a shutter banged, nor a floorboard creaked. No one had come upstairs. The floorboard at the top of the stairs, the one that Althea had been trying to get Liam to mend, had been silent all the time that I had been in the linen room, and there was only that one way upstairs. If anyone had come they would have had to step on that floorboard, unless they knew about it. Of course, only the family knew it was there and I was certain none of them would ever climb the staircase again. Althea had complained about there being only one way up or down from the upper floors. "In case of fire," she had warned, "we will all be trapped in our beds—except Luanne!"

I was wearing a winter silk in a lovely shade of orange. Irish said that orange suited me, that it set off the black of my hair and the pale of my skin. I pressed the skirt close to my sides holding it with one hand as I opened the door slowly, quietly, and stepped into the upper hallway on padded feet. Liam had always complained that you could never hear me coming, that I would simply pop up around a corner or into a room or by a chair when he least expected me to do so and that somehow it was an invasion of privacy.

I made my way on those same padded feet down the long, dark corridor past the room that Eugene and Liam shared and past Uncle Stanley's room. The doors were both open and the rooms were empty and as I turned and looked down the corridor I could see Mary Agate's and Althea's rooms at the far end; both stood with their doors closed. I held my breath a moment but could not hear any sound from behind those oak doors. Irish had a room adjoining the attic, really two rooms that he had converted himself. He had moved up there when Uncle Stanley came to live with us, so that Mary Agate could have his old room and therefore neither Althea or I would have to share one with her or each other. The door leading up to his quarters was latched.

I listened but there were no sounds overhead. I made my way cautiously down the corridor to the stairway. It was late afternoon but moonlight already shone through the overhead skylight. I stepped widely over the loose floorboard and took each succeeding step slowly, quietly, pausing and listening each time before continuing my descent. I stood in the downstairs reception hall for what must have been several minutes before I managed enough calm to walk past the dining room and to the great double doors of the front reception room. They were closed. The shiny brass door handles were cold to my touch as I turned them.

All I could see was the design of the white molding bordering the high ceiling. Then, as I gradually lowered my eyes, there on the manteltop, exactly where I had placed it, was our mother's Dresden Lady, still bowing down at all who entered, and turning her aristocratic back on the print of Gainsborough's "Blue Boy" which hung above her. I shifted my glance to the deep blue velvet of the winter drapes on the bay window and then to the slim stripes on the fresh wallpaper that had only been hung that spring. Finally, I lowered my eyes to the piano.

The crystal lamp that had stood on the polished mahogany piano top for all the years I could recall, had toppled and splintered into a thousand pieces. I had been very fond of that lamp. On sunny days, placed on top of the piano at a proper angle and rubbed shiny and free from dust, it had caught all the light from the bay window. I looked down to the floor beneath the piano. Althea was hunched over like yesterday's wash and slivers of crystal shone like fresh raindrops from her deep auburn hair. The tea cart was at her feet and Miss Pansy's arms hung loosely over its side. Miss Pansy was sprawled across the cart as if she were guarding our mother's silver tea service with her body. Uncle Stanley was slumped in his chair beside her with Mary Agate's head on his shoulder, the back of his wheel chair a prop for her limp figure. Eugene and Liam were burrowed into the corners of the settee, their overturned teacups on the rosewood table before them.

I took a step toward Althea so that I could remove the crystal from her hair and I stumbled.

Irish was face down on the floor, his arm extended as if he had been reaching out for something, his fingers grasping the fringe of the carpet. I stooped down and carefully loosened the carpet from his grasp and then held his beautifully bony hand in my own touching it to my cheek to wipe away a tear. Then I gently lowered it to the floor and rose and went back into the hallway, first closing the great doors after myself.

I made my way back upstairs as quietly as I had come down and sealed myself in the cedar wardrobe and remained there until I could stop sobbing. I never thought to ring the police. Finally, I decided to ring Miss Pansy's sister because she was the only other next of kin.

I was in the bathroom when the maid entered to turn down my bed. Had I realized anyone else had a key and could enter, I know I would have managed to fight back my nausea. I told her I often was train sick after a long journey and that it was nothing. She stood watching me as I washed and dressed and was hesitant about my leaving the room but I assured her I would feel greatly improved after a light supper.

I went downstairs to the hotel dining room. The captain led me to a small table near a rear window but even so, I kept my glance averted so that I did not have to look at anyone at the adjoining tables. I had not been in a restaurant since I was a young girl. I felt ridiculous and awkward and out of place. I was sure all eyes were studying me, calculating my age, my background. I ran my hand over the hard gold surface of my mother's gold wedding band. (I had worn it since the day they had died to remind me that once there had been a Woodrow family.) There was a fire going in a vast hearth. The woods of the room glowed. There was the sound of spirited conversation, of laughter. I slipped my hands into my lap and watched the candle flicker in the lamp on my table.

I was immediately conscious that Hans was standing by my side. I studied his hands for a moment and then breathed deeply to fill myself with the already familiar scent of his tobacco.

"Miss Woodrow," he began.

It startled me that he knew my name and though I raised my eyes to look at him I must have had a rather frightened rabbit expression—the kind of look a rabbit gets before you shoot it. (I had gone hunting with Liam once behind the Heath, though it is not permitted, and I remembered that look, though many other things about that day had long since faded from my memory.) His eyes softened and a reassuring smile flashed across his face.

"The hotel register," he explained gently. "I am an old bachelor who travels a lot. I am afraid studying hotel registers is a rather distasteful habit of mine." He was leaning toward me now. There was a trace of a foreign accent in his speech. He bowed slightly. "Hans Aldik. I assure you I am thoroughly reputable—and practical. Which is exactly why it seems like such a waste of time for each of us to occupy a separate table." His hands were resting on the rim of the table and he was so close I could feel his breath. "It would make the Weisshaus and myself quite happy if we sat together."

I mumbled something to the effect that he was welcome to join me. Then I did a most curious thing. I slipped the wedding ring from my finger into my open pocketbook on the seat beside me. I did not want him to think I was married and I did not want to explain why I wore a wedding band if I was not.

14

"You haven't ordered," he said as he sat down. "Let me." He called the waiter over and the two of them discussed the menu and the wine list very seriously in German. The waiter seemed pleased when he departed for the kitchen.

"What are we having?" I asked, forgetting my former indisposition.

"The specialty of the house. Each night it's the same with a slightly different sauce. The waiter knows it and I know it but I make his evening a little happier by pretending I don't. It is generally good, however. The Swiss are not terribly inventive but once they learn something their standard is high. Luckily, the wine is French, white, and quite exceptional."

He sat back and his face grew pensive. There was a silence between us and yet I felt we were saying more to each other at that moment than most people could say throughout an entire evening. If the silence had remained it would not have mattered. I was not afraid to answer his steady glance. I knew that unless I wanted it, he would not ask any questions which might be difficult for me to answer.

"I also saw in the register that your Christian name is Luanne. Would you mind if I called you that?"

"No, of course not."

"And you call me Hans." I nodded my head. He smiled again, this time softly. "Luanne. What a lovely name. I don't believe I've heard it before."

"I was named after both my grandmothers. One was Luisa and the other was Anne. I never knew either of them, but my mother's mother, Luisa, was Italian and she met my grandfather, who was Irish, when he was in Rome. He was studying to be an artist at the time." I stopped, surprised at myself for speaking so casually about family history that I had only heard about from Uncle Stanley and had never discussed with anyone before.

"And did you inherit your grandfather's artistic talent?" he asked.

15

"I used to paint. Well, of course, it was only a hobby."

"You should start again. This is spectacular country."

"There is no way really of duplicating the beauty of nature. The best one could do is imitate. That is why I painted imaginary things." Again I was telling him the small secrets I had kept since childhood. "Anyway, I haven't painted in ten years."

"I'm sorry," he said with true concern.

I thought back to the last time I had painted. I had always used the trunk room in the basement of the great house where I could be insured privacy. I would paint by candlelight, my canvas resting on an upright trunk propped against the basement wall. It gave me an unnatural light that helped me to retain a sense of illusion as I painted. This last canvas was little more than a fusion of colors. From an exploding mass of yellows and oranges, flesh-like extensions appeared. I had heard the door behind me swing open and knew it was Irish before I turned to face him. "You must not dream about a man and a woman," he had told me, sensing the meaning of the painting even when I had not been conscious of it myself. "I want you to experience it. I want you to live with life, Lululu, not dreams," he had continued quietly but with an intensity that had caught me unawares.

"Have you ever skied?" Hans was asking.

"No. Never. I suppose it seems stupid to come to a ski resort when you don't ski," I told him, "but you see, the photographs in the brochure that Cook's sent me—I don't know if you will understand this—but this village—the snow—the mountains—they suited my mood." I managed a smile. "But you came here to ski, of course?"

"I came here to write but I am weak and so I ski too much and I write too little," he said, with a touch of laughter in his voice.

"Oh! you are a writer. How wonderful!"

He pretended to scowl. "Why?"

"Well," I began clumsily, "it must be an exciting profession and my brother was a writer." Then the thought came to me that I should have known his name when he introduced himself. "I'm sorry. You are probably well known and I didn't recognize your name."

"I am just as likely to be unknown, unpublished and then there would be no reason for you to recognize my name." He grinned.

"I don't think so." I could never explain to him how he stood and sat and walked and smiled with the assurance that only a successful man, a man who was accustomed to acceptance, could have. Then there was his face. It was the face of a man who had fought a brave battle and had won. "Do you write books?" I asked eagerly, wanting to know as much about this man as I could. He smiled and nodded his head. "How terrible! I should have read them!"

He pretended to scowl again. "Everyone should have read them so that I would have received big, fat royalty checks." I laughed at him and that seemed to please him. "I hoped before the evening was over I would see you laugh," he said gently.

I told him things I was surprised I had remembered, books I had read, pictures that had stirred me in galleries I had been to with Uncle Stanley, the games I had played as a child on the Heath. It all spilled out, all the happy memories, all the funny anecdotes. Yet, I was conscious of all I had not said, knowing it is the unsaid things which constitute the truth.

Two hours later we were still sitting there. "We'll take a walk," he said, as he helped me up. "I'll send to your room for a wrap."

I walked past the crowded tables still timid of the open glances from their occupants. People called out to greet Hans and he smiled, waved, and holding my hand tightly in his, never paused until we were out of the room.

We walked in silence until we had turned away from the village. We made our way up an incline, past wide-balconied houses and thick clusters of snow-laden trees. A large dog

17

appeared in the center of the road and barked at us. Hans held my hand tighter.

"Don't be frightened," he said in an even voice. "Keep up the same gait." As we passed the dog he came up to us and walked uncertainly beside Hans for a few steps. Hans paused then and spoke in that same even tone to him. "Good boy." He leaned down and stroked the dog's head. The dog sat down in the road and we continued on our way, but the animal just sat there watching us move farther out of sight.

"You're out of breath," Hans commented.

We stood on a high rise looking down at the village. It was set in the mountains like a spray of jewels. There was a deep cleft between the two nearest mountains which extended all the way to the next village. We could see their night lights shining as well. The sky was a dark blue but there was a bright moon and more stars than I had ever seen at one time before. A soft wind touched my face. "It's the beauty of it all," I finally said. "I believe it is making me a bit dizzy."

A bench rested between sheltering trees. I had noticed several of them tucked into side paths along the way. "We'll rest here before going back," he said.

We sat down, silent now, both of us in our secret worlds. I was thinking about the nights I had dared to go to the Heath alone trying to capture the very feeling I was now experiencing. Irish had often joined me and we would run breathlessly up and down the small rises of the Heath, weaving between the trees, catching glimpses of each other lighted by the moon, shadowed by the night.

"Even in war," Hans said at last, his eyes tearing from the soft wind, "there are nights like this when a great stillness will surround you and the universe seems more commanding than the enemy's nearness. Then it begins again. Guns. Answering shots. The shouts, the cries blocking out the sound of the wind. "I began as a war correspondent," he explained seriously. "I wrote to keep the rest of the world informed. But they could never know what it was really like. How could you expect them to? They had never known that great stillness which makes a man aware of his lowly rank—heard that stillness broken by the pitiful exchange of man's stupidity and frustration. That same stillness returning long after the guns had stopped. If they had, they would know how futile war—mass murder—is. No one shall ever be able to conquer that great stillness."

A car was coming up the road. We sat there until it had passed. I studied his face in the glare of the headlights. He was staring out at the near mountains, the far village, but I was sure he was seeing something quite different. "I could have been done with it. Written of other things. But I keep returning. Wherever there is a war, I return. I keep saying I am first a reporter, second a novelist. But I don't return to courier the news. I return to remind myself of the great silence that the guns can only interrupt but not destroy."

I knew in that moment that he was the one human being I had ever known who would understand. We had shared man's greatest evil—the facility to kill. And we had shared the omnipotence of the great silence. I waited for him to rise. He took my hand again. It was growing colder and he wore no gloves but his hand was as warm as if he had just risen from a well-blanketed sleep. We walked without speaking for a time. Then, as we turned with the road, we saw the dog still sitting in the middle of it as if he had been sure we would return to him. Hans let go of my hand and the shaggy animal came up to him and stood on his hind legs so that his front paws rested against Hans's chest.

"Good boy," Hans said as he stroked him.

The dog followed us down the hill but when we reached the edge of the village, he turned and walked back up again.

The hotel was gay. There was music and dancing. Hans sensed my inability to share the evening with any outsiders. He saw me to the door of my room and leaned down from

19

his great height and kissed me on the forehead, a light sunspot kiss. Then he crossed to his room and opened his door, never looking back at me as he closed it after himself.

I always rose earlier than the others so that I could have the downstairs to myself for nearly an hour each day. It was Boxing Day and Irish was still with us. I had not been in his room, when he was in it, since I was twelve and he was eighteen and had just moved there. However, I would often go there when he was not home to put his clean clothes away after Miss Pansy was done with the ironing.

I was careful not to awaken the others as I went upstairs to the linen room to fetch fresh sheets for my bed. The door leading to his quarters was open and I could hear Irish turn over in the old iron bed that Althea had insisted he get rid of but which he refused to relinquish.

"Lululu?" came the familiar voice. "That you, Lululu?"

I climbed the narrow staircase to the very top. I was standing right outside his open bedroom door. "It's me," I said in a whisper.

His tousled head appeared in the doorway. "Come in then," he told me.

I had to bow my head to enter because the doorway was set in the side of the room that was under an eave. There was the comforting smell of tobacco and spiced after-shave and the pungent remains of the oranges and cloves which I had made for him myself and hung in his wardrobe. The room was furnished sparsely, one chair and the bed, with shelves crammed with books and papers. Very few of the books were leather bound like the ones Father had left in the library. Instead they wore bright paperback jackets, cracked and creased because they were more read than cared for. There

20

were books of the Russian Revolution and the Civil War in Spain and books by the Marquis de Sade and Oscar Wilde and Jean-Paul Sartre, all books our father would never have permitted in the house. Our father had, for that matter, burned all our mother's books on the Irish Rebellion after her death.

There was no desk, but Irish had taken a plank of wood and placed it across one entire side of the room and supported it with some bricks that had been left over when the garden-house had been repaired. The top of the wooden plank was cluttered with pipes and paperclips and rubber bands and pencils. Papers were strewn about as if left wherever they had fallen from his hand when he had done reading them. There were no conventional objects, just a cracked saucer that sat on the floor next to his bed filled with ashes and burnt out tobacco, and several rocks on the windowsill which we had collected together as children. There were only two pictures, unframed and thumb-tacked to the wall. One was a Picasso print, the other a calendar with a drawing of a blond girl with her hair blowing against the Irish coastline.

The small room which adjoined this one had no doors and contained his wardrobe, a chest with a mirror over it, an old chair that had been given a bright coat of orange paint, and a washstand. (Irish called this his "recovery room" since he went there, he said, after intellectually bleeding.) There was no rug on either floor. It was another point of great dispute between Irish and Althea (whose room was directly below), but the floor remained bare, the old mellow wood a warm golden honey color like the sloping walls and the slanting ceiling.

I sat on the undersheet of the bed because he had drawn all the other covers about himself and tucked them tightly around his body. The bed creaked loudly even though I had sat down very carefully.

"Everyone else still asleep?" he asked. I nodded. The bed was not far from the door and he reached out and eased it shut. "There, Lululu, we are now in our own little castle turret, eh?"

He eased himself up, leaned against the iron bedstead and looked seriously at me. "What is to become of you, Luanne? Will they ever let you leave this castle?" I stared at him with a lack of comprehension, tasting the bitterness behind his words in my own mouth. He leaned toward me, his wide, broad forehead now furrowed and gathered together like rain clouds before a storm.

"You can't really see it," he said. "You think this house truly holds life? It doesn't, you know. It is just preserving us all. But eventually preserves have to be taken down from the shelves like Mary Agate's spring fruits and be eaten. Otherwise they mold, they rot, they turn gray and green and return to the earth as surely as we do."

I must have looked frightened for he reached out and took my hand and held it tightly in his own.

"Lululu, you are the only one there is hope for. By some miracle there is still a real woman inside you, giving you a good fight for her own existence. Remember the game we used to play on those train rides to Cornwall when we were children? We would turn all the words on the posters backwards as we passed them. In this house, to LIVE reverses to— EVIL! Don't question me with those sad, disbelieving Tchaikovsky eyes of yours. It is true. Your Irish says it is true. Change only exists outside this house. We have petrified ourselves. Even I, who when I was younger, had the great courage to leave the castle and cross the moat. But it was too late for me. I still must come back whenever it becomes too real out there. The rest of us are lost, Lululu, but not you. Not yet."

The familiar hand was moist and the eyes were set and unrelenting. I could feel his breath on my cheek. "Have you never thought it odd that there are no newspapers delivered to our door? No television in our house? No radio? The voices, the only voices we hear, are our own." He released my hand and fell back against the hard steel of the bedstead but he seemed to feel no impact at all.

"The lot of us are like the teacups on the shelf that clatter in their saucers each time a footstep draws near," he continued. His eyes no longer looked at me but stared at the ceiling. "And Althea? Our most hideously enticing Althea is like the white stone lion that has stood guarding this great house coldly, implacably, cemented in the front gate since the house was built. At twenty-three she has never blushed at a man's glance, never exposed herself, for that matter, to such glances. Her beauty is frozen in her looking glass." He turned back to me. "But I have stood back and watched you—oh yes, at times I have followed you on your short excursions into the world outside this front door—and seen that you are not immune to such glances."

I looked away and he touched my shoulder. "I've frightened you. I'm sorry. But I think there is no other way." He waited a long while before speaking again. His hand rested on my shoulder and my back was to him. I knew he could hear my struggle for breath—the irregular beatings of my heart. "Get into bed with me," he said softly. "I will hold you." I shook my head. "There is nothing wrong and everything right in it if it takes the fear from your eyes and if it can keep that woman inside of you still fighting to exist."

"We are not children any more," I said, still away from him.

"All of us are children, Lululu, and all of life is really only a child's game."

He had moved to the far edge of the bed and thrown back the covers. He took my arm and turned me toward him and helped me into the bed. Then he drew the covers over us. We lay that way for a long time before either of us spoke.

"What is she like?" I finally asked. His arms were still around me. Our bodies were touching so that I could feel his warmth through the soft flannel of my robe.

"Who?"

"Claudia Mitchell," I managed to answer, though the name was barely audible.

"She is a woman," was all he said. He released me from his arms.

I sat up. "If I could cook I would make you the most glorious breakfast you have ever had!" I told him.

"What would we have?" He smiled.

"All things shiny and golden. Crystal sugar on golden grapefruit. Honey on crisp golden waffles. Golden toast and golden scones. Golden butter and golden preserves and tea as warm and as golden as the sun!"

His face clouded. "Go get dressed. You and I are going out where we can eat from everyone else's grease and share a morning paper stained with words of man's injustice and take a crowded tube to Earl's Court or Lambeth." He pushed me off the bed and swung his legs over the side. "You and I are going to walk the streets of the living," he announced.

But it was just then that we heard the stirrings below and I cautiously went downstairs to find Mary Agate in the kitchen preparing kippers and onions and steeping thick dark tea. I went to my room and dressed and waited, but Irish never came down to fetch me.

HANS...

Hans stood at the top of the Gotschna, the Swiss Alps in a breathtaking three hundred and sixty degree circle around him; and contemplated his descent down the long pass that was still light powder. He was above the clouds. Klosters, Kublis, Jeñez were all lost below. This was the incomparable moment before he started down. He held it as long as he

could, then his huge body leaned forward and he and his skis
were one as they cut fresh tracks in the early morning snow.
He skied well and hard, with a grace that only the best skiers
have.

Hans had been an athlete all his adult life. His shoulders
were so broad that he seemed oversized in doorways, but his
stomach was flat, his legs pliant. War had taken him many
places. He had caught the big fish off the alligator's back that
was Cuba, shot game in Africa, played football with the
American boys in Vietnam, rugby with the English in Cypress.
He had swum in Italian waters, sailed in Greek waters, learned
judo in Japan and spear fishing in the South Pacific. Skiing
was the only "luxury sport" that had reached him. He was
competent at tennis, surfing, skin diving—but the first day he
strapped a pair of skis to his body, he knew he had found the
merciful escape for which he had been searching.

Yet his athletic prowess had come late in life. As a child
Hans had not even known how to throw a ball. He had been
born into poverty in the Hague and spent his boyhood in
orphanages and hospital clinics, a survivor of at least two
childhood diseases that should have killed him. Minus one
lung by the time Hitler was on the march, he was physically
unfit to fight. He went to work for the Red Cross. He placed
the displaced, tended the injured, brought small hope to the
captured, and buried the dead. He began to write, and submitted what he wrote to the wire services. He was hired.

It was one thing to write about war behind the lines, another to be sent to the front. He was obsessed by the horror,
haunted by the waste, and driven by the need to use the one
shake-up pill he possessed—words—to bring home the truth
that no one ever won a war.

When the war ended Hans had been sent to Dachau to
cover the liberation of the Jews. There they were—survivors—
free. They were clothed. They were fed. They were given new
numbers. He had interviewed a man named Scheiner who
had lost his wife, his mother, and his four children. His only

son had died two days before the liberation. He spoke to Hans in a voice that was no longer human. "In the Book," he said, "it says that only understanding divides love and hate. That would keep a man alive. He could be dignified in a fight for understanding. But to live just for survival . . ." He had thrown up skeletal hands in hopelessness. He was discovered dead—two hours later—his head in an oven in the Red Cross kitchens.

Two weeks after "the end of the war," Hans was sent to another front. For over twenty years he had not known more than a few weeks of each year when he was not at one war or another. Even after his novels were successful, bringing him fame and money in quick succession, he had returned. The last time it had been Vietnam. It could have been Korea, the Congo—no difference.

One day he had ridden in an allied reconnaissance plane over the rice fields rimming Sweet Water Bay north of Qui Nhon. Below him, in swamp water that had to be chest deep, were hundreds of dead Viet Cong and North Vietnamese, one body leaning against the other, their heads grotesquely still above water. In a war where finding the enemy was not an easy task, those dead were like trophies from a deserted shooting gallery. They had been flushed out of hiding when they took potshots at a helicopter of the United States First Cavalry. Behind them was the sea, and the guns and rockets of the United States Navy. Across their watered grave had been an open rice field.

The reconnaissance plane had swooped in low stirring up the dark, red stagnant waters. The flies and maggots were wrapped around the dead like thick beards, their movement shifting the current so that heads were disappearing beneath the thick, debris-filled water. In the distance there was the stutter of machine guns. Two helicopters had risen from the tops of trees on the nearby shores. They buzzed the reconnaissance plane: a signal which meant—"All's well! The survivors have been located and eliminated." That had been over a year ago and he had not gone back. Somehow he knew he would never go back again.

This was a warmly familiar pass to him, one he had taken so many times that he knew each turn, each clump of trees as you know the bones and flesh of a woman who has shared your bed for a long time. He had skied this pass in early snow and late snow, in light powder and heavy powder, yet it had never lost its power to excite him.

There had been a great many women in his life but he had trouble remembering their names. They had been The Photographer, The Editor, The Actress. There had been Marlane, of course, The Collector of Injustices, born too beautiful ("I have no one to talk to. Men refuse to let me be intelligent and women resent me."), too rich ("I attract the 'leaners.' It's terrifying! Now you must let me pay for a secluded place where you can write and I can take care of you."), too American ("Well, if you go with a man for nearly a year there comes a time when it has to be marriage or—good-by!"), too often married ("All four of my husbands were beautiful people—weak, twisted, sick, beautiful people.") He hated everything that made Marlane what she was, yet he had been with her for over a year—until that last trip to Vietnam.

He did not know when he had made his decision to write a "non-fiction novel," but the story of the Woodrow mass murders had haunted him since the day it appeared on front pages throughout the world. The night of the murders Hans had been reading a book written by one of the victims. It was not a book that was well known and Hans had only come upon it by chance. Someone had left it behind in the train compartment he was taking from Brighton to London. The photograph of the author, Ira Sean Woodrow, on the back cover of the jacket looked familiar. Somewhere Hans had seen or met that man. He could not recall more than that. He had read the book to see if it held any clues. It had not, but the book had stirred him. It was an allegory, impeccably written in a style that was almost lyrical, about a girl who lives in a castle and is immortal unless she leaves the castle for the world outside. A dog comes to her window. It cries. At first she resists his cries but the next night and the night following he is back again. She finally unlatches the castle door and calls out for him but he stays still crying beneath her window. She steps outside to fetch him and the door latches behind her. Then the dog stops his crying and turns on his tail and disappears from sight leaving the girl alone and mortal. In an epilogue the dog ends his life in a horrible fight in which he remains passive while being mutilated by a pack of wild dogs.

The book had been dedicated: To Lululu.

All but one member of the Woodrow family, which included an old family retainer, had been poisoned by strychnine in sugar they spooned into their own tea. All but one had died almost instantly. The one survivor, the sister Luanne, claimed to be upstairs at the time, insisting she never joined her family for tea, preferring that time of the day to herself. She said she had heard nothing—nothing but a terrible silence, and that it was this silence which had driven her downstairs to investigate. She had not called the police simply because the thought had not occurred to her.

Luanne Woodrow had been taken into custody and tried, but found "not guilty." The final verdict was suicide and murder, by the deceased Ira Sean Woodrow. There had been many photographs of the young woman in the papers and Hans had studied them all.

28

He could not believe the girl guilty any more than the jury had but he also knew very well that the author of that book was incapable of a mass murder. From the book one sensed that he saw himself as the sacrificial lamb, capable of martyrdom but not of murder. If he had been guilty he would have left conclusive proof. Nothing had been found except some old prescriptions for a nerve stimulant he had once taken that contained small amounts of lethal strychnine.

Luanne haunted Hans. He did what was for him an unprecedented thing and attended her trial. Even more out of character, when she entered Laurel Groves he sought out the head matron, a Mrs. Pritchett, managing to convince her to keep in touch with him about the young woman's progress and pledging her his help in any way it might be needed.

The letter had reached him during the summer. Mrs. Pritchett reminded him of their conversation ten years before —the kind letters he had written from time to time, and extended the hope that he was sincere about his original offer to help. She wrote that Luanne refused to leave Laurel Groves although she had been quite well for years. She was concerned that the young woman might remain in the insular society of the nursing home forever, and was trying to interest her in a holiday as a first step toward a final break. Since Hans traveled so much she wondered if he might be kind enough to suggest a place where she might accompany Luanne. As he knew Luanne's special problems she felt assured he could recommend a suitable holiday.

Hans did not reply right away. He knew he had to be very sure. He let the summer pass and began the "non-fiction novel" on the murders. Once into it there was no way back. He wrote Mrs. Pritchett suggesting a winter holiday, adding that if the girl could be convinced to travel alone he would remain close at hand. He was sure she would feel, as he did, that leaving Laurel Groves meant leaving Mrs. Pritchett as well. He would be in London within a week, he told her, and they could discuss the matter privately at that time. He had not planned a trip but he went and Mrs. Pritchett finally agreed to his plan. He had not told her about the book, knowing she would never have allowed Luanne in his care or company had she known.

Hans brought himself to a sudden stop on the slope. A spray of snow hit him in the face. He took off his glasses and wiped them vigorously on the inside of his scarf. He did not know what he had expected but he had been totally unprepared for the young woman whose fate he had forced into his own hands. He asked himself a few tough questions. Why had he been so driven to write the book? Why had he felt so passionately that it had to be his *best* book? Why was he using the girl for this purpose? Money didn't enter into it. He had as much as he ever cared to have. Success was already his, as was the notoriety a successful author naturally receives and this was not a murder that altered history.

It seemed irrational to a man who, at forty-nine, had rarely felt more for a woman than reflex and physiology demanded, but those sad, beautiful eyes—that voice that trembled—the hands that constantly grasped each other because they were trying so hard to hang on—had reached him in the same way that skiing once had, and he could not let go. He could not let *her* go would be closer to the truth.

Perspiration poured down his face, although the wind was up and the snow carried particles of ice. He should have shoved off and continued down as quickly as he could. She should not be left alone too long, for one thing. But for the first time since he had worn skis, he could not concentrate on the descent.

There was a hut he could stop at almost a mile from where he was. He would have a beer and some thick, black coffee and crusty bread with old Herr Grass and his Frau.

30

LUANNE...

I wore mauve because it is an undecided color, and made me feel less conspicuous. The guests of the Weisshaus had been on the slopes all day. They were returning now, their voices still pitched to the outdoors as they went into the dining room for afternoon refreshments.

It had been a day clouded with doubt. I had walked in all directions. Everywhere there were family groups and student groups and skiing groups. The older folk were huddled together in the cafés over glasses of hot coffee and mugs of dark beer. The streets had been filled with skiers going to and from the slopes in a solid parade. It had been strangely satisfying. Groups of people remain anonymous. I was not sorry I had come.

The decision had not been an easy one. Most of the residents of Laurel Groves were elderly and their children seldom came to visit, but I was always there and they looked forward to our daily chats.

Who would have time for silent old Mrs. Sydney who searched the corridors for me each morning? When I approached she sat contritely in the center of the corridor, blocking my passage, and I would relate small inconsequentials to her. Then she would reach for my hand and hold it for a brief moment before spinning her chair away, dismissing me and yet unable to watch me go. How could I ever desert Mrs. Sydney or Laurel Groves and the other residents? They had become my home and my family.

After the trial I had returned to the great house in Hampstead but I had not been well and I could not cope with the sightseers and reporters who constantly rang the bell and, if I did answer, (which I never did) would peer through the windows. I took to keeping the drapes drawn all day. Miss Pansy's sister, Mrs. Devlin, was a kind soul and after hours at Laurel Groves, where she was employed at the time, would come to me. I suspect she came more to see that I was not totally alone than to assist me. It was only a short time, however, before her arthritis made it impossible for her to work. Her visits soon became infrequent. She fussed about my being alone and, in the end, I decided to go to Laurel Groves.

The house was put up for sale with all its furnishings and it brought a better price than the estate agents had expected. Unquestionably it was because the house was considered a place of interest. It was bought with all its contents by a well-known mystic. I gave Mrs. Devlin a half share of the sale price. It was a gesture which relieved me of the responsibility I felt toward her, and filled her with slightly overpowering gratitude. After that, no matter how damp the day or how painful her arthritis, she never failed to visit me at Laurel Groves on Saturday afternoons.

There was that about Laurel Groves which made me feel as if I was still in the great house in Hampstead. Perhaps that was why I continued living there. But it was more likely because, once behind its high brick walls, the world forgot me and I lived in welcomed anonymity. How could ten years have passed? But they had, and not unhappily either. There had been the old folks for a start. I was the daughter, sister, friend—who no longer visited them. There were the gardens I dearly loved, the Sisters I could help, and Mrs. Pritchett, a woman of wisdom and sharp intellect. She gave me books on philosophy and religion and would discuss them with me tirelessly. She brought me portfolios of great artists and discussed their work enthusiastically. In every way she kept trying to help me find more to occupy my life at Laurel Groves.

I resisted her first suggestions that we take a holiday. The truth was—I had been somewhat depressed at the time and the thought of a holiday secretly cheered me and brought back the memory of days in Cornwall when I was a child. I was apprehensive about it at the same time. I am not sure I actually agreed to go, but suddenly plans were being made. When Mrs. Pritchett found she could not join me it seemed more advisable to put off the idea entirely. I had never in my life traveled alone. However, Mrs. Pritchett convinced me I would be doing the residents, most of whom would never go on holiday again, a good turn. The plan was that I would share with them as much of the journey as I could recall on my return. Then—somehow, there I was on the plane to Zurich! Cook's had arranged for a representative to meet me on my arrival. He made sure I boarded the proper train for Klosters. And now, here I was, waiting for the second evening of my holiday to begin.

I sat down at the same table Hans and I shared the previous night. A late sun had set over the top of the mountains and I could feel its warmth on my shoulder as I studied its golden stripe along the outside of my arm. I had not been there long before Hans entered. He crossed to me and took my hand in his cold, weathered one. I wanted to hold it there to transfer my warmth to him, but I did not. The sun was causing a glare on the window behind me and his wide forehead was wrinkled into narrow trenches as he faced it to smile down at me.

"Tea time?" he inquired as he rubbed his hands together. He sat across from me. "Would you mind if I had something a bit stronger?" he asked.

"I don't drink tea," I said, feeling ridiculous as soon as I had spoken. "I hoped you might." I realized instantly he would assume the truth—that I had been sitting there waiting for him. I glanced down, clasping my hands together and keeping my eyes fixed on the tight white skin on my knuckles.

"What we both need is a brandy," he informed me. I shook my head but he held up that huge hand of his and pointed two fingers at the waiter, who seemed to understand what that meant for he soon brought two brandies to the table.

33

"Drink it. It's good for you." Hans insisted.

"I'm not used to brandy."

"Drink it anyway." He sat watching me until I had lifted the glass to my lips and managed a token swallow. "There, that's better. Well! What have you been doing today?"

"I walked a great deal."

"Did you make any friends?" he asked lightly.

I shook my head negatively as I interrupted him before he had a chance to disapprove. "But I really had a most beautiful day!"

"That's good. My day was not." I must have looked concerned because he was quick to explain. "It was just that the skiing was bad. Next week it will be better. It's still early." He finished his brandy. "Would you care for another?" he asked.

"Oh, no! Thank you."

He signaled the waiter for one more. He was looking at me now. The sun was at the foot of the mountain and the room was at that hour when days begin to die. "I never like this time of day at Laurel Groves," I said, before realizing he did not—*could not*—know about Laurel Groves. I grasped for words as if they were air and I was drowning. "I work at a nursing home," I told him, hating myself immediately for the lie, but fearing more what he would think of the truth. I avoided his glance feeling sure he already knew me well enough to tell what I was thinking merely by the expression on my face.

"That's rewarding work," he said. His voice passed lightly over the words.

I breathed deeply. The sun was nearly gone but its last warmth was on the back of my neck. He was smiling casually. I suffered small stabs of anxiety. He had accepted my lie easily.

"It's the old people who make it worthwhile," I said. I could hear the nervousness in my voice.

"I know how it is," he replied. "Most people don't have time for the elderly. They are like children when someone does find the time."

34

"They are like my family," I began. "Mine are dead. All of them. Ten years now. Not one of the Woodrows I told you about last night is still alive." I was ill at ease thinking— now he would remember the murders and be horrified he was at the same table with Luanne Woodrow. He would be too much a gentleman to show it. His voice would merely detach itself into politeness and he would remain courteous throughout this meeting, but he would avoid any further confrontations.

Instead his eyes filled with compassion and he reached across the table and separated my hands. I had been clasping them together, one holding the other as though I was holding on to myself for support. He took them securely into his own hands. "I'm proud you could share those bits of yourself with me, Luanne," he said with such intensity that I had to close my eyes to fight back the blinding tears of relief. I had been wrong! He did care! And he did not know!

A chill passed over me. I would have to tell him. Not now. But—*eventually*. If only he would come to trust me first—so solidly, so unflinchingly that he would be able to look at me and see nothing but the woman Irish said I had inside me!

I opened my eyes. He released my hands as if he were saying, "I know! You have passed the crisis." He leaned back in his chair and his face eased into an attempt at lightheartedness. "We'll have to find you more to do tomorrow," he said.

"I was happy today," I assured him. "Really."

"It's not good to be alone too much. Thinking is an exhausting sport," he mused.

"It was a pleasurable sport today," I told him without hesitation.

"Oh?" He smiled and raised an eyebrow.

I could not help my embarrassment. I knew the kind of thoughts he might believe had occupied me. "I kept thinking about my Uncle Stanley," I managed to say, as I prayed silently the burning in my cheeks had not turned their color. He was waiting for me to continue. There was only interest in what I was about to tell him in his expression. It gave me

35

the courage to continue. "I loved him very much," I said softly. "Next to my brother Irish, I always loved him the most."

I had been twelve when Uncle Stanley and Mary Agatha came to live with us. Mary Agate (Liam had given her that name because her eyes and her hair were the mottled color of the agates he collected) was an awkward eight, as was Liam. When Liam teased her, which was often, he would call her, "Semipellucid variegated chalcedony!" which was the technical name given to the agate. When he was angry, he would contract that into, "Pellucidony!" But it was difficult for him to get the desired reaction of hurt and fury from her. Mary Agatha so wanted to be accepted by us that she was pleased when one of our members even threw her his abuse. Soon we all called her Mary Agate and she never appeared to object.

I am sure Uncle Stanley loved his daughter. He was gentle and kind to her. Perhaps, somewhere in her gray putty face there was a resemblance to the woman he had once loved, who had so mysteriously disappeared. I never heard Mary Agate call Uncle Stanley, "Father." She always addressed him as "Sir," but she said it in the tone of endearment one would use for the word "Father." She never joined the excursions Uncle Stanley and I took together. They were unattractive to her and she often was quite verbal about telling us so. ("I can't bear to see the animals in cages at the zoo. Their droppings make me ill." . . . "Art galleries make me dizzy. All that color and nowhere whatsoever to sit." . . . "It's dirty down by the Thames. There must be great rats there.") The places Mary Agate liked to go, Uncle Stanley never visited—Madam Toussaud's Wax Museum, Hampton Court, and Westminster Abbey. Uncle Stanley called them all "Ghostantics."

36

There were other divertissements Uncle Stanley would arrange for the two of us. He called these, "Visits to the Human Galleries and Zoos." They included Parliament (always when some inconsequential was being debated) and Old Bailey (when a case suitable for the ears of a minor was being tried). He would brief me first on what was about to happen and explain why we were there. I was thankful to Uncle Stanley later when I sat in the dock myself. I had seen the great melodrama of justice so many times I was not frightened of it.

"Old Bailey," Uncle Stanley would say, the trace of Ireland still in his voice, "is the people's zoo, Luanne. We come here to study the various species. That way we learn that life should never be taken too seriously, for it is a farce and at its best a poor imitation of the animal kingdom."

We would go early to insure our having front seats in the gallery. It must have been most disturbing to whomever was seated behind us. Uncle Stanley was an exceptionally tall man and, if that were not problem enough, he was in constant movement. He would shift his position every few minutes to gain the best view or a new angle.

"Now you are to watch the judge, who is more concerned with his own wit and weary with his own boredom than with anything that is said in his courtroom. Carefully study the two barristers who wear their wigs and their robes as proudly as peacocks! Have pity on the usher, who is a dutiful dog, but not upon the prisoner in the dock. Guilty or not this is his one moment in life to learn that 'civilization' does not mean he cannot steal what he does not own, but that the qualities he has come to believe mean 'being civilized' can be stolen from *him*. Pride, dignity, privacy. He will lose all these before he leaves this arena."

Uncle Stanley usually forgot that he had told me the same things before, in much the same manner. He would speak softly and his eyes, which were normally a lively green, would gentle into a mellower shade. "You must be silent and you must not laugh," he would continue. "Not even when the

37

judge looks up to the gallery for laughter and everyone about you is laughing. You must not cry either, for whereas laughter might be overlooked, tears would not and we would be asked to leave as your tears might influence the jury. Now—the twelve men and women you see in that box have come to believe they suddenly have been crowned with the wisdom they were heretofore unable to apply to their own lives."

Althea never approved of Uncle Stanley taking me to Old Bailey, but I quite liked it. For all of Uncle Stanley's attempts to bring me face to face with the inequities of life, it seemed unreal to me, with the flowing black robes and seventeenth-century wigs and the Elizabethan language of the courtroom. It was a farce, a tragedy. The entire spectacle made each inequity a bit of overdrawn theater. I always hoped Uncle Stanley might take me to a theater, for that matter, but he did not like it and he was not a man who would go anywhere not of his liking.

After one trip to Old Bailey, we went to the Robin's Egg, a restaurant Uncle Stanley had mysteriously found on the top of a building that otherwise housed theatrical outfitters. To reach it, since there was no lift, one had to steer a dark course through rooms of knights in armor and Indians on the war path and Canadian Mounties on the march. The restaurant perched on the building like a bird's nest balancing on the end of a branch. It contained only eight or nine small tables all of which looked down into a giant wasteyard filled with broken armature and decaying props.

Uncle Stanley was filled with reminiscence that day. He talked about my mother and my maternal grandparents, as well as his own youth which was excitingly filled with war and rebellion. Finally, he spoke of Father (he had never done so before). "He was a hard, cold man, Luanne, but I never held it against him. I knew, you see, the great burden that he carried." He leaned forward and his voice became serious. "His father, your paternal grandfather, had been convicted and hung as a traitor during the First World War. It branded

38

the Woodrow name and your father found the inheritance bitter, indeed! It was the beginning of his withdrawal from society."

Uncle Stanley shook his head sadly and I waited for him to continue. "My sister was a beautiful woman and an intelligent one, much before her times. But she was still a woman in love and as women in love all think foolishly, she was no exception. She married your father believing she could change him. Ah, well, she had been a fighter since girlhood. She knew no other way than to take the devil by his horns with her bare hands. Her husband was convinced his father had been libeled and was innocent and she insisted he devote all his efforts to proving it. They worked together with a feverish drive but, in the end, proved nothing. If he was hard on your mother after that one might not forgive him but one could understand."

The waiter brought Uncle Stanley's trifle to the table but though it was his favorite sweet he could only smooth the cream with the back of his spoon. "He kept to himself after that, trying, but never succeeding, to quench your mother's high spirits. But he did manage to isolate her from the world he thought he could no longer trust." Uncle Stanley was thoughtful. Compassion creased his face. "I cannot be too hard even against his memory. He was a driven man and the guilt was heavy upon him."

I heard once again the pacing on the floors above my bedroom when Mother died, and the cries that had slipped through the opening in the chimney. I must have looked as if I would cry myself for Uncle Stanley took my chin in his supple hands. "No tears, little Luanne. No tears," he said soothingly.

But there were tears in Uncle Stanley's eyes and he let them fall shamelessly onto the tea-stained linen on our table.

I shared these confidences later with Irish and he told me more. Father had not wanted us to attend school because Thomas Woodrow's act of betrayal was printed in all the

39

school history books. We never told the others, and as far as I knew, they never learned the Woodrow secret. Shortly thereafter, Uncle Stanley suffered a stroke and when, for several months, he hovered between life and death, I would spend the half-hour the others took for tea, in his room by his bedside, reading to him. When he was well enough to sit in his wheel chair he joined the others (the only part of the day he usually spent with them), but I never did. I had found a certain peace in those newly acquired half-hours away from the others and I was not willing to part with it.

The sun had disappeared completely. The day had passed. Hans was still silently listening to me. A suggestion of a smile played at the corners of his mouth. "Uncle Stanley was quite a fellow," he said.

I nodded, unable to find the words that had slipped out so easily only moments before. The tables about us were empty. Tea time had come to an end. I wanted to turn the clock back to that first moment he had entered the room. Never before had I been so loathe to see time pass. He would surely choose to leave soon. I could not hope to detain him any longer. It came to me that on my return to Laurel Groves I would be expected to share what I was feeling this moment and had felt all the moments I had been with Hans. How foolish I would seem. In their elderly wisdom the residents of Laurel Groves would think I had reverted to schoolgirl romantics. It would be impossible to tell them. I knew I could not bear their patronizing smiles either, or their expressions of sympathy. "A holiday romance!" they might say. "A girl should know better than expose herself to that kind of hurt!"

Of course, it was true. I would only be here ten more days. At the end of that time he might be kind enough to see me to my train and wait politely until it had pulled out of the station before finding other companionship. A terrifying thought occurred to me. "How long do you plan to be in Klosters?" I asked. I said it easily, as if the answer was not the most feared answer to any question I had ever asked.

"For the season," he replied. "And you?"

It was difficult for me to speak. He had brought such overwhelming joy to my heart. "Ten days," I managed to reply.

"We might have you skiing by then." He smiled.

"I think not!" I laughed nervously. "I would be scared silly!"

"Well, we can't have that," he said. "Would you feel better if I took you to the slopes myself? The lower ones, of course."

"Oh, no! I mean . . . that's kind of you but I really don't want to ski. But there is something. . ." He leaned forward as I spoke and it was not easy for me to continue. "I thought, perhaps, if you had one with you . . . you would lend me one of your books . . . one you had written . . . to read." I ended in a rush, adding, "I would be very careful with it."

"You are not supposed to spend your holiday reading my books! You must get out and enjoy yourself! Tomorrow I will spend the entire day seeing that you do," he said. My face must have had several reactions on it; great pleasure at even the thought of an entire day with him, pride that he wanted to spend it with me, and fear that he might not want to give me the book. He glanced reassuringly at me as he rose from his chair. "And tonight I will make you a present of my first book and can only hope between my work and myself you won't become too bored."

"I don't think that could happen," I said surely.

He helped me to my feet and smiled down at me. "Promise me you will tell me if it does?" he asked.

I just shook my head doubtfully and we crossed the room. The tables were now being laid for dinner. I had kept him at tea over an hour. "Go up to your room and get into some ski pants and warm clothes," he ordered, when we were in the vestibule. "I have a surprise for you."

41

"I didn't bring that sort of clothing with me." It sounded stupid and I was moved to explain. "It was not the activities that drew me here." And since that sounded even more inane I went on. "I came to rest." Then I was frightened he might change his mind and not include me in his surprise if he thought I was an invalid of sorts. "It was a silly idea. I don't know now what ever possessed me to think I needed a rest." I beamed a healthy smile at him.

"We'll have to hurry and buy you some clothes before the shops close." He ignored my protests, threw his own ski jacket over my shoulders and hurried me out of the Weisshaus and across the street into the nearest shop where he bought me a pair of ski pants and a bright red sweater and some fur lined boots.

When I was dressed in them he stood back and admired his selection. "Just right, now you are ready for the surprise."

It was dinner at the restaurant at the top of the Gotschna. We had taken the cable car up with groups of gay young people and the restaurant was already filled with them. There was music and dancing and a roaring fire in the massive fireplace. No one was left to dine alone. The young people all knew Hans and his work and asked him a million questions, led him into a thousand youthful arguments. The girls flirted with him and I was certain the young men envied him. He treated them all with a slightly professorial though not a condescending manner. After a while, when the fire was all low embers, they left us alone. "Do you suppose anyone ever died of happiness?" I asked.

"No! But they have of over-exposure!" he replied. The room was cold now and the others were deserting. He hustled me out and into a waiting cable car and we rode back in silence, listening to the others, but pretending not to notice their impatience for love-making.

Before parting, Hans fetched the book. As we stood before my door he wrote on the inside cover and then handed the book to me closed. He kissed me lightly on the forehead and returned to his own room.

"To Luanne—With Gratitude—Hans," he had inscribed. I could not put the book down before I had finished it entirely. It was about Hans's childhood and the early days of the war. Then I reluctantly closed the cover. Across the corridor Hans was typing. I could hear him working half the night.

LUANNE...

When I awoke there was a winter sun. But had the day been gray and overcast it could not have dampened my spirit. I was in love for the first time in my life. Sensibly, I knew I was approaching middle age, but first love must have the same sweet taste no matter when it happens. I felt I would never again be the same. The past was a still and unfaltering shadow, with shadows even beyond it. It stirred in me. The pain lingered, and yet there was a new sensation that gently anesthetized the old nearly out of existence.

Hans had written a number of books, yet he had chosen to give me this one which was so much a part of him. The biographical sketch inside the jacket confirmed my feeling. It referred to him as, "a child of our times" and mentioned that even before the book's publication it had won an important award.

I wanted to believe that by giving me this book, Hans was sharing his childhood with me as I had been sharing mine with him the past two days. I wanted to interpret that gesture as a first true gift-giving (for material things such as the gifts of the previous day are of a different nature). He had, I told myself, given me a bound copy of some measure of himself.

The book still lay beside me on the bedside table. I watched the sun spread over it and felt the same sun caressing me. The Weisshaus was silent. I glanced at my watch and saw that it was not yet half-past six. I wondered whether Hans was lying

43

there as I was, awake and yet not willing to part with the night. Then, I remembered that my last conscious memory before falling asleep had been the steady tap of his typewriter. It had been past three in the morning then. He might have worked all night.

I propped up my pillows feeling more awake after my own short three and a half hour rest than I had ever been after a full night of sleep. I picked up his book from the bedside table and opened it.

"To Luanne—With Gratitude—Hans."

It was written in a large hand, bold and certain. I could not turn away from the word—"Gratitude." Gratitude could be only a passing reaction to a small kindness. Yet in my case, oh, yes! I was overwhelmed with gratitude. His kindness to me had roused me from a long sleep. It had stirred the woman I had given up as dead. My gratitude was a residual of love. I yearned to know what he had felt when he wrote those words.

I closed the book and turned to the back cover. There was a photograph of a younger Hans, still untouched by gray, the dear lines that now etched so deeply around his eyes were missing. The mouth was still slightly petulant with youth. It seemed unfair that I had not known this Hans, the face on the book was not the familiar face that now lay in the shadow of the far mountain. Somehow I must learn more about this Hans. But I had to be patient. I could be sure of very little, but I *was* certain of one thing. First love was to be taken gracefully or it might, through inexperience, slip out of one's grasp.

Even reading his book left much untold. Whether he had ever married. Or had children. He was the sort of man one knew had had many affairs yet I wondered if he could still recall *his* first love. How clumsy, how unknowledgeable I must seem to him!

I was overwhelmed with the frightening thought that all this was a mere fantasy of a nearly middle-aged spinster who had come to a late awakening. Maybe Hans had given me the book out of mere politeness and had chosen this one simply at

44

random. He was a man of generous nature. He would easily give one book or even one evening to a lonely woman as something for her to remember. I recalled the flirtatious young girls, the admiring and envious young men, the brilliance and talent contained in his book. How could I even imagine that a woman like me would interest him? I tried desperately to concentrate on the view outside my window, to erase such thoughts from my head. Then I shifted my glance to the little cupboard where my clothes were stored.

The doors were closed and for some reason I did not understand I arose from the bed, crossed to the cupboard and flung it open. Perhaps I was afraid the clothes he had bought me would be gone, some figment of my imagination. But they were there, neatly folded and in their proper places.

I went into the bathroom and ran the water for a bath. The room soon filled with the consoling warmth of the steam from the hot water. The mirror over the sink was lost in its vapors so that when I passed there was no reflection. I was thankful because I did not think I could stand the look that would be there—waiting, in my eyes. I took out the ski clothes and laid them carefully across the bed and then stepped into the steaming bathtub. I concentrated on the warmth that soon enveloped me and after a while lulled myself into less agitating thoughts.

I was already at breakfast before I allowed my mind to come back to Hans. I ate heartily and was in no hurry to leave my table. I lingered over the thick, bitter coffee and felt better by the time the small pot was empty. I had come to a decision. I would make it easy for him to accommodate his manners and still not forfeit his day.

Yet I was unprepared for the sight of Hans when he entered. I thought I had memorized all there was to remember. But here he was, crossing to my table, and I discovered I had not. There was his step, so light for a man his size. Then, there was the set of his shoulders, whipped back, braced for the day and all comers.

"Good morning." He smiled across the table at me. I had

not remembered the sincerity with which he spoke even such casual exchanges. Nor the way he emphasized certain syllables. Nor the inflection his voice could take—up or down—immediately telegraphing his mood. He was happy this morning.

"I heard you working until all hours," I said, unable to keep the concern from my voice.

"My typing kept you awake!" Then, as if he was angry at himself, he hit the open palm of one hand a hard blow with the closed fist of the other. "Bad habit of mine. Working at night. Damned selfish, too. I'm sorry."

"Oh, please. Don't be! You didn't keep me awake! I read your book, you see, and when I had finished and was ready to switch off the light, I could hear you at the typewriter. That was all. I went straightaway to sleep." I looked at him sincerely now, dropping the bantering. "Thank you for the book. It was wonderful." I forced a smile back on my face and gaiety into my voice. "I have a wonderful plan for this morning! I hope you won't disappoint me."

They had served him his coffee and he was pouring it. He drank it black and unsweetened and he had motioned for them to take back the rolls and preserves. "I told you," he said, "it's your day." He looked past me to the warming sunlight on the snow-covered mountains. "I don't think the sun will be there much longer," he commented.

"I hope it will," I said, "because. . . ." My smile felt frozen to my face. I thought my words might crack it. He was waiting patiently. There was a thick vein on the side of his forehead that throbbed as his heart must. I found myself watching it, fascinated. "I would like you to take me up to the top of the mountain with you," I managed to say at last. "I can watch you ski down and after you are gone spend some time watching the other skiers. It must be wonderful up there! Another world! I can take the cable car back and we can meet for lunch and if you are not back by then—well—I thought I might do a bit more shopping. As you see, I am very fond of your gift, but I can't wear it every day!" I was talking rapidly,

46

not giving myself a chance to back down. "If you don't return until the same time you did yesterday, I will have a new outfit to greet you with!" He had narrowed his eyes and was studying me. "Please, don't say no," I finished.

He was slow in answering, as if trying to make sure what answer I truly wanted from him. In the end he smiled and patted my hand. "All right, so it shall be. We will go to the top of the mountain together." Hans was silent as he drank his coffee, watching me, waiting for some giveaway sign on my face that would tell him what I was truly thinking. I hadn't fooled him completely. He knew I was playing some kind of game. He stood up as soon as he had finished his coffee. "I'll get my skis," he said. "I won't be long."

I nodded and watched him cross the warm wood-beamed room and bow his head to pass beneath the low doorway. I had not meant to follow him. I had only thought to fetch a warm jacket and some gloves from my room, yet I was on the step, just before turning to our landing when I saw him come out of his room. I drew back into the shadow.

The maid was outside his door sorting linen. I could not distinguish what he was saying to her in his soft Schweizer-deutsch, but saw him take her to his door and show her it was securely locked. Then he put the key in his pocket, as if asking her not to go into his room nor let anyone else into it. He stood for a moment looking at my closed door and then started toward the doorway. I went back a few steps and retraced them as though I had just been coming up.

"I forgot something," I smiled weakly and ran up the stairs past him, not daring to meet his glance. When I returned to the reception hall his skis were tall against his broad body. We went out into a fading sun and made our way, side by side, up the street to the cable station. We walked down and under the railroad tracks and came up directly in front of the cable station. The sun had suddenly disappeared completely from the sky.

There was already a good-sized queue. We stood in silence

47

as the queue moved in the direction of the lift. I was unable to keep up the pretense I had started. I wanted to tear away, run back to the privacy of my room. But we were now alongside the entrance of the cable car, and Hans had his hand securely under my elbow helping me over the threshold and inside. We sat down together on the wooden seats. The car was crowded with skiers in heavy sweaters, most of them carrying bulging packs. It had not been like this the night before. People crushed in on all sides of me. I could smell their morning coffee and after-shave and the heavy odors from their lunch baskets. There was a babble of languages as we rose above a cluster of trees and the car started up the side of the mountain. I could not speak. Neither could I look out or down. I pressed closer to Hans and smiled nervously at him. It had seemed fun the night before. But then it had been too dark to realize the great distance that was growing between us and the foot of the mountain.

"You all right?" he asked.

"Just somewhat overwhelmed."

"It will take a while yet. You're not going to be sick?"

I shook my head denying any such inclination, and forced a smile back on my face. I listened to the gay voices of the young girls who were flirting with boys their own ages, and the hearty laughter of the men. Most of the people in the cabin either knew each other or became immediate comrades. There were fragments of sentences like: "Didn't you go to Stowe last year?"—"How was the skiing on the new pass yesterday?"—"Someone said they might close the Parsenn."

A voice called out to Hans in German from across the cabin. He searched over the heads of the skiers and found the girl belonging to the voice. Immediately there was an exchange between them. Then both of them laughed. I straightened and drew away. This was not at all what I had intended. Before we even had a chance I was embarrassing him with my silence. I should not have come at all. Some young American girls in gay ski clothes, their shining hair tossed carelessly about, their shoulders drawn back in pride of their youthful bodies, smiled boldly at him. He smiled back. I wondered whether he would have spoken to them if I had not been with him, maybe helped them on with their skis at the top, perhaps, even skied down with them.

"Only a few more minutes." He consoled me with a gently reassuring pat on my shoulder. I turned away and kept my glance out the window at the slanted snow and the arrows of tall pine trees.

Finally we came to a halt and Hans prodded forward and helped me out of the cabin. He led the way through the station and then onto a snow-dusted ledge in the mountain. I had not been able to see it well the night before. Now, I could see that one side was sheer ice covered rock that fell dizzily for hundreds of meters. The other side dropped more gradually and was smooth with the night's untouched snowfall. Hans stood on the edge looking out.

"Come over here and see the world from a skier's view," he called.

I started toward him slowly. "Don't be afraid," he said. "I won't let you fall." I took the few steps to his side. He gestured out across the great expanse of snow and slope and mountain and valley. "This is one of the greatest feelings there is!" he exclaimed. He breathed deeply. "And that was a deep breath of freedom!" He was grinning widely and I answered it with a smile. "You really aren't enjoying this," he said. "Why did you want to come here?"

"Oh, but I am!" I insisted, though even I did not hear the right enthusiasm in my words.

"You are a funny, small animal. I think I shall call you, 'Squirrel.'"

A shadow appeared behind the shadows. It clouded my vision. I thought about Irish and his habit of thinking of people as various animals. "Please—I like you to call me Luanne," I said.

"All right, Luanne." He roughed my hair as one might a

49

young puppy's. "Let's go back to the restaurant and have some coffee and some breakfast conversation. I'm not much of a talker over my first cup of coffee." He started back but I could not move. I thought of all those gay, young beautiful people that would be inside. All the languages that would be spoken that would be foreign to my ears. All the intimate exchanges that I could not share. He paused when he saw I was not coming. "What is it?" he asked.

The words tumbled out. "I would rather you went down the slope. Right now!" I said, shocked at how it sounded once it was said. A cloud had been moving across the top of the mountain. It was turning cold and I pulled my jacket tighter about me. Hans stood, his great wide shoulders rising, mountain-like themselves, from the mist that seemed to be engulfing us as we stood.

"I'll wait for the mist to lift," he decided.

"No, please—now," I said. My voice had lost any attempt at lightness. I watched him closely to see if he suspected the terrible twistings in my heart. I had to turn away, unable to look at him any longer. "You must think me a silly woman," I said, the tremble in my voice almost cutting off my speech. It was hopeless now. He knew fear had brought me to this spot with him, not a desire for a happy day. I would ruin everything. He would hate me for my stupid dramatics. I could have told him I wanted to take a bus tour of the surrounding villages by myself rather than engineer this disaster. My pride disappeared and before I could stop them, the tears broke through and I had to stand there humiliating myself, embarrassing him.

"I've never been able to endure a crying woman," he said softly. He tried to turn me back toward him but I stood solidly frozen in the snow. "I won't look at you," he promised. "It's all right." I was riveted to the spot. He stuffed his handkerchief in the side pocket of my jacket. "It's cold enough for tears to freeze," he went on gently. I wiped them away but I could not face him. He took my shoulders tightly between his hands and spoke close into my ear in a soft, intimate voice which, nonetheless, held more authority than had he shouted at me. "Luanne, what you think you feel and what you fear *cannot* be, *is* real and *can* happen. Don't ask me how these things occur between two seemingly ill-assorted people, they just do. It will be all right. I promise you that."

Some skiers drew close to us and we both waited until they were gone, voices and sprays of snow trailing behind them. "We could go back down in the cable car," he said when we were alone again. "It's good we know how we feel. It is better to have it out in the open. I could hire a car, Luanne." His words were now so close they exploded in my ear. "We can go any place you wish."

I thought the tears might come again. I shook my head unable to utter even a small two letter word like "no." He would think me an idiot. He might even doubt his instinct as to how I felt toward him. But what he had just said were all the things I ever wanted to hear and it was too much coming so unexpectedly. I had to have time to become used to it. I could only pray he would understand.

"All right, Luanne." His voice was hushed but farther away. He stepped closer again. My back was still to him and he put his arms around my waist and pressed his face against my hair and he drew me closer to him. We stood there a long time, my shoulder touching his chest, no words between us. I did not hear the other voices, the birds, the whoosh of the skis. The cloud lifted though and I could now see all the way across his snow world. It took my breath away. I loosened his hold and held his hands as I pulled away. Then I turned to look at him.

It was as though, for that moment, no one else existed. "Now!" I whispered, hardly hearing my own voice.

He leaned forward and then swept downward and began his weaving, curving descent. Once, it seemed he would be lost in a giant snowdrift. And again, he might fall a hundred meters to the sharp ice rocks below him. Then he was gone.

A light but insistent rain began to fall. I blinked back the water from my lashes and made my way to the waiting cable car. If I could have crawled down the great face of that mountain I would have done so, so overwhelming was my fear of the cabin I must enter.

It was empty. The door closed after me and I was alone. The snow outside became sheets and table linen. The smell of the wood benches was of cedar. I tried to open the door but the car was now rising over the top of the station. Then it started down with me in it. Down—*down* the long rugged side of the far mountain.

L U A N N E . . .

It was the sound of the birds that awakened me. I had gone straight to my room upon returning to the Weisshaus. I must have been asleep for hours, because when the sound of the birds cut through my dark dream, the moon was high in the sky and the room was lighted as if by a candle's breath.

I dreamed I had returned to our summer cottage in Cornwall. It lay in a small valley over a rise from the sea. I could see myself as a child playing on the sand alone. It was growing late in the day and the others had obviously deserted me. I was occupied with digging moats and building sand castles and had apparently not even known I was by myself. The tide came in and the castle I had just completed dissolved into grains of sand that were swallowed by hungry water.

I retreated toward dry land and made my way to the white cliff which divided Sleepy Hollow, our cottage, and the valley from the sea. The water washed me back again and lashed me to the cliffside. I clung until the tide relented and then scrambled up the pale white precipice that was so like dried bone, but great, white puffins were on the top. They flew at me and drove me down the other side of the cliff where I slid and cut my wet flesh. I could see my blood stain the rocks as they raked my knees and elbows and the flanks of my legs.

Sleepy Hollow was about a hundred yards away and once I had reached the bottom of the cliff, I ran as fast as I could toward the familiar white picket fence entwined with its ring of red bramble roses. But when I reached it, the bramble bushes had grown taller than I, and the tender pale green thorns were now great brown spikes and there was no way for me to enter. Then the white birds came again. I dared not turn but I heard their cries and then the angry flapping of their wings. The dream had ended when I stood frozen— waiting—fearing retreat against the giant thorns as much as attack by the puffins.

I had awakened to see the two birdlike shadows on the low eave outside my window. I rose from the bed now, not bothering to put on my slippers, and with the quiet step that had disturbed Liam so much, I approached the window ledge and opened the window as carefully as I could. The birds were alert to even this small foreign sound. Their wings fluttered and they rose over the roof and lighted on the chimney of the building across the way. I could see them outlined against the clear blue-white of the evening snow. They were blackbirds and the knowledge greatly relieved me. The village church steeple stood sentry to the cold winter night. It was eerily light; the snow reflecting the white of the moon. The sky was an incandescent blue. I could read the time on the church steeple clock. It was just past nine o'clock.

I glanced down and saw the bright reflections on the ground from the lights of the Weisshaus. There were sounds below me. The others were still at dinner. I shut the window. The birds moved farther up the stilled, deserted street.

The outside handle of my door turned. Slowly, then impatiently. A fretful knock. There was the babble of querulous voices close—then across the corridor a door opened. It would be the maids on their evening rounds. They had gone into Hans's room. I opened my door soundlessly and stood behind it peering out the narrow slit, knowing that all the maids could see was my door ajar if they chanced a glance my way. They came out of Hans's room without looking in my direction, closing his door and then making their way up the winding staircase to the floor above. They had left his door unlatched.

I was still wearing the ski clothes I had put on in the morning. I found my shoes and made my way deliberately but inaudibly across the corridor to Hans's door, opened it, entered the room quickly and then closed the door behind me. The maids had turned off the light when they left and the room, looking out to the far mountain, cut off from the moonlight, was in blackness. I leaned heavily against the closed door, catching my breath, accustoming my eyes to the darkness.

There was no logical explanation for my behavior. The maids could return with soap or linen and find me. Hans could come up from dinner. Still, I knew I had to see his room. I straightened and made my way to the open door that was to my right. It was the bath. I turned on a light and then half-closed the door as I went back into the bedroom. Enough light came through to help me make out the objects on the tables and yet not cast a reflection on the rug that might be seen from under the door and into the corridor. I crossed to the bed closest to the window and sat down on it. It was the bed they had turned down, obviously the bed Hans slept in. I carefully studied the objects on the bedside table.

His pipe was still warm in the ashtray. He had not taken it to dinner with him and he had not been gone long enough for it to grow cold. I breathed easier. He would not return for some time if that were the case. There was a book beside it, a bookmark inserted to secure his place. I glanced at the cover. *The Woman by Claudia Mitchell*. A warm flush burnt itself into my cheeks. I turned the book over and in the half-light studied the face that had once, I supposed, looked tenderly upon my Irish.

It was a face that held no compromise. Wide, wise forehead. Clear, straight eyes. Set, firm mouth. And yet, surprisingly, a terribly feminine face. A face more French than English. More woman than authoress. A delicate hand pushed a stray lock of hair from the wide forehead. A locket buried itself in the soft curve of the long neck. I read the short biography below the photograph though I had to hold the book at odd angles to do so.

Mrs. Mitchell says this of herself, "I was born in France and raised in various parts of the Continent. My education was rather do-it-yourself. It was the group I met in Paris during the sad days of the Occupation and immediately thereafter who are responsible for my advanced education. Millet, Frocound, Alain Detre. All the finest literary talent France had produced in many years. Marriage and motherhood brought me to England and afforded me the great luxury of writing my first novel." That novel was the brilliant *Fountain of Love*. Since then, Mrs. Mitchell has become equally famous for her short stories and articles, as well as for her novels and biographies.

I replaced the book exactly as I had found it on the table. Claudia Mitchell was a revered and famous writer. This was her latest book. It was not at all unusual that Hans should have it in his room and be reading it. I sat for a moment and then lay back upon his pillows. I looked out the window to the view he would awaken to see and the view he would close his eyes to before sleep enveloped him. "Why am I truly here?" I asked myself. The answer came with the echo of remembrance.

It was the scene that morning in the corridor. His insistence that no one enter his room. His glance to my door. There is a secret place in everyone's life that one guards from strangers. But, when I thought about it, my fear was that Hans's secret was only meant to be kept from me. Had I not done the same thing? What possible ghost in Hans's past could compare with the horror in my own?

Somewhere there was a memory he could not extinguish. Footsteps that echoed. A face that haunted him. What would she have been like, this woman I was so sure he did not want me to know about? She might have been a member of the Resistance, a refugee from war or a writer like Hans. She could have been all three. They had shared a memory. What would that memory be? I thought about our first evening together. Could I in some way remind him of *her*? She could have been English, had my coloring, something just that simple.

I sat up and eased the drawer of the bedside table open, looking for what? Letters, I supposed. Instead I found pens, pencils, a writing tablet. I took out the tablet. All the pages but one had been torn from it. I studied the only line that appeared on the one remaining page. It was written in that same bold handwriting of his: "A *Pyrrhic victory at best.*"

From a hidden chamber of youthful reading I recalled that King Pyrrhus of Greece had won a battle in ancient Rome at the price of the lives of all his soldiers. I replaced the tablet and closed the drawer as quietly as I could. I got up and went over to the bureau. I suppose when I opened the top drawer I was looking for a jewelry box. I thought it might contain a wedding ring. The bureau was a large, old chest that had nearly outworn its use. The drawer creaked unmercifully, like a cry from a small injured animal. I stopped and looked up. Silence. I went into the bathroom and got some soap and came back with it. I managed to squeeze my hand through the opening I had made and rubbed the soap along the top of the drawer as best I could. It opened with a soft moan. Torn pages from the tablet were strewn over the tops of his stockings and handkerchiefs.

I heard the door open behind me and I held on to the rim

of the chest for support, looking down into the drawer for a long moment before raising my glance to the mirror above it. Hans stood reflected in the doorway, the light from the corridor shining into the room and framing my frightened face next to his in the mirror. I could not move. He closed the door and came inside and turned on the light. There was a sinking feeling inside of me. Stabbing pains of anxiety. I was certain I would faint if I did not maintain my grasp on the bureau.

"Whatever you are looking for would be easier to find in the light," he said. His tone was casual, as though there was no surprise in finding me in his room. I was working desperately to put all the stray fragments together in my mind. He started toward me. I simply could not move. He paused just behind me and looked into the mirror, into the reflection of my eyes. "I knocked at your door earlier. You didn't reply. Are you all right?"

I nodded my head. He was reluctant to turn away from the mirror. "I had a headache." My voice sounded as if it did not belong to me.

"The aspirin is in the bathroom." He turned toward the door, seeing that the light was on in that room. "Oh, you looked in there and couldn't find the bottle. I keep it in my little traveling kit on the shelf." I shook my head in agreement. He crossed and picked up his pipe from the ashtray and knocked the ashes from it. The sound put a strange chill in me. I turned away from the mirror as quickly as I could. The drawer screeched shut behind me as I leaned back against it. He never glanced up. He was taking a tobacco pouch of tanned leather from his pocket and was filling the pipe as he talked. "I've waited dinner for you," he said. "You'll feel better after you've eaten."

My back was still against the closed bureau drawer. "I had something sent to my room." I lied. "I'm sorry." He came over to me and helped me over to the side of his bed.

"You don't look well at that. I'll get you those aspirin." He left me sitting there as he went to fetch them. "One or two?" he called out.

"Two . . . please," I said numbly.

He came back and sat down beside me. "Here they are." His voice was soft and low. I could not look at him. He placed the aspirin and a glass of water down on the bedside table and let me take them myself. He sat quietly until I had done so. "Did you find anything to upset you?" he asked. His voice was filled with warmth and concern. I was too confused to measure his sincerity. He was waiting for a reply and I did not know what I could tell him.

"I am so ashamed!" I finally blurted. The tears welled up in me. "I know I had no right in here." The words now coming between sobs. "But, it has all happened so quickly. There has never been another man in my life before. Oh! I know that must make you think I am hopeless, but there have been unusual circumstances. I didn't want to go back to London a complete fool." I was shaking and he sat quietly—not touching me—waiting for me to continue. "I thought you might be married," I said at last. "I came here to see if there wasn't some proof. A letter, a picture . . . a wedding ring."

A soft smile spread across his face. He touched my shoulder lightly. "No. I am not married. Never have been. I don't even have any illegitimate children that I know of—so you see, there was nothing for you to worry about." I had lowered my head so that I would not have to look into those earnest eyes. He lifted my chin with his hand. "I love you, Luanne. Believe in that."

I could no longer control myself. The sobs erupted and I flung myself at him, burrowing against the warmth of his chest. He let me cry myself out, stroking my head from time to time. I clung to him, my face wet against the rough wool of his jacket. After a time he placed his hands solidly on my shoulders and pushed me back from him, keeping his hands there to hold me erect.

58

"All right?" he asked gently. I nodded my head and he released me and gave me another of his white linen handkerchiefs. The scent of his tobacco clung to it. His expression was serious and he was looking directly into my eyes. I dried them. For a moment he studied me. His hands moved back and rested on the bedstead behind us. I glanced away. "I may never have married . . ." he began, in what he attempted to be a reassuring tone. He spoke quietly, easily, his voice sincere and not marked with any passion that he thought might in some way make me wary. "But, I know a little bit about women. Only a little, mind you. No man can ever know a hell of a lot. But I know you haven't had any experience with men. If you had—you would never have doubted what I told you this morning. And you would know that you need not be ashamed to ask me anything, nor be humiliated at anything you might do." I was trembling. He brushed my shoulder with his hand and a chill went through my body and I straightened. "Thank heaven," he continued, "I do have some small knowledge. It keeps me from laying a hand on you now, for if I did, Squirrel, you would go scurrying further up the branches to the tree-top," he ended, using the small-animal name though I had asked him not to. Hans crossed to the door and switched off the overhead light, then he came back to my side. He propped the pillows up behind me and lifted me back on the bed so that the pillows were right behind me. He leaned over, stroking my cheek. "When the time comes, Luanne, I promise you patience and understanding."

I could not reply. He stretched out carefully on the bed beside me and took me gently in his arms, holding me without saying another word, without moving. It made me think about Irish, and the times. . . . I buried my head in Hans's chest and he held me tighter. It was a long time before he spoke.

"Would you like to sleep?" he asked. I shook my head negatively. "You should eat something then."

The words began to come painfully to the surface. "Yes . . . I think I would like that." He could have no way of knowing how desperately I hung on to that idea. How frantic I was to get out of that room. How it was suffocating me. How I wanted to get as far away from that chest of drawers as I could. Close his door. Never go back.

He rose from the bed and went into the bathroom and returned with a cold, wet towel. "Wipe your face with this," he ordered softly. "It will make you feel better."

I took the cool cloth and pressed it against my burning skin, before refolding it and placing it on the ashtray beside the bed. Then I rose and crossed to the door where he was waiting for me. In a moment we were in the corridor and the door was shut behind us. I excused myself and told him I would meet him in the dining room. I went to my room and latched the door. But nothing could erase the indelible image that was torturing my thoughts. I could still see the bedside table. The tablet with the missing pages. The bureau with those pages scattered over his belongings in the top drawer. They were notes written in his undeniable hand. Notes about the murders. *Notes about me.*

The day of the funeral the first snow of the year had fallen. Mrs. Devlin stood iron-faced beside me. She shed no tears, for which I was grateful. I will never forget the way she was dressed. She looked a birdlike creature, tiny wren hands, blackbird eyes, veil and cloak, the umbrella she leaned upon resembling black raven wings. Her gaze was frozen upon the tops of the seven coffins which were lined up as if they were a set of black dominoes. Behind them waited the seven open graves. I looked with despair at the markers on the coffins. Althea was to rest with only Mary Agatha, whom she disliked so in life, beside her. I had not thought to give instructions on the final arrangements. Had I, I would have made sure that

60

Mary Agate had an outside grave with Uncle Stanley beside her and Irish next to him, then Althea and the boys with Miss Pansy at the other end. I did step forward as if to speak, but the wren hand pinched mine and I held my peace and so they were laid to rest with Althea separated from the others by Mary Agatha. I have never forgiven myself for this dreadful oversight and though it seems a strange compensation, I have already drawn up my own desires, should no one be present upon my death, and requested that I should be laid to final rest beside my dear Althea.

The funeral gathered a great crowd but they were kept back behind the stone walls of the cemetery. Still, fathers lifted their young onto their shoulders so that they could see, and as the wall was only high enough to reach the average adult chest, it was difficult not to be disturbed by the sight of those two-headed monsters with legs in the middle. At the graveside there were only Mrs. Devlin and myself, the minister, the cemetery officials, and selected members of the press. The press were, at this time, a respectful and pleasant lot and confined their picture-taking to moments of the greatest discretion.

. . . *glorious, glorious brother* . . .

There was a soft downy comfort of snow upon the seven coffins by the time they were lowered into the earth. There is a lovely smell to fresh snow. All is good and clean and new. Dark autumn has passed and has been finally put to rest.

. . . *somehow we shall meet again.*

HANS...

He studied her closely throughout dinner. She had changed. It could have been attributed to many things but Hans was certain there was only one possibility. She had seen the notes.

Damn the maids! After all his precaution. There was no way of knowing how the revelation had affected her. He was stirred by her face now in the flickering half-shadow of the lighted candle on the table. She looked like a child might look who had just been deserted by its parents. Her eyes were the eyes of abandonment.

He had not intended to fall in love with her. It had simply happened that way. There was no questioning the depth of his feelings for her and he did not doubt the depth of what she felt for him. It was exactly why she sat there looking cornered, frightened, deceived. She would not know what to think or believe. Mrs. Pritchett had warned him something like this could happen and had held back her agreement to the plan until he had dispelled her fears.

"Mister Aldik, if I may say so, you are an attractive and romantic man," she had begun. "Not the ideal prerequisites for dealing with a thirty-one year old woman with the intelligence of her years but the retarded emotions of a young girl. More than that, a young girl who had, it would seem, been born in another time, another civilization. Confronted by a person such as yourself, Luanne, in her simple naivety, could misconstrue any small kindness you might show her for an indication of a commitment. And Mister Aldik, if she then had to be faced with the truth, she could crumble into a pitiful ruin."

He had understood and he had assured Mrs. Pritchett that he had no intention of even engaging the young woman in the most casual of friendships. She would only identify him as a fellow guest. But, he would be there in case the unexpected happened. If, for instance, there was really a man who could not and would not understand the seriousness of any flirtation. He would be there for any number of reasons, too. A faithful, unseen watch dog. The main objective was for her to take that first step out of her unnatural seclusion. She would have the opportunity of a choice. Someone had to give her that chance. It had to be Mrs. Pritchett. He was only insurance.

62

In the end Mrs. Pritchett had consented. But not until she had looked at him with uncommon wisdom and asked, "Why does she mean so much to you, Mister Aldik? Your interest has lasted a decade. Very little in today's world lasts that long. Not marriages, not power, not trends. This is a transitory world we inhabit. You know that better than anyone, and yet you remain constant in your desire to help a young woman whose life has never in any way crossed your own. Why?"

He thought he had known why. The book he felt possessed to write. The seed had buried itself in his mind when he first read of the murders and saw that photograph of Luanne. Only writing about it could rid him of that compelling image. But he could not tell Mrs. Pritchett that. And even if he had been able to, he knew the answer himself. "The book could be written from research. There was no need to ever meet Luanne Woodrow."

No reason—except something not explainable. It was a crime that would always, no matter what the jury's verdict, remain unsolved. Mass murder had been committed and there was no logical explanation for it. The one survivor could not comfort herself with a knowledge that would lead her to feel: *They died for that reason. I live to give that reason cause.* Gypsies, Jews, Hungarians, the survivors—had reached for similar security of reason. From the very beginning these murders had taken on an unusual significance to him. He had never been able to pinpoint *what* it was. The girl had been the key. She still was. Research could give him the facts but it would not tell him what any of these people thought. The girl could. And somewhere in those thoughts was the logical—even if insane—reason for such terrible butchery. He could not tell Mrs. Pritchett that either.

He told her, instead, a basically honest story. Luanne Woodrow had been a victim just as surely as the other seven. Their torture had ended swiftly. Luanne, alone, had been left to suffer all these years. He had seen this with all the survivors of the wars he had witnessed. He had felt helpless to aid *them,* but he could, he knew, in some small way help *this*

63

young woman. It had been a painfully long time before Mrs. Pritchett had agreed to the plan—but agree she finally did.

From the moment he had seen Luanne that first day he knew the truth. No matter what his other motives were, he loved this haunting creature so deeply that he had to become a part of her life. He realized in that instant that she had been a part of his life for over ten years. And he knew, undeniably, that he would not have gone to such great lengths for another living soul. She had walked up the stairs that day and past him, like something out of a Greek myth. He had thought of Artemis, the daughter of Zeus, goddess of the world when it was wrapped in darkness. The cypress was sacred to her. She was the floating huntress from the moon-world, Aphrodite in her immortal raiment. She was the myrtle and the dove and the swan and the sparrow. Or, no, perhaps she was really Zeus's sister, Hestia, the virgin goddess whose fire was always tended by six virgin priestesses. It was his destiny to love this woman and her destiny to be loved by him.

And yet, she sat before him now, on the brink of crumbling into that pitiful ruin Mrs. Pritchett had feared. And he was the cause. The color drained from her face, her shoulders drooped in defeat, and her hands no longer grasped even themselves for support. She had lost her will.

"Luanne," he whispered. She drew farther away from him. He leaned all the way across the table and grabbed her hands and held them vise-like in his own. There were no more tears for her to cry. She seemed empty, void of the human frailties. Her hands were lifeless in his own. "Oh, God, how do I say this, Luanne?" He could not tell her here. They would have to be alone. He would have to get her to trust him again. "I have to talk to you alone, Luanne. Away from here." He looked behind her to the lighted terrace. "There is a terrace right outside. It will be all right. You can face these windows and know how close people are to you. I won't touch you if you don't want me to but I have to tell you something very important—the truth, Luanne, to clear up the distortions that are confusing and frightening you now." She had not moved.

64

The candle flame had not flickered once from her breath. He released her limp hands. "This is very important, Luanne. Perhaps the most important moment in your life in many years. If you turn away from me now what we could have together might be lost forever. You might never again be able to find the road back. You knew this evening, before you came to my room, that there was a future out there somewhere with me. You *wanted* to believe that. You can. I love you. I love you so much that I have acted like an idiot. But there was never one moment, and there never will be, that you could not and cannot trust me. You believe me, don't you, Luanne?"

She did not reply and she remained motionless. Hans rose from his chair. "I am going out on the terrace." He offered her his hand. She got up and stood there a moment looking into his eyes. He patted her hand, holding it, and turned away, breathing with relief as he led her to the terrace door. He let go of her hand as he opened the door. She went past him and walked to the far end of the terrace and leaned against its low wall. Then she turned, watching him. He came quickly to her side.

"Thank you," he said humbly. He reached out for her hands again and she drew back. "Please, Luanne, it will give us both more courage." She considered it for a time and then, slowly, extended them to him. He took them in his own without glancing away from her face. He held her slightly away from him holding her hands firmly.

"I am aware that you know about the notes." He noticed only the faint tremble of her hands in his. "I have gone about the thing all wrong. I took the unnecessary chance of harming you and it was the last thing I wanted to happen. I am writing a book—about the Woodrow murders." He had said it in a clear, straight voice. His eyes never once turned from her glance—for that was all her impersonal look was. But her hands were telegraphing a more urgent message. They were moist with fear.

"I did not choose the subject arbitrarily," he continued. "I

65

was in London when the crime occurred. I was at your trial. I have been in touch with Mrs. Pritchett throughout the years simply to chart your progress. I am here in Klosters because you are here. I have, I know now, loved you for years, and I *have* to write this book—to dig up the bones and free you once and for all from the darkness that has surrounded you."

She turned aside now. The life had come back into her eyes and the hurt and confusion were showing. She clung to his hands. He pressed in closer to her but never removed his hands from hers. She looked chilled and he ached to take her in his arms and warm her. He spoke softly, gently into her ear. "It's the only way I know of bringing you back to this life where I am. Help me, Luanne."

She turned back to him, searching his face before she spoke. Her voice was controlled. There was a sobering maturity to it. "I trust you," was all she said.

His entire body trembled with relief. He clasped her hands tighter. Thoughts and plans spun through his head. Their time was shorter now. They could not go on as they had been for the past two days. She would be self-conscious now about talking about the past. He would have to unearth something that would stir her, something that would trigger her remembrances and make the book possible. That would mean getting to London for a day. That part was not difficult. The flight from Zurich was only an hour and thirty-five minutes. He could go in the morning and be back before dinner. But should he tell her he was going? No. She might be frightened he would not return. But if he went, could he leave her alone?

He released his clasp now and placed his arm around her waist and walked back with her toward the restaurant. "What I think you need," he said warmly but as lightly as he could manage, "is a day without me. Then you will appreciate me more when we are together." He paused with her before going inside. "This time I have a plan. They have marvelous tours which travel this area every day. There will be friendly people on them, mostly tourist types. You can go to St. Moritz and

66

back if you like. They stop along the way and you will eat at some pleasant café. It will be a nice change for you. I can put you on the bus early in the morning and meet you when you return in the evening. They are usually out about nine or ten hours. You can tell me all about it at dinner. In the meantime, I will spend the day on the slopes and have something to tell you."

He waited for what seemed an eternity. Finally, she nodded her agreement. She smiled weakly but it encouraged him and he opened the door and led her back inside.

HANS...

They had breakfast together early the next morning. She had been reflective and somewhat distant but there was a spark in her eyes that could have been defined as anticipation and there was now a lightness to her step as he walked with her down the short incline from the Weisshaus to the Verkehrsburea from where the bus tours departed. She was wearing a tweed coat and her hair was caught back with a gay scarf. There was a high wind and she walked with her head turned way from it so that he could not see her face. It was cold and gray but there was no fog and the wind tasted fresh and the air carried the scent of pine. The church clock struck eight and the milk wagon turned in front of them headed for the Molkerei. The large tin containers on the rear of the wagon clattered and broke the morning stillness as the wagon bobbed along the snow-rutted street. The bells the donkey wore rang out a happier sound.

There was a large group waiting to board the bus and Hans was thankful that many of the tourists were English. "I know you are going to enjoy this," he told her when it was time for her to board. "You return about six and I will be right here waiting for you."

Luanne replied, "It's only a block to the Weisshaus. We might be delayed. I would rather meet you in the dining room at the table at half-past seven." She was smiling and he detected a new warmth in her smile. The driver started the motor. "Well," she said, "it is time." She stepped into the bus and then came back again. "You were right. We both need today to ourselves. But I want you to know how very much I am looking forward to this evening." She raised herself up on her tiptoes and kissed him lightly on the cheek and then turned away before he had a chance to say anything to her.

He stood watching through the half-steamed windows as she settled into a seat beside an elderly English lady, school teacher variety. She sat with her back to the window but when the bus began to roll she turned, a moment of panic on her face as she searched for him on the sidewalk and then relief when she found he was still standing there. She raised her slim, gloved hand and waved at him. Her smile returned briefly to her face. Then she was gone.

Hans fought the wind as he ran up the hill to the Weisshaus to the waiting taxi he had ordered the night before. He would take the helicopter service from Klosters to Kloten Airport in Zurich and be there in plenty of time to board the nine-thirty-five plane to London. That would get him to London Airport by ten past eleven and with luck he would be in the West End by noon, giving him three and a half hours before returning to London Airport for the journey back. Her new plan to meet him at half-past seven in the dining room meant a safer margin for him.

He would carefully plan his time after his first meeting. He had decided during the night (which he had spent virtually without sleep) that the first person he would seek out would be Claudia Mitchell. She was certainly a person who might be able to chart some direction for his next move. It had been a long way back in her past, but she was a very bright and seemingly sensitive woman and, according to several news articles at the time, had known Ira Sean Woodrow very well indeed. She had never appeared in court, but a private deposition had been taken. However, it had not been read at the trial, nor had a word of it reached the press.

Hans reached Claudia Mitchell without any problem. She had a listed telephone and he rang her from Kloten and made an appointment to see her immediately upon his arrival in London. Now, as Mrs. Mitchell entered her own reception room to greet him, he wondered at his own impetuosity. They had never met and knew each other only by their respective literary reputations. He was surprised by her femininity. It threw him off-guard for a moment. Her work was terse, uncompromising and quite masculine. As the petite, electric figure crossed to him, and extended a light, small-boned hand for him to shake, he began to feel this meeting ill-advised. One does not query a married French lady on her lovers—even though they may be dead.

"Hans Aldik!" She took his hand and held it warmly between both of hers. Hans was aware of her perfume. It was not a scent that he could identify. "We should have met years ago!" she said sincerely and squeezed his hand slightly.

"I wish we had," he told her.

She smiled delightedly and let go of his hand. "Incredible! Less than three hours ago you call me from Zurich—and now! You are here! A drink perhaps? Coffee? Tea?"

"No, thank you." He was feeling awkward—not knowing where to begin. He had told her nothing when he rang her. Simply that he had been an admirer of hers for years and was going to be in London for one day and wanted to speak to her about a matter that much concerned them both.

She sat down on a graceful, green velvet Victorian chair. She curled her legs beneath the soft fabric of her wide skirt. Her head, resting against the velvet, made her blond hair like golden wheat upon green fields. "Sit down!" she said, with welcome more than command. Hans sat opposite her on a blue silk couch across the room.

The room was highly individual, each piece carefully and personally selected. It was, though, above all else, a woman's room, of gentle colors set in rounds and curves and graceful sloping arches. There was no sign of her husband, nothing that might hint that a man lived here with her. A seascape hung over the carved wood mantelpiece. It set the color scheme for the room, blues mottled with grays and greens accented with frothy whites. The woods had been bleached to their lightest tones, resembling driftwood, and the rug was the color of shifting sand. There were fresh, heavy greens wherever you looked and huge bowls of shaggy yellow and white daisies and asters. On the walls were a number of good paintings, French Impressionists. There was a Degas dancing girl on a pedestal backed by a hand-painted silk screen. One wall was lined with books, their covers impeccable, their arrangement exact. They were not jammed or crowded into the shelves. They were kept orderly with numerous white dolphin marble book-ends, and the spaces between housed Wedgwood china and Dresden figurines. There were large windows along one side which overlooked Hyde Park. On them were hung gossamer panels of white lace which were drawn back so that the thick greens of the park were brought into the room. There was a double window on another wall which overlooked Park Lane and carried the eye as far as the gardens of Buckingham Palace. Nothing in the room was worn, or soiled, or disordered, and Claudia Mitchell appeared to be much the same kind of woman as her room.

"I quite liked your last book," she said, her green eyes appraising him, her voice throaty and accented as if she were speaking her native French. "Oh, I have read all your books. The last was the only one I truly liked." She made no apologies for saying exactly what she thought. "You are a strange writer. You never commit yourself politically. Your books have suffered from this."

"I am not a political writer," he said without apology either.

"A shame!" Her head was angled so that the light fell along one side of her face. It was an exquisitely molded face. She had the kind of bones artists and photographers sought to capture but there was not one portrait or photograph of her in the room. It was as if this woman was so sure of herself that she intended to dominate the room with only her physical presence. She had been quite correct.

"I believe that when a writer becomes too involved in making a political statement he loses his power as a writer. You are talking about the ability to sway people. I write to involve them. Whatever action they take is then entirely of their own making." He watched her closely as he spoke. Her smile remained fixed. She was being the hostess who, though she thought her guest's statement ridiculous, would in great dignity refrain from making him *feel* ridiculous.

"Are you working on a novel now?" she inquired, her interest sincere enough to make Hans aware there were only two of them in the room and that her attention was entirely on him.

"Yes, I am."

"And somehow that is why you are here?" Claudia Mitchell caught the small nervous smile on Hans's lips. "Come now! There is no reason for you to be ill at ease with me. We have never met. There is no one between us. No past memories." She sat up now, swinging her legs around in front of her and placed them close together, her small feet only touching the floor with her flexed toes. Her elbows rested on her slender thighs as her hand cupped her magnificent fine-boned chin. It was difficult to think of this woman as in her fifties. She appeared timeless. She raised one natural, unplucked eyebrow. "Or are there?"

"I am here primarily because of the novel I am working on," he managed to say—unable to bring himself yet to the subject of the Woodrow murders and Ira Sean.

"Primarily. Ah! That is the operative word." She thought for a moment. "Are you going to tell me what your novel is about?"

"It is still vague," he replied.

"Better now than after it is published." She laughed. But there was no mockery in the laugh. She was sharing the dangers of their mutual profession with him. Poking fun with him at the pitfalls.

He returned the laugh, conscious of the sound of it, fearing it might sound hollow. "Well, I am basically a war correspondent," he began. "This new book is no real departure. A minor one though. It is not about the same kind of war as generals plot, though it is still about violence." He stood up, glanced over to her. She sat there patiently waiting for what he was about to say. He began to pace the room as he continued. "It is a 'non-fictional novel' based on an incident that occurred a long time ago. I never forgot it and I guess I knew all along I would eventually write about it. I said it was still vague because it deals with real people and until I begin to have some true inkling of what made those people tick, it will remain vague."

Claudia Mitchell seemed suddenly weary. Her eyelids lowered for a moment and her thick lashes swept the high cheekbones of her face. He waited for her to look back at him. "Oh, the Woodrow murders," she said softly. "You want me to tell you what I know about Irish. What *can* I tell you, Mister Aldik? He had it in him to be a great writer. He was devoted to world peace. He was against nuclear warfare because the innocent were involved, but he could well have murdered all of them to keep them from breeding monsters like themselves. He thought them monsters, you see. But I have no more idea than you if he in fact did kill them."

"I am not a detective." He smiled. "I did not expect you to know if he did or did not commit the murders. I simply want to find out what made him—and the others—go round." He lifted a small side chair and crossed the room with it, putting it down within a few feet of her, and sat backward on it. He was very much aware how the action, and the sight of him sitting as he was, disrupted the studied grace of the room. He noticed her disapproval but simply went on speaking.

72

"You were very close to him, Mrs. Mitchell. Even if he was not guilty, something must have been happening in that family just prior to their deaths that would give some clue as to why anyone would have killed the entire family. From what I have already learned there seemed little chance at the time of any of them breeding at all. They kept much to themselves—except for Irish."

"I am afraid I cannot help you much, Mister Aldik. I had not seen Irish for weeks before the incident and it had been months since we had been close. In plain language—since we had slept together," she replied. She was not self-conscious in the least and spoke about herself as if she were talking about a total stranger.

"I am sorry. I have overstepped my . . ."

She interrupted his apology. "You came here. See it through." She was smiling.

Hans was caught by the courage of the woman. "Had you been seeing him very long?" he asked, embarrassed to put the question to her.

"Our affair lasted two years," she said without hesitation. She relaxed now, her smile easier. She reached out and touched Hans's cheek for a moment, disarming him completely. Then she smoothed out her skirt as she began to talk. "We met when he came to work on the Committee for Disarmament. I was very active at the time. He disarmed me but we did very precious little as a committee. Not enough to stop them making bombs, nor even testing them! He was an exceptional person. You could always feel that about him. But it surprised me when I did go to bed with him. Our first meetings were so asexual. He came home with me one night after a meeting to borrow some books. My husband was away on business and Irish simply stayed on for a fortnight while he was gone. He had not yet published anything. Still, he was being subsidized by a publisher who sensed the same thing in him I did. Real genius." She leaned back now drinking in the warm noonday winter sun. She was remembering now.

"Irish hated this flat. He said it made him feel clumsy. He thought it was a room set up to castrate any man who walked through the front door. In the beginning he thought that about me as well! The next time he would not come here. I bought a barge and we used it as a sort of floating lover's hideaway. But, to our surprise, we both found that we wrote unusually well there. It was an added bonus. He began to spend longer periods of time on the barge writing. Writing was never easy for Irish. He wrote slowly, painfully. Always in longhand. My husband never suspected. We were together —working—mostly during the daytime, in the evenings—only when my husband was away. But he often stayed alone for long periods of time on the barge." She reached farther back into her memories. "I would work at the desk and Irish would be seated in a nearby chair. He was like a small schoolboy. He would hand me each page and insist I go over every word and we would discuss each nuance. I am not saying you could ever 'lead' Irish. But he listened. If it was advice he agreed with, he would alter his work—but only then. I did not like the first book. I made that very clear. I don't fancy the ambiguity of allegories. It never stopped him from completing it. His second book, however, I did like and believed it held great promise."

"What was it about?" Hans asked.

"A group of men—like the United Nations—who annihilated anyone anywhere by fair vote, naturally, who might trigger off a nuclear war." She smiled again. "I didn't really approve of that plot. But the writing was vital and outspoken. At least he was saying what he really thought."

Hans returned her smile. "Do you know what happened to that manuscript?" he asked.

"No. I made inquiries after the incident but I never could locate it. He had never submitted it to the publisher. The police did not list it among his effects in the house. (They were kind enough to allow me to see the list.) It is possible the girl has it. But I never contacted her," she said.

"Luanne, you mean?" he asked.

74

"Ummm." She passed lightly over the name. "It was not listed among her effects either. The police allowed me a glance at that as well. But she could have hidden it before—or burnt it after. She had time."

"But you never went to see her or spoke to her about it?"

"I am not one to exert unnecessary energy, Mister Aldik. If she had it, she never would have given it to me of all people. Purely a feminine reaction, of course. I was the enemy. She had been having an affair with her brother, you see."

The room seemed to close in on Hans. The possibility had never crossed his mind. Now he knew, with a sickening honesty, that it was not only possible, but probable. The act did not revolt him. Anyone who was brought up with the Bible was also brought up on the simple acceptance of the incest within its pages. This explanation could account for almost everything about Luanne's seclusion, her guilt, her fear. But she had been nearly seven years younger than her older brother. If incest had occurred, seduction had been used —possibly rape—and the brother had to be the one who sustained the relationship. There was an entirely new picture of Ira Scan Woodrow in his mind now. "Are you sure?" Hans asked, but he had already accepted it as fact.

"He told me about it. He seldom spoke anything but the truth," she said. Hans was filled with questions he wanted to ask but he could ask none of them. She continued on. "He talked about his family only once. It was not a subject he cared to discuss with me and so I let it go at that. He thought of them as members of a class which no longer existed. A decadent society, but Irish, no matter how he fought it, was always one of them. He would run away to me—but if one must run from something you may be assured one must return. Irish often did."

"Why did you stop seeing each other?" Hans asked quietly.

"He stopped coming. That was all. I represented truth you see and, as I said, he demanded truth of himself. He understood he had to come to terms with his family once and for all before returning to me. I never contacted him. I felt he would do so when he was ready and not before." She sat up brightly for a moment. "Are you sure I cannot offer you a drink of any sort?"

"No, thank you," he replied. She immediately relaxed. "What did he look like?" Hans asked. "Oh, I have seen the newspaper photographs, of course—and the study on the back of his book jacket, but what did he look like to the people who knew him? To you?"

She leaned back in her chair again and closed her eyes. "A poet," she said quickly. She opened her eyes and sat up straight but her gaze was fixed across the room as if Irish Woodrow was standing there and she could see every detail of the man. "He was terribly myopic. It gave his eyes a far-off, always misty look. I could sit for ten and fifteen minutes at a time studying his eyes. Great black pools in a lean, pale face. He had a great deal of hurt in those eyes and a great deal of tenderness. He was tall, but too thin and almost hungry looking, to be an imposing figure. He was loosely put together, like some string-tied puppet. Yes"—she said as if seeing him again before her—"his face caved in and his fingers were tied together to his hands with knots! He was very beautiful!" She sat there quietly for a moment. "I loved him." She sat back now and considered that. "A part of me passed with him, at any rate." She turned to Hans now. Her face clouded. "Why do you want to write this story, Mister Aldik?" she asked almost crossly.

"I read about it a long time ago and I never forgot it," he replied.

"Not enough reason. It has been ten years." She studied him closely and his face reddened as if he was a lad whose teacher found him cheating. "What is she like?" Hans started to protest. "Come now! It must be the girl! What is she like?"

"How can I really tell, Mrs. Mitchell? I am in love with her," he finally said.

"And you are writing this book because you want her but must exonerate her first?" she asked in a harder voice than she had used throughout the entire meeting. Hans rose quickly

76

from the chair. "Oh, don't bother to get angry, Mister Aldik. I had to ask that question, but as soon as I said it and saw your face I knew it was wrong. However, I am sorry to say to you that there is nothing more boring than an author who turns detective, unless it is an author who falls in love with the subject of his own novel." Hans stood there still angry. She smiled patronizingly. The forgiving teacher. "Would you mind replacing the chair where you found it?" she asked gently.

He turned away and replaced the chair. When he faced her again she stood gracefully in the center of her room, her small hand extended to him, a warm smile across her face. "Come now—we shall have a drink together after all." She took his hand. Hans felt the sensation through his entire body. When she cared to be, Claudia Mitchell was one of the most sensual women he had ever met. She crossed with him to a hidden cabinet below the bookshelves. She did not release his hand as she opened the bar. The decanters gleamed, the glasses sparkled. She finally let go of his hand. "Sherry," she stated as she poured some out into two glasses. "I hope it is all right. I find drinking hard whisky makes me drunk and makes others terribly unreliable." She handed him the glass. "Until we meet again," she whispered.

"Until we meet again," he repeated.

"Soon, I hope." She smiled.

They drank their sherry in silence, very much aware of each other's presence.

HANS . . .

Laurel Groves could not be seen from the road. It squatted behind a tangle of trees that were strapped back by a long brick wall that was seven feet high and was covered in thick, green moss still damp from an early morning raining. Branches of bramble roses now bare in the early winter of St. John's Wood, trailed along the foot-wide shelf at the top of the wall. The overhang of shrubbery kept the sun from drying the small droplets of rain water that clung like small thorns to the barren brambles. Hans opened the front gate and walked up the brick path, but did not see Laurel Groves until he was virtually at the front door. It was a two-story building but the two groping arms thrust out as if reaching to grasp the nearest clump of trees, were only one story high. Smoke rose from the chimney. A frail light shone through the tightly drawn front drapes. Those old, thick brick walls held back all sound.

It was his first visit. The one time he had seen Mrs. Pritchett they had thought it advisable to meet outside of Laurel Groves. Now he was glad he had come as it would give him a greater insight into what Luanne's life had been like these past ten years. Mrs. Pritchett had been surprised when he rang. He noted the disapproval in her voice. He knew he would not be in for an easy time since her tone indicated that she thought him derelict in leaving Luanne alone in Switzerland even though he had carefully explained that she was safely on a bus tour for the day. He had not intended to contact Mrs. Pritchett. It was Claudia Mitchell's mention of the unfinished manuscript that had been the deciding factor. If, in fact, it existed—and if Luanne had held on to it—Laurel Groves seemed the only logical place for it to be. He thought about asking Luanne directly, waiting until he returned to her, but then he would have to tell her about his visit with Claudia Mitchell and he felt the time was not ripe for that.

The thick oak door opened and a Sister, immaculately dressed in a starched uniform, faced him. She wore a tight expression of annoyance at having been interrupted. "Yes?" she impatiently greeted him.

"Hans Aldik. Mrs. Pritchett is expecting me."

"I see." She let him in and closed the door and turned on her heel. There was a crunch of stiff shoe leather on the polished floor. "This way," she said curtly over her shoulder.

78

The interior of Laurel Groves came as a pleasant shock. It was cheerful and well-heated and—above all—light. Hans could see that the daylight came from wide panels of glass at the rear of the building which overlooked the gardens. The drapes were not drawn across the windows as on the windows in front. It was obvious that Laurel Groves did what it could to seal itself off from the outside world. The reception hall was filled with print chintz sofas and bowls of fresh-cut flowers. There was a fire in the fireplace and the smell of dry logs burning. There were, in fact, no damp or musty odors. "Our guests entertain for Sunday tea in this room," the Sister told him with pride.

"It's very nice," he said sincerely.

"We grow our own flowers. There is a hothouse for those of our guests who enjoy that sort of thing," she continued, turning now and offering him a smile to tell him she had thought about it and finally approved of him.

They were now at the rear of the building standing mid-way in a long gallery that rimmed the entire ground floor. The gallery appeared to be a fairly new addition. The sun gleamed through its wide sliding-glass doors and warmed Hans as he waited for his guide who had momentarily paused to consult with another Sister. The grounds were vast and rolling but in the area just beyond the gallery were patches of separate gardens. Laurel Groves at one time had been a private estate. During the war it had housed a hospital. After, it had been taken over privately. The gallery and newer decor were probably added at that time.

The Sister motioned for him to follow her again. Opening onto the gallery were large private and semi-private rooms. Their front shades were tightly drawn, but the rooms were lighted well and had double doors flung open now to catch the warmth of the midday sun. The bedridden turned their sunken eyes to Hans as he passed and held out a hand gesturing for him to come visit their bedside. All eyes were on Hans—watching him. He glanced away.

The Sister continued her conversation. "They all dress on

Sunday," she confided. "Most of their friends are gone. Some have not had a visitor in over five years, even those with living children. I would prefer they did not come at all. Creates a terrible do after they leave. It sometimes takes a month to get them back to normal after one of those visits." She paused. Then she turned to him. "I hope I didn't speak out of place. You aren't a relative, I trust?"

"No, I'm not."

The Sister smiled with relief. She craned her head, looking out to the grounds beyond, sighting something out of the corner of her eye. There was a soft wind that had risen and it hummed at the corners of the sliding doors. "Oh, my! Jenny again!" A small, withered gray form, clad only in a thin silk dress, her stockings fallen like two great tears around her spindled ankles, stood securing some green vines to a post in one of the garden patches. "Those doors ring a bell whenever they are opened but Jenny manages to elude us anyway!" She took a few steps forward. "Sister Kennedy!" she called. A young nurse appeared in a doorway. "Jenny is outside again, without a wrap and her legs bare." She shook her head.

"I have Maude on the bedpan, Sister MacGibbons," she replied. Sister Kennedy was a youngster. No more than nineteen. Her face was free of make-up and her hair was neatly drawn from her radiant face and held back partly with her cap.

"Where's Sister Markle?" Sister MacGibbons asked.

"Writing a letter for Lady Eastbrook," the young Sister replied and took a step closer. She smiled at Hans—then quickly turned aside.

"There is no one left for her to write," the older Sister commented dryly.

"It's to Mister Churchill to tell him about the roses," Sister Kennedy confided. "I told her yesterday that he was no longer living but she just said, 'nonsense!' to me and insisted I go on with the letter. She didn't trust that I had posted the letter. She has Sister Markle rewriting it now."

"Oh, all right." Sister MacGibbons turned back to Hans

as the young nurse spun quickly on her heel and went back to her patient. "Mrs. Pritchett's office is at the far end of this corridor. The only door on the right." She did not wait to get a cloak for herself but slid open the door nearest to them. A bell sounded down the full length of the corridor and another Sister with a pad and pencil in her hand peered up the corridor from a doorway. Then, seeing it was Sister MacGibbons, she disappeared again. Hans stood for a moment watching the brittle Sister MacGibbons, unbending in the wind, walk across some patches of dirt garden to the little old lady's side. The small figure leaned childlike against the Sister's sturdy body and they both started back toward the sliding doors.

Hans continued up the corridor. A hunched figure in a wheel chair blocked his path. He smiled uneasily. "I'm sorry . . ." There was no response. "May I pass? I have an appointment with Mrs. Pritchett." Two dead eyes looked out of yellow parchment skin at him. The thought that the woman was paralyzed and could not move the wheel chair, occurred to Hans. "Perhaps I could wheel you where you would like to go?" He took a step forward and as he did the woman reeled the chair so quickly out of his path that it seemed she would surely tip over. The Sister with the pad had appeared in the hallway and moved quickly enough to save an accident.

"Mrs. Sydney! Now that was very naughty. We are not rude to our guests. Come and visit Lady Eastbrook. She has a lovely rose from the hothouse she wants to show you." The Sister took hold of the back of the wheel chair and piloted it down the long sun-streaked gallery and presumably into a room belonging to Lady Eastbrook.

He continued on, starting past a room which contained a television set. The room was filled with wheel chairs, their occupants all wearing headsets, privately tuned into the sound. None of them looked up at Hans as they were too engrossed in the program they were watching. Hans glanced at it for a moment. It was a children's program, typical of the BBC's afternoon fare.

The door to Mrs. Pritchett's office was slightly ajar and Hans rapped lightly. "Come in," Mrs. Pritchett called in her clear, unruffled voice. As he entered she drew the curtains so that the room lost most of its light. Then, as she crossed to welcome Hans, she flicked on a lamp and pushed a buzzer.

"We'll take lunch in here, Mister Aldik, if it suits you," she said.

There was a feeble knock at the door. "Come in, Ada," Mrs. Pritchett called. A maid with small eyes and a meek manner, poked her head into the room. "Luncheon for two in here, Ada. And tea for myself." She turned to Hans. "Tea, Mister Aldik?" she inquired.

"That will do fine," he replied.

"Two teas."

"Yes, Mrs. Pritchett." Ada departed, closing the door behind herself.

Hans was impressed again with the handsome woman who now crossed to the comfortable sofa and motioned for him to join her. "Do sit down, Mister Aldik." She waited until Hans had done so. "Now suppose we dispense with any small conversation and get right to the heart of the matter. There are obviously things you have not told me about yourself and your interest in Miss Woodrow, Mister Aldik. That seems like a good place to begin." Her gray eyes were flinty, her silver hair impeccably groomed. She sat in an uncompromising position, her back straight, her head high, her long tapering hands folded in her lap.

Hans decided the only approach was a counter one. He ignored her opening remarks. "I am glad we met here this time, and I have to compliment you on an unusual establishment. But it is no place for a young woman like Luanne Woodrow to have spent ten years of her life. Why did you allow that, Mrs. Pritchett?"

"I see." She smiled weakly. "Well, Mister Aldik, suppose

82

we play the game your way for a time then?" She wasn't really asking a question and she smoothed out the smile on her face and looked rather sharply at him. "Miss Woodrow *chose* to reside here. It was never a case of what I would allow."

"I'm sorry. I didn't mean to offend you, but I just find it rather appalling. Look, let me start over again." They both settled back. "Was she ill when she first came to Laurel Groves?"

"Not physically. Mentally—perhaps."

"Was a psychiatrist consulted?"

"This is not a home for residents who need psychiatric care. Every applicant must be passed. We are one of the finest establishments for the elderly. There is a doctor in daily attendance. Our Sisters are all highly qualified. We have a psychiatrist on our Board of Directors and we do not take any applicant whose needs could only be properly treated in an institution. Laurel Groves is not an institution. It is, as I said—a home. When Miss Woodrow came here, what she needed was exactly that. She had been under terrible emotional stress. She had had a strange childhood and been through a bewildering experience. She was given a thorough psychiatric examination before we admitted her. There was never any question of her sanity, or her potential for final adjustment. A year after she came to us she was qualified to leave. But the question was where—and to what? England had not forgotten the tragedy. Newsmen still attempted constant ruses to see her and interview her, even here, and a bad experience could have shattered what we had repaired. The decision, not just mine, Mister Aldik, but the Board of Directors', was to allow her to remain here until it was thought she had been forgotten. In four or five years time the newsmen stopped coming—except on the anniversary of the tragedy. I began to prepare Miss Woodrow for her departure at that time. By then, unfortunately, she refused to go."

Mrs. Pritchett sat thoughtfully for a time. "Which brings me to you, Mister Aldik."

At that moment Ada entered the room with the luncheon trays and the conversation was left in abeyance while she set them on a table before the sofa. She stood smiling over the hot dishes for a moment as if she had prepared the food herself and was admiring her handiwork. It did, indeed, look very appetizing. It was served on good china and was garnished to please the eye. There was poached turbot with hollandaise, brightened with a sprig of watercress; small new potatoes delicately buttered and sprinkled with parsley; and fresh-cut green beans placed symmetrically along the side of the plate.

"Lovely, Ada, thank you." Mrs. Pritchett approved.

Ada beamed with pride. "Thank you," she said and bobbed up and down in a quick curtsy and then quickly left the room, making doubly sure she had secured the door behind herself.

"As you were about to say," Mrs. Pritchett said, as she spread her serviette carefully over her knees.

"I wasn't about to—but I shall." Hans's voice was severe. "I took a look around this room, Mrs. Pritchett. No pictures of your family. I venture to guess you have none. But somewhere in your past there was a husband. You have known love—and somehow lost it. Luanne is a proper age to have been your daughter." He rose from the sofa. "You should have forced her to leave, Mrs. Pritchett, and you know that!"

The cloud of Luanne was between them for a long moment. Hans turned away and looked out the far windows to the thick brick wall which was green with its heavy moist growth of moss.

"You love her," Mrs. Pritchett said matter-of-factly. "I should have guessed. And you want to make sure . . ." Hans turned angrily and looked down at her. "As I just assured you, Mister Aldik, I have my other guests to consider. Miss Woodrow would never have entered these doors if I had any question about her—responsibility."

Hans sat down again—closer to her this time. "Neither have I," he said earnestly. "But I understand things now I did not before. She feels guilty. Responsible. I am certain she thinks her brother did it *for her*." He grabbed one of

84

Mrs. Pritchett's hands without being conscious of the action. "I have to prove he was not guilty," he said.

"But the court found him so," she replied calmly.

He let go of her hand, embarrassed, but he pressed on. "If that is true, then I mean to find out why he did it."

"And if he did it, believing in his sick mind, that it was *for* Luanne?" she asked, not continuing her noonday meal. A more intimate atmosphere had been struck. Mrs. Pritchett had dropped the formalities of last names: Miss Woodrow was now—Luanne.

"Then we have to show her how sick his mind was," he said.

She picked it up immediately. "We?" she inquired.

"We, Mrs. Pritchett. Because we share the mutual responsibility. We, and only we—love her."

Mrs. Pritchett placed her fish knife and fork carefully on the edge of her plate and pushed the plate farther from her. She was quiet and thoughtful as she carefully refolded her serviette back along its original creases. Hans waited patiently for her to speak. "How was it you thought I might help?" she finally asked.

Hans got up again and began to pace slowly as he thought about it. "I don't know," he told her. He stopped. "I did find out one thing. Her brother had been working on a book at the time of . . ." He paused before continuing, "The tragedy. The manuscript was never found. But Luanne might have kept it. She could have hidden it." He sat down on the edge of the sofa. "It was a novel that apparently had nothing to do with the murders. But it *was about* murder. That manuscript could have something in it that could prove *something*. I just don't know what yet."

"If Luanne had kept it," she said logically, "it would seem it would have proved something *already* to her, if indeed, it proved anything at all."

"Not necessarily. She might never have read it. Never summoned the courage it would have taken for her to read it," he said.

"Well, I don't see . . ."

He interrupted her. The thought just came to his conscious thinking—though it had obviously been there since he rang Mrs. Pritchett after leaving Claudia Mitchell. "Would you allow me to search her room here?" he asked.

"It is quite irregular," she answered immediately but there was not the ring of stubbornness in her statement. She was already considering the alternative herself.

"But will you allow it?" he pressed.

She stood up. He was aware that she was nearly as tall as he. She was looking him almost directly in his eyes. "If you find a manuscript here I will have to refuse its removal from these premises," she said precisely.

"I give you my word." He was sweating. He took his handkerchief out of his pocket and mopped his brow. He glanced up at the clock on the wall. It was almost two. She crossed over to her desk and unlocked a side drawer and brought out a key and handed it to him. He took it eagerly. "Thank you," he mumbled, as he stuffed the handkerchief back. He turned, then faced her again. "You'll come with me, of course?" he asked.

She shook her head. "No, Mister Aldik. I won't. But I would be grateful if you would stop by here on your way out to return the key."

"Naturally." He turned to go.

"Her room is not on the ground floor. It is now in the main building where my own is. She moved there five years ago. If you will return to the reception room, you will find a door on your left. Beyond it is the stairway. Luanne's room is at the far end of the upper corridor, facing the front. It is a room that looks beyond our gates." There was a coolness in her tone, as though it was there to wash away any corrosive emotion.

Hans thanked her again and went out. He made his way swiftly up the gallery. The Sisters, assuming he was leaving, gave him curt nods of dismissal as he passed. The young nurse, Miss Kennedy, smiled at him. "Come again!" she trilled.

86

He was aware that Mrs. Sydney was approaching him in her wheel chair. As it came close Hans pivoted to one side, sliding past and then quickly continued on until he reached the reception room. Then he ran up the stairs.

The key turned easily in the lock but he hesitated before opening the door. He caught his breath and swung it inward, stepped inside and closed the door. He stood there for a long while. It was not the sort of room he had expected. It was as though Luanne might materialize at any moment, her essence so filled the walls. It was extremely large, made up into a bed-sitter. There was an old sewing machine carefully stored in a corner and Hans could imagine her there making the delicate robin's-egg blue silk spread, and the incredibly fragile, putty-white silk covers on the sofa and the two pull-up chairs. The sofa and bed each contained about six small petit point pillows; each with a complicated original design. She would have worked on them in front of the bay window where a rocking chair stood, a small sewing table beside it.

Hans crossed to the window and glanced out from the vantage point of the rocker. It looked over the top of the wall that held back Laurel Groves, to the wide road which fronted it. She would have sat there in winter and watched the children in their bright green uniform coats as they made their way to the school at the top of the road. In spring, the gardens across from Laurel Groves would be red with rhododendron and the trees pale green with bud leaves. If she turned her head—just so—she could have seen the high black roofs of the taxis and the gay red and green buses on the High street—and yet, heard nothing, for the distance kept out the sounds. He was less critical of Mrs. Pritchett now. Luanne had, at least, achieved a half-life of her own. He turned away and back into the room.

It contained only one wardrobe, one double chest of drawers and two bedside commodes in which the manuscript could be hiding. He started with the wardrobe and systematically worked his way through it. There were clean clothes, hung neatly and primly, and boxes smelling of camphor which held carefully sorted clothes that were out-of-season. The bureau drawers held a musky perfume which lingered for a long while after they were closed. It was a scent that Luanne carried with her. One he liked.

There was no manuscript in the drawers. He crossed to the bed, he started to sit down on the silk cover and then decided against it. He leaned over the first low commode. It contained a few books. He examined their covers. Collected works of poetry and a much-read volume of Shakespeare. The other commode was empty.

Hans fought back his disappointment. Where else? Where else? He kept asking himself—the question throbbing in his brain like a pulse beat. It came to him almost instantly.

The police had taken inventories of all items in the house, on Luanne, and on the bodies. But one other person had seen Luanne *before* the police had arrived. She was never suspect. She was never searched. He conjured up an immediate picture in his mind of all the chars and household ladies he had seen walking the streets in London. They all wore the same low, broad ugly shoes which gave them an identifiable walk, and they leaned to one side weighted with thick, worn carrier bags, which held their change of clothing and their meager purchases and gratuities from their employers.

Mrs. Pritchett would have Mrs. Devlin's address. That is where he would go next.

LUANNE...

The bus stopped at a small village, and I remained on board where all the other passengers disappeared into a nearby guest-house for lunch. I watched them all hurry across the fresh snow that had been falling, leaving their great boot tracks in it. The driver came back and told me we would be there an hour and that the rest of the passengers had gone in for their lunch. I smiled winningly at him and said I wasn't hungry and assured him it was all right, I would rather sit where I was and read for the time. He shrugged his shoulders and left me there. I heard him call out in Swiss-German to a friend as he stepped down from the bus. He was answered by loud laughter and enthusiastic greetings. I sat there in the growing cold, a traveling rug about me, until the sounds had all faded away.

It had been true. I did think both Hans and I needed the day to ourselves. There had been so much that had happened in a span of so few days. *He knew and he loved me.* All night long that had repeated itself over and over again in my thoughts. It was as though the end of a nightmare was in sight. But the end was the most terrifying part of a bad dream, so fearful it caused you to awaken.

Would he still be there if I finally awakened from this nightmare? The answer rushed at me. It was like the cascade of water down a steep fall, or the voice of the wind in a roaring blizzard. "Yes! Yes! Yes!" My heart was singing now. It could not contain itself to the confines of my body. I thought, "People will think me mad. I will leap from this bus. Dance in the snow. One of those ritualistic dances. The rites of spring. The reaping of the harvest. The coming of the rains after a long, stifling drought.

"Mad," they would say. "Obviously bonkers!"

I tossed the travel rug aside and stretched until I could feel the breath going out of me. I knew I could not stand an entire afternoon in the bus talking with Miss Winthrop, the teacher who was riding beside me, about horticulture and the breeding of basset hounds. Hans was on the slopes. If I returned to Klosters we both would still have the afternoon to ourselves. I had an overwhelming desire to reread his book again and to see that sensible handwriting on the inside cover. I decided I would go by myself to the top of the hill where we had gone the first evening we had been together. I would spend the rest of the day in thoughts of him, of the two of us. There was so much for me to get used to, so little time to fortify myself for the end of my nightmare.

I found the driver at the table nearest the door just inside the café. I was grateful I had not had to pass Miss Winthrop and make excuses. I told him I had remembered something terribly urgent I had left unattended in Klosters and that I would have to return. He glanced at his watch. There would be a train in less than five minutes, he told me. It would be a one hour ride by rail. I thanked him with a great deal of profusion as if he was personally responsible for the train schedule that would return me so soon to Klosters. I would be back at the Weisshaus just past one. I could sit at our table and have lunch seated in his chair, looking out to the terrace where we had stood the night before.

I ran down the road. The train was coming around the last turn into the station. I boarded it almost before it had stopped, almost before the passengers for this village had disembarked. I walked through to the second-class car and sat down on a wooden seat. The train was only in the village for a minute. I pressed my face to the pane, so glad to see it growing smaller in the distance. The conductor took my fare, smiling widely at me. I was sure my childish excitement must show, like a youngster with the remains of the jam on his face! I settled back and carefully scanned each slope we passed, knowing well enough that if one of the tiny figures I only saw as dots on the slopes had been Hans I could not have known it. But when you are truly in love for the first time in your life you are highly illogical.

"Balmy," they were probably saying. "Look at that insipid grin on her face!"

I was so impatient when the train arrived in Klosters, I nearly knocked over some children who were standing in the gangway. I felt I was home from the moment I stood on the station platform and I looked out to the welcoming arms of the mountains. I walked briskly down the main street to the Weisshaus. The shops were closed as they would be from twelve until two p.m. The street was quiet. It was as though I had our entire world to myself. For no accountable reason when the Weisshaus was in sight I began to run toward it and was breathless by the time I stood just inside it before the reception desk. I could feel the healthy red in my cheeks, the tiny tears the cold had brought to my eyes, the numbness of the tip of my nose. Still, inside me there was a deep, delicious warmth.

I removed my outer wraps and approached the dining-room captain. "Do say my table is free?" I asked, a smile that was almost a plea on my face.

"It is, madam." He smiled back and led the way through the room to the table.

He pulled the table for me to sit beneath the window but I was already settling myself in the outside chair which Hans had always occupied. "I am dining alone," I said. He bowed and handed me the menu and waited for my order. I was looking out to the terrace and to the Gotschna beyond. "I do hope Mister Aldik has good skiing today," I said.

"Mister Aldik, madam? I believe he left for Zurich early this morning. Now—may I suggest the Bundnerfleisch first. It is a speciality of the Grisons and perhaps after—the fondue?"

". . . for Zurich." The words spun around inside my head. Why would he have lied to me. Why? I got up quickly from the table. "I'm sorry," I managed to say, "I'll—I'll be back directly." I thought I would never reach the reception desk. I arrived there out of breath and impatiently interrupted the clerk's conversation with a waitress from the dining room. "Mister Aldik," I said. "What train did he take for Zurich?"

"I don't know. He ordered a taxi for eight this morning. Perhaps they drove there," the clerk answered swiftly.

"When do you expect him back," I asked—my heart hardly beating.

91

"He reserved a table for two for dinner," he said in reply. "But the dining captain's brother owns the taxi. Perhaps he can tell you." He turned away from me and back to the young waitress.

I did not wait to ask any more questions. I rushed out of the Weisshaus and stood ridiculously lost in the middle of the street. I was confused. I did not know what to think. He had lied. But why? He had gone to Zurich, but for what reason? I don't know through what process of thinking I arrived at the conclusion that I had to go to Zurich. But before I was aware of what I was doing I had walked back to the railway station and boarded the waiting train for Zurich. I remember nothing at all of that journey.

I suppose I hoped to see his face among those waiting for arrivals—rushing for a train. I knew I could not return to Klosters without him. I was standing at that part of the Zurich Bahnhof where all the gates lead to the incoming and outgoing tracks. I found the gate to the Klosters-Davos train and turning my back on the track so that I would not miss him if he approached, I began my vigil. There were trains within an hour of each other at this time of day. The ski-specials. I could not know if he was even planning to return by train. If he had hired a taxi one way—it could be standing by to take him back. Still, I stood there with certainty, as if we had made a previous appointment to meet on this very spot.

I had been standing there for a long while though I had no idea of the exact time. I had not eaten since morning and I began to feel dizzy. I started to make my way toward a sign marked "Information." I don't really know what it was I intended to ask. It was then I began to think about the buzzards. Perhaps I thought about them because of all the people in their heavy flapping winter coats who rushed past me stirring up the air between us into little steady gusts of wind. I could not erase the image of the buzzards from before my eyes.

The shroud of night had come to Sleepy Hollow. Althea breathed heavily in her sleep. Small gasps—as though sleep was strangling her. I rose from my child's cot and crossed to her side and leaned in closer.

"Althea . . ." I whispered.

She stirred but that was all. The moon cast a strange light in the small back room we shared that Whitsun holiday. Althea's tangled red hair spilled over her pillow looking like rivulets of blood. I made my way quietly across the room and went out into the old hallway and started toward our mother's room—down the warped and creaking floors. Irish appeared in his doorway. He motioned to me and I went to him and he drew me into his room and then closed the door. Neither of us spoke. He knew I was afraid of the night. He took my hand tightly in his and we walked the short distance to his bed. Both of us got beneath the covers and held tightly to the other. I was shaking but soon that passed and I was able to concentrate on the warmth that Irish brought to my body and the scent of the sea that came through the window above us. Then we heard the sound of footsteps approaching his door. Irish helped me over the back of the bedstead and out the window. The moon was light enough to see the ground.

I don't know why I made my way from the cottage toward the cliffs. I reached the ring of bramble roses and stumbled and the thorns caught on my summer nightdress. I had frightened the night birds and they fluttered their black wings angrily as they resettled themselves. Somehow, in my childish ignorance I thought they were buzzards—and I knew buzzards were always hovering whenever death was near at hand. I screamed and then there stood our father, and behind him, all clothed in night shades of black, our mother holding Liam in her arms and Althea was hiding behind her skirts. Irish was the last one I saw—standing behind them—near the cottage, before the birds shrieked and then flapped their wings close to my face. I began to run from the birds, away from Father, away from Irish—toward the rising cliffs and the sound of the sea which I knew was just beyond, but I stumbled and fell and Father caught up with me and angrily scooped me up from the ground and carried me back into Sleepy Hollow.

HANS...

It had suddenly begun to rain. Gently, only a faint tapping on the roof of the taxi at first. Then great drops streamed down the windows and made the rest of the world look distorted. The sun still shone, its brightness now a watercolor wash for the background of the day, its warmth cooled and dampened. There was the smell of wet pavement and wet greens. Rain bonnets and umbrellas dotted the Finchley Road and the people were moving more quickly, in strange sidesteps, as if they were attempting to walk between the drops.

Hans glanced impatiently at his watch. He had very little time to spend with Mrs. Devlin and he had a premonition from his short conversation on the telephone with her that she would not be easily swayed into giving up anything that might have been entrusted to her care. Time and patience would be required and he had neither. The taxi had been crawling along the street behind a beer lorry for blocks. Hans rapped on the glass partition between himself and the driver and then slid it open.

"Where would Hillside Crescent be from here?" he asked.

"Straight on to the next lights. Left on that turning. I don't know which side of the crescent twenty-seven would be, guv," the driver replied. He was relaxed and unperturbed by the thick lane of traffic.

Hans looked at the meter, added a shilling to the fare, handed the money to the driver and then stepped out on the curb side. He began to dodge in and out of the hurrying crowds with the brim of his hat down and the collar of his trenchcoat pulled up. He glanced back as he reached the turning at the traffic lights and saw his taxi behind the same lorry a good block down in traffic. He sped up the incline of Hillside Terrace to Hillside Crescent at the top, hazarded a guess that twenty-seven was to the left, and breathed a sigh of relief that he was right. He ran up the front steps and under the front stoop and rang the bell. After a moment the door opened a narrow slat.

Mrs. Devlin's head perched on her shoulders like a bird on top a scarecrow. She appraised Hans through small eyes that narrowed myopically. He introduced himself and she finally opened the door but waited to greet him until he had removed his coat and wiped his feet thoroughly on the rubber mat in the entry. Then she lent him her hand but only allowed their hands to brush before quickly pulling hers away and burying it, as a dog with an old bone, in the pocket of the ancient smock she wore. Her clothing fell limply over the sharp bones of her thin body like damp wash might hang from a peg. She closed the door then, and stood with her back to it making no move to lead him to any other room in the house. It was clear Mrs. Devlin seldom received guests and that she did not intend Hans to stay long.

"As I said when I rang you," Hans began, "I am a friend of Miss Woodrow's. Mrs. Pritchett was kind enough to give me your number and I was hoping you might not object to my having a few words with you about Miss Woodrow."

"I don't recall hearing any mention of you before," she commented sourly.

"It has taken me a long time to step forward," he answered quietly. He looked toward the door to the sitting room. "May I please come in?" he asked.

"I guess I could put the kettle on," she mumbled.

"No, thank you," he assured her.

She did not press the offer and led him into her sitting room where she left him standing in the doorway as she sat herself down. The room was small and once they were both in it, it seemed to be overcrowded. Every table and every chair had a hand-embroidered doily. The overstuffed horse-hair sofa and the two sofa chairs in the room were a matching suite. There was an electric fire going in the fireplace. All the windows were closed and the room was unbearably hot. Hans noticed the woman's body for the first time. The hands were knotted and she looked somewhat hunchback. He recalled now hearing from Luanne that Mrs. Devlin suffered from acute arthritis. She leaned back in the brown stuffed chair which was part of her living-room suite. "How good a friend?" she chirped.

He crossed the room in only a few steps and sat down on the sofa opposite her. "Very. And I know you are, too. I am counting on that. We can both help Miss Woodrow, you see." He spoke to her as you might a young child. And like a youngster she sat there waiting for him to give her some proof of the words he spoke. "I have kept in touch with Mrs. Pritchett all these years," he began. "It was I who finally convinced her to talk Miss Woodrow into taking this holiday she is on now. I would like to see Miss Woodrow able to leave Laurel Groves permanently, very soon. I would like to help her find a life outside Laurel Groves for herself.

"Are you one of them head doctors?" she whispered.

"No. I am a writer," he told her. She drew back instantly. "Not a reporter. I write books," he added quickly.

"Do you now?" She smiled for the first time, impressed with Hans. "I never met a lit'ry type gent before. Well, there was Mister Ira Sean but . . ." Her voice trailed off for a moment. She stood up but it took her a long painful moment to do so. Hans rose quickly to help her and the idea rather pleased her. She smiled fatuously at him, leaned heavily on his outstretched arm and gingerly took a step away from him. "Arthritis," she confided. "Painful, I can tell you! Trying to make an invalid of me long before the old gal's ready. But you can't give in to it, can you? I haven't missed one Saturday night at the Cross and Bow in ten years. Nice place. Highly respectable lot there." She nodded her head in agreement with herself. She started toward a table which Hans could see had a giant scrapbook on it. "I have pictures of the entire family, if you want to see them," she said.

Hans followed her over to the chest. He was aware of something for the first time. The room was so cluttered he had not noticed it when he entered. Though the upholstered pieces and some small oddments were not distinguished, there were pieces of furniture that were terribly dear antiques. He glanced around the room, studying them beneath their garish tasseled and embroidered doilies. There were a pair of small Queen Anne tables, a fragile French lady's desk and stuffed in a corner—the chair which obviously belonged to it. You could not help but see the ugly brown suite first, the lino-topped cocktail table in the center of it, and the cheap calendar art over the electric fire in the plastered fireplace. Now he could see that the chest with the scrapbook on it was also a lovely thing. And over it—so badly lighted that one did not see it until just beneath it—a small painting that was most certainly an authentic Turner. Hans ran his hand thoughtfully over the side of the chest and felt the grain of the fine wood and the curve of its well-crafted line as one might a fine piece of sculpture. The gesture did not go unobserved by Mrs. Devlin.

"That's a good bit of work." She grinned proudly. "From Miss Luanne's own bedroom in the great house. That's all she took. The furniture and bits and pieces from her own bedroom. Give them to me to look after for her. Not one scratch in ten years. Nothing ever had to be mended. That

97

vase over there arrived mended like that. But nothing else has a mark on it." She turned back to the scrapbook and opened it with her talon-like arthritic hands. "I never showed this to none of them reporters. Not one." She stood over the first picture in the album studying it wistfully. "This here's me sister Pansy." There was a large photograph of a rather sweet-faced woman already past her prime. "There was three of us. Daisy, she was the oldest, Pansy and meself. Me name's Violet. Mum called us her 'spring flowers'." She giggled and then controlled her laugh. The smile dissolved in a flash. On the next page was a family group picture taken at Christmastime.

Luanne was a young woman in the photograph. Probably no more than nineteen or twenty. She was gazing dreamily past the camera. All of them were as she had described them to him. It was as though he had seen each of them before many times. His glance held on Irish Woodrow. He was smiling. A strange smile. Almost a smile that said: "I am above all this, but I will humor you."

"Oh, Miss Althea!" Mrs. Devlin continued. "She was a real Christmas cracker! And Mr. Ira Sean—a mite too much gray matter for meself, but quiet-like. That's Mr. Eugene. Looks like a girl, don't he? And Mr. Liam? Never could get a smile on his face. And this here's their uncle, Mr. Stanley, and their cousin Mary Agatha. Not nearly the lady her cousins were, mind you, but respectable. She liked to cook but Pansy cooked *that* goose, you can be sure." She peered closer at the picture. "Ummmm. Yes. Pansy cooked that one." She looked up rather wearily. "There was a proper carry-on for years after the murders. Reporters, people who would have done better to mind their own business. They followed Miss Luanne wherever she went." She closed the scrapbook, tired of looking at it and leaned on Hans as he extended his arm again and helped her back to the same chair she had been sitting in. "I found her sitting on the top step of the staircase that day. 'Would you care for some raspberry tea, Mrs. Devlin?' she asked. I didn't know at the time, mind you, it was tea what had killed all those people, but I thought something with a nip in it was called for, if you know what I mean—so I went down to the dining room where they kept their store." Hans sat on the sofa now, facing her, waiting for her to pause. "She was delicate. Always was. Impossible to consider she'd had anything to do with it. Well, meself I never did, that was all!" She glanced up now. "I kept an eye on her for as long as I could," she said apologetically.

"And the older brother?" Hans asked softly.

"Likable for all his high and mighty words. Different from the rest. He didn't like any of them very much. You could tell it in his voice. Sort of stuck-up when he spoke to them. But he was fond of Miss Luanne. Only came to be with her. Pansy said . . ."

"Yes, go on," Hans urged.

"*News of the World* offered me ten thousand pounds. Not one word. Not one glimpse of me pictures." She rubbed her hands together as if they were kindling sticks. "Of course, Miss Luanne took good care of me. I got no need to worry for the rest of me days." She craned her neck and spoke softer as if afraid someone might be listening. "The house brought near twenty thousand pounds! Even after the estate people was paid! Miss Luanne split it with me." She wrinkled her nose disdainfully. "Taxes!" She breathed deeply. "Left me enough to take good care of meself but with that extra ten thousand pounds I could have gone somewhere where they get sun all the year 'round. But not *one* word. Not *one* glance at me album. I'm only speaking to you on Mrs. Pritchett's account." She nodded her head, again agreeing with her own words.

"You were talking about the older brother," Hans prodded.

"The Woodrows was all refined." She moved into the shadow and flicked on a small light behind her. Its thick shade turned her face a sallow yellow. "Mister Ira Sean was a good man. Against war and the bomb. Always believed the police was wrong there, I did!"

"Was there someone else you thought it might have been?" he asked.

"Not me business to think about such things," she snapped.

The afternoon was fading. It was growing late. Hans had to get her around to the subject he was really here for. He leaned forward and smiled encouragingly at her. This was a woman who had spent most of her life in service. Her one pride was her employer's trust. "Miss Woodrow," he began, "trusted you more than anyone else she knew. She was always grateful to you, as well. She told me only the other day about how you always gave up your Saturday afternoons to be with her and that it was you who first brought her to Laurel Groves." It was an outright lie. Mrs. Pritchett had told him that when they were about to ring Mrs. Devlin only an hour before.

"I'd do anything for Miss Luanne," she said.

"Well, you see, it was Miss Woodrow who really asked me to come see you. There was no time for her to write you a note, which is why Mrs. Pritchett rang you. It has been such a long while since the tragedy. Miss Woodrow was in a state of nerves at the time. But as you know there were many things she did want to hold on to for a time when the tragedy was behind you both. She trusted only you to have these things. And she was most certainly right! Not one scratch, as you said. But she seems to have forgotten what *exactly* she did give you to keep for her. Lately she has been thinking about a book that her brother had started and which she had thought to preserve from the police. She cannot remember if this manuscript might be among the effects you have." He was sweating nervously. "Warm in here," he commented.

"It's me arthritis. Painful when it's cold. I keep the fire high." He thought she had forgotten what he had said. But then she spoke again. "That time was terrible confusion. I

100

hardly remember anything from the time I found her until the time she was let free. I made a full inventory, though! I pride meself on being very business-like. And there is a box of papers and things in the attic. Can't remember what's in it."

"Miss Woodrow was sure you might remember this. She thought she handed it to you to put in your carrier bag just before the police arrived," he said.

He could tell nothing from her face. It had no reaction and looked waxen in the yellow light. "Is it something she wants right away?" she asked.

"Yes," he said hopefully.

"Maybe I could 'phone her in Switzerland, then. Might be she could jog me memory."

His heart sank. If she did have it she was being cautious. "Well, yes, that might be a good idea. Perhaps in the morning. No rush before then. In the meantime maybe you could be kind enough to have someone take down that box in the attic. If you like I could do it for you now?"

Her telephone rang. She rose slowly and he got up to help her. Then she went on by herself into the hallway where the telephone was connected to the wall. He sat there trying to figure what he should do next. He had so little time. He was hopeful that she might let him take the box down from the attic because with her indisposition it would not be easy to do it herself. He would have to make the time to do it, that was all. She was standing in the doorway when he turned. Her eyes were narrowed even more, glancing around the room for a moment as if to see if anything had been disturbed.

"Mrs. Pritchett," she said. "For you."

He went to the telephone.

It seemed inconceivable! Luanne had collapsed in Zurich in the railway station. The manuscript would have to wait.

He turned back to Mrs. Devlin who had been watching him. He told her nothing about Luanne. "Business calls me, I am sorry. Perhaps in the meantime you could have someone take the box down from the attic and then when you speak to Miss Woodrow you will know if the manuscript is in it or not."

"Yes sir!" she said. "Be happy to."

LUANNE...

The day had been gray and damp, as Boxing Day seems traditionally to be, and none of us had left the house. The Christmas spirit of the day before had dissolved into the fearful awakenings of all aftermaths. Everyone had kept to his or her room and though Mary Agate had prepared a festive supper we all partook of it silently on trays in spots of selected solitude. I chose to have mine later than the others. I ate in the kitchen after it had been cleared and deserted, though there was still warmth from the great oven.

It was a room I came and sat in often by myself for it contained a large window which looked out to the swollen hump of earth that was our backyard. As a child it had seemed like my own private mountain. The mound was terraced and in the spring the narrow shelves were bright with delphiniums and hyacinths. They were gone now and a light snow was there instead. Beyond our land was the Heath, but it was too far below to be in view. On some October days, when the wind was on the rise, leaves from the Heath would blow over onto the crest of our land, and pile up on the terraced earth and cover the late summer flowers. As a child, I liked to walk on top of the brown and red intruders and hear the delicious crackle beneath my feet, and scoop them up and scatter them in great handfuls. It was a very painful sight to Irish who truly believed they felt pain. He would frown at me and disapprovingly chastise me for breaking their slender backs.

I could hear the trees in the Heath bending in the wind. The only other sound was an occasional dog's bark as some child perhaps threw a rock or a twig for him to retrieve—a last game before Nanny took a warm, small hand and led the child behind it through the chill of late day to supper and to bed. It was a time of day I never liked, though a time more bearable on days like these, when twilight could not be seen through the heavy gray and so the death of a day was not so clearly discernible. It was a time, maybe the only time, I thought about our mother and our father. I would close my eyes and evoke before the inside curtain of my lids their familiar faces. It would only be a momentary glimpse—then, I would lose them again, though their voices would often linger in my mind like the voice of the sea in a conch shell.

Irish had gone out that morning and not returned. I could not forget the gentle soul in those eyes when he had leaned down toward me as we stood in the doorway of the great hall to say good-by. He had held my shoulders loosely in those large bearlike hands of his and brushed his lips against my forehead.

"That's especially for you, Lululu. Keep it until I return," he said. Then he turned, hands thrust deep in the pockets of his tweed trousers, shoulders shrugged together under the dark blue turtleneck sweater he had worn for years, and was lost to the gray day before he reached the front gate. I suffered great loneliness each time Irish left me. This day there was an unaccountable foreboding. The grayness had enveloped him like the mist enfolds the sea. It was as though he had walked into the sea and was lost to me forever. I remember closing my eyes that moment (as I did later that day at twilight, by the warmth of the great oven), and trying to bring back those gentle soul-filled eyes. I remained to myself the rest of the day.

The fog was settling in now for the night. A moment and there was nothing beyond the kitchen window but a heavy gray blanket. I watched—fascinated, nearly terrified, as the gray came into the room like a dragon's breath, between the window and the sill. It was like some living, writhing thing. I rose, almost certain it would attack me, and advanced to close the window and shut it out. Acrid vapors filled my nostrils and smarted my eyes. I could see the child lost to his Nanny now—a call, a cry, a whimper. I slammed the window tightly shut and the gray coiling thing inside the room with me rose once and then was gone, but its rank sour breath clung. I had to leave the kitchen as I now felt chilled through and uneasy about being alone. I went out into the hallway to see if any of the others might be in the front room.

Althea was just coming down the stairway, a strange triumphant smile on her lips. I always liked the sight of Althea descending a staircase. She did so with her head and shoulders high, never looking down, moving swiftly, her auburn hair a flag.

"It's peaceful without him," she said in a queer voice that made me back away. She was at the foot of the staircase then, just a few feet from where I stood. It seemed a small pain had passed through her body for it creased her face. "But, he'll return." She came to me, not touching me physically and yet holding me to her with her eyes. Her voice now lowered for only my ears. "You could keep him away, Luanne," she said. "It is really up to you."

"This is his home, Althea," I whispered. "It always shall be."

"His home!" She spoke harshly, her mouth strange to me as the corners dropped and her bowed lips stretched tautly between them. "He desecrates it each time he returns." She took me by the arm and walked with me back to the rear of the hall near the kitchen, next to the door to my own room.

The wind came up then, making a sullen sound as an unlatched shutter rattled against the side of the house nearest us. "I don't want to discuss this with you now, Althea," I said with great calm. "The holiday is depressing to all of us. Most holidays are when you have lost people you love. But it isn't *his* fault things are not like they once were. Irish suffers their loss, too, Althea."

104

She was looking at me curiously. "I never noticed how greatly you two resemble each other," she said. She leaned against my door, twisting the knob in her hand. "He confides in you, doesn't he? Tells you of his passion for this Mrs. Mitchell?"

"Althea!"

"You know as well as I that he has been sleeping with this woman for over a year now." She sneered, "She is married, you know, and old enough to be his mother. What a fool he is! Unworthy!" She reached out and took my hand tightly in hers. She was frightened. Althea was so seldom frightened that it alarmed me.

"Althea, dear, you must not upset yourself," I said, stroking the hand which gripped me tightly. "She has just been a good friend to him." She wrenched away.

"The house is all we have. The only protection. I think of it as Noah's Ark. We mustn't leave it, Luanne, until all the storms have passed. Irish knows that, but he left and now he must not come back or you or Liam or Eugene might be lured from safety by him."

Her eyes held something in them that I wanted to forget and yet felt I must dispel. "The others will hear us," I said lamely.

"Mary Agate is reading to Uncle Stanley in his room and Liam and Eugene are in their room. Liam is listening to a rather poor recording of Beethoven's Fifth and Eugene borrowed my book on the life of George Sand and is deeply engrossed." Althea pressed her beautiful face closer to mine and I could feel her short warm breaths upon my cheek. "They are my responsibility, Luanne. You do realize that?"

She did not wait for me to reply but opened the door which led to my room and drew us both into the dark interior. She closed the door before she flicked on a nearby bedside light. "I don't know why you stay in this room. You should be upstairs with the rest of us. What we could do is redecorate the two rooms in the attic, break through the wall. I have been very careful this year on the household money and we could manage that."

"Those rooms belong to Irish," I said firmly.

"Nothing *belongs* to Irish. He has proved himself unworthy." She sat down on my bed and looked up at me, her face half in shadows. "I have bolted the front and rear doors. He has no key. He will come here—to your window. You are to forbid him to enter, Luanne."

"I shall do nothing of the sort and you had no right to bolt the doors against him," I told her sharply.

"Every right. I am the protector of this house. It is dark and silent and hostile out there. Outsiders will know they dare not intrude," she replied harshly.

I stood looking down at her and I thought, "Althea is a stranger." You can know someone all your life and then suddenly, in one painful moment, discover that you never really knew them at all. She was a bitter woman and I had not seen when and how it happened. She sat there, discontent resting heavily on her shoulders, the great ache of dissension gnawing so voraciously inside her that it was sucking in all her flesh. Disenchantment had turned her mouth into a sneer. The smell of anger had dilated her nostrils and narrowed her eyes. This Althea had been unknown to me until this very second.

"Oh, Althea!" my heart cried. "Oh, my dear." The thoughts rushed through my head. A sharp pain cut across my brow, and in my breast, fear for Althea stabbed me so that I could feel its blade turn within! There is nothing I would not have done to bring back the Althea I had lost—I knew not when! Nothing I would not have tried to bring relief to this suffering unfamiliar form which sat hunched together on my bed. But I was helpless.

We both heard the footsteps on the gravel path beneath my window at the same time. Althea leaned over and turned out the bedside light, her voice was a warning on the wind as she stood up, and then went past me. "Forbid him to come in, Luanne," she whispered. Then she was gone but through the darkness I saw her stand beside my wardrobe. She would not be seen from the window, but from where I stood she was directly opposite me. I had grown accustomed to the dark and could see her silhouette clearly. She was breathing fast and the dress she wore clung to her body. I thought how beautiful Althea was, even when the dark obscured her features. Now she was like some magnificent black leopard about to leap on his prey.

I turned on the bedside light. I was sure it would be Irish and yet fearful it could really be an intruder. With the front and back doors bolted from the inside by Althea, my first instinct was to turn out the bedside lamp again and run from the room and bolt my own door leaving Althea and whoever was there to face each other. A second handful of gravel scratched the window. There was a rap. Three short taps. It was Irish.

"No scene, Althea," I said, before crossing to the window. "This is my room. I can have in it whomever I wish." She made no sound whatsoever.

Irish stepped over the sill in one long, loping step and closed the window behind himself. "Not gone seven and the doors bolted already," he said, the familiar arched tone and humorously raised brow accompanying his words. I could have run to him and hugged him so glad was I to see him.

I tried to keep my eyes from straying to the wardrobe. "I believe Althea is apprehensive of visitors during a fog," I lied lamely. "People lose their way so easily around the Heath. One never knows what sort of person might come to the door."

He smiled warmly and had just turned to light the fire and warm his hands when Althea stepped out of the shadow from behind the wardrobe and confronted him.

"I bolted the doors against *you*," she said in a high, rasping voice.

"Really!" he replied, obviously undaunted or surprised by

her presence. He wore a soft smile. I wanted to warn him for he did not smell the danger so close to him, but the words froze in my throat.

"Don't be smug, Ira Sean!" Althea's uncomforted body twisted angrily and she spun away and took measured steps to my bed. She turned. She was standing before the door to my room, apparently to stop Irish from proceeding any farther.

The room was hot and oppressive. Outside the window was an impenetrable mass of gray. I looked from one to the other—Althea's body frozen with all her breath still in it, Irish's face a solid rock of decision—and I could feel the perspiration rolling down the slope of my brow. Yet my hand was too paralyzed to wipe it away.

"Did you bolt the doors," he asked in a voice that instantly cooled the temperature of the room, "to keep *me* out or the *others* in?"

"I'm fully prepared for you, Ira Sean," Althea hissed. "This moment has been a long time coming. The answer is both. You are the enemy and we both know that. You won't stop until you destroy this home, scatter all of us to the four winds. You come here just to unsettle us. I won't let it continue. The others rely upon me for their well-being."

"You are destroying this house, don't you realize that, Althea?" he asked in that same hard, cold voice that was stranger to my ears. "You fancy yourself queen here, the others your subjects. You did even when you were a child." He was moving closer to where she sat on the bed. I believe both of them forgot I was there. "Don't you know you hated Mother? You shed no tear, silent or seen, when she died. You moved onto the throne even before a decent period of mourning." Althea sat still—feet now digging into the carpet as if preparing to support a leap. "Then, there was Father. In your childish fantasies you wished him dead, too. And he died." Now—when I thought they might leap at one another—Irish walked away and across the room and sat down in my small desk chair. He leaned back and balanced on the slender rear legs. "But alas, here I am. A threat to the safety of your reign."

Althea stood up, calmer now—a small smile twisting her mouth up at the corners against the desire of her face. "You are quite mad," she said quietly.

"You are *very* sick," he replied.

Althea froze in the center of the floor. There was a long, painful moment and then she started out of the room. She paused by my bedside table and turned for a moment back to him. "It is the world outside which is sick," she said, "and each time you enter this house you contaminate these walls with that disease. You are not to come again, Ira Sean. *Never* again. And if Luanne chooses to see you she shall have to leave as well."

It was not until that moment that Irish looked at me. It was the first time he had been aware of my presence since he first saw Althea. He was asking me to leave—that moment— with him. His eyes asked it of me. There were no words. No words were necessary. Instinctively I felt I must do what he was telling me to do. I felt the urgency and as he stood and held his hand out to me I moved toward him and took his hand and then his arm for support. Neither of us was aware of Althea in that split moment. But she could not restrain the inner scream her lips were trying so hard to bar from escape, and, as she picked up the Wedgwood vase on my bedside table, I turned and Irish pulled my arm. Yet, when the vase hurtled past the place I had been standing, I was still close enough to feel the air it stirred. (It was not until long after that I realized Althea had hurled the vase at me—purposely—with perfect aim.)

The vase hit the wall just behind me. It had once sat upon our mother's dressing table and had always been a favorite of mine. I cried out when I saw it break and shatter into a thousand pieces, though I knew the breaking of the vase was inconsequential in view of what had just happened between these people I loved. I could not help tearing myself away from the firm grasp of Irish's hand on my arm. I ran to squat in the corner and began to retrieve all the tiny, delicate blue fragments into the safe hammock I had made of my skirt.

When I turned they were both staring at me. For a moment, as I looked at Althea, her face began to crumble as the vase had done. I saw her leave the room and felt Irish's arms lift me to my feet and help me to my bed. It was as if I had passed into a world of deep, blue water.

It was raining now. Steady and insistent. The lids of my eyes were too heavy to open, but I could hear the rain falling on pavement. I was in a bed, a window was open at my side. The smell of the rain was good and familiar and I turned my head toward it. I tried to open my eyes but the light made them water and I had to close them again. There were footsteps beside the bed. The smell of antiseptic. Someone closed the window, then patted my arm. "Fräulein." It was a woman and her voice was Swiss and uncluttered by emotion. "Someone will be here soon."

She slipped one strong arm beneath me, propping my pillows with the other. "You've had a good rest. You should feel better now."

I opened my eyes. A woman in a nurse's uniform patted my shoulder and then turned away and drew a white curtain around one side of my bed before she disappeared.

My bed was between the curtain and the closed window. I turned to look out the window. It was night and it was raining hard. The fat, round drops hit the sill like small water pellets and exploded. The wet pavement reflected the neon lights above. I could see some signs. They were in German. I was still in Zurich. The linen on my bed told me I was in Red Cross Headquarters in the Zurich Bahnhof. There were muffled sounds beyond the white curtains. I closed my eyes again. I was warm and safe and sleepy. *Someone* would soon be here, she had said. I never stopped to wonder who it might be.

Irish turned off the light and drew the covers over me. He closed the door and came and sat on my bed, by my side. We listened to the rain together. I had always liked the rain. Often in the late spring, when the rain came to wash away the winter snows, I would open my window wide and let the rain come in and splash upon my face. Or lie in bed (as I did now) and wait until the thunder ceased and the gentle first drops became sheets of fresh-smelling rain carrying the scent of the Heath into the room . . . then, you could hear it! As Irish and I did now. No sound except the falling of the rain.

My thoughts were like pieces of a complicated jigsaw puzzle. So many of the pieces seemed to be missing. But I felt nothing would ever again be the same. Althea had said Irish must leave and if I allowed him in my room again I must leave, too. "I can't leave," I finally whispered. "There is no place to go." I was trembling. "I am afraid, Irish!"

"Shhhhh." He placed a finger over my trembling lips.

I was quiet until the shaking had left my body. It must have been a long time and Irish just sat there patiently waiting. "She was not Althea," I said at last, my voice controlled. "I looked at her and she was a total stranger. Oh, dear Jesus, I don't understand it at all!" I turned to Irish. "You do believe in *Him* don't you, Irish?" I pleaded, wanting him to assure me that he did.

"Originally, but not recently," he replied.

"I want to very much," I said. "*Very* much," I repeated. "At this moment *He* is all that seems to be left."

"I'm here," he said gently.

"Yes, of course." I smiled as best I could for I kept thinking about the watered graves of the dead terrace stones. The watered moss on our parent's graves. The stripped trees and the Heath unprotected against what was now a lashing rain that slanted and struck the window unmercifully. No sound of wind. No other sounds but the rain. He placed his hand upon my shoulder.

"You have a chill," he said.

I nodded my head and took his warm hand and held it close to my cheek.

"You are trembling again," he said softly.

I could not speak.

"Remember," he began in the voice I loved the most—the end of a whisper, "when we were children and we were both terrified of night sounds and night people? We would make our way through darkened corridors and find each other and give our warmth and life to the other." He had drawn back the cover.

"We aren't children anymore, Irish! We're not! It's wrong. Don't ask me why—because I don't know. Once it wasn't wrong. But it is now. It just is!"

He had slipped in beside me and then covered us both and held me close to him, both of us feeling the other's warmth beneath the clothes we had not needed to remove. "Love is never wrong, Lululu. Love heals." He began to stroke my hair back from my forehead. "If you must remain," he whispered into my ear, "then I shall always come back."

Outside was the rain and the night and the world. For the first time, I yearned to run out into it, but Irish held me to him in a close vise. He kissed my throbbing neck and then placed my head into the curve of his shoulder and held me tightly there. Soon he was asleep but I never closed my eyes for the entire night. I just remained there like a woman buried in a state of catalepsy, waiting for someone to pry open the coffin lid.

LUANNE...

It would be a clear morning of gentle sun and soft breeze. The rain had stopped but the smell of wet pavements and washed air remained from the night. I don't know how long Hans had been standing beside my bed. He could not have been there long, however, because it seemed impossible I could smell the lost night rain and not the familiarity of Hans's tobacco which I now inhaled.

"Luanne," he called softly, leaning in close, his clear blue eyes studying my face with endearment. I could not mistake the look in those deep-set candid eyes. He took my hand and held it tightly in his own. "You fell asleep last night before I arrived." He smiled. "I thought it best not to wake you."

Feeling returned to me. The hard, stiff Swiss mattress was unrelenting on my spine. My legs ached, my cheeks felt warm and my lips dry. He had been here an entire night and I had not known. I had slept away the hours. I thought for the first time about the previous day. The confusion rushed back at me and he leaned down and stroked my forehead as if trying to ease away the lines of pain that had creased it. I tried my best to shut it out of my mind. I glanced past his rough tweed shoulder to the drawn white curtain, swaying erratically as hurrying figures brushed by it. The white was like the snow. I could feel the morning sun on my shoulder. I made an effort to block out everything but an image of the mountains and the snow where the sun now warmed the early skiers.

"I have rather messed up your ski holiday," I told him— unable to answer his straight glance.

"Not to worry." He straightened. "I am taking you out of

here," he said in a voice of great authority. "I have been assured you will be all right. You think you could dress and leave now?"

I nodded my head unable to speak, to tell him how thankful I was that he had come, how sorry I was that I had been asleep the night before. There were so many things I wanted to say but at that moment I could say nothing. My eyes were lowered as he started out of my little curtained room. He parted the curtains and was almost gone when I finally found my voice. "Hans!" I called out feeling it must have been a shout but knowing from his slow reaction that it had been barely a whisper, and that he had not been sure any sound had passed between my lips. He stepped back into the room and I looked up at him. He knew immediately. He came to me and reached out to take me into his arms at the same moment as I thrust myself into them. I had never known anything quite so wonderful as the harsh wool of his jacket as it scratched my cheek when I rested my head against his chest. I thought I would cry with joy but the tears did not come, instead, there was a bursting feeling inside me. "I love you so much," I breathed.

"I love you, too," he said surely. Then he tore me from his embrace and held me away from him. "Now do as I tell you. Get dressed. I will be waiting for you in the next room." His face softened into a gentle smile. He could see the fear that was clouding my eyes. "I promise," he said quietly.

I nodded my head and watched him disappear through the curtain. I could hear his heavy footsteps on the old wooden floors. His muffled words (though I could not quite hear what they were) as he paused only a few yards away and spoke to a woman who had a voice with the texture of smooth stones. The voices stopped then and only her footsteps drew near, solid, sensible—while his became an echo which I thought I could still hear, but which I knew had been lost beyond the sound of a closing door. I threw my legs over the side of the bed and braced myself to stand. Neither my arms nor my legs could hold me and I fell back on the bed. The curtain parted again and for a brief moment I hoped it might be Hans. It was the nurse I now remembered had been in the room the night before and earlier in the morning. She approached me with a broad smile on her face. She was carrying the clothes I had been wearing the day before.

"Hallo!" she said brightly. "What have we here?" She crossed to me and placed my clothes neatly at the foot of the bed. Then she came alongside me and extended the same strong arm I could recall from her night visit. I took it and lifted myself to my feet and as I did she supported me against herself. "You will be all right in a moment. We will walk." She placed one arm around my waist and held the other beneath my elbow in support, and we walked back and forth behind the drawn curtain for a few moments until my legs could support me. She let go and I stood alone for a time and then took the few steps to the bed to reach my clothes. I was steady on my feet. The weakness had past.

"Hans is waiting for me," I told myself over and over as I dressed. Everything seemed to take longer than it ought. I fumbled with all the fastenings, buttoning things lopsided and having to redo the task, putting my jumper on wrong side out and having to take it off and slip it on again. I was like a child in too great a hurry to attend to such a simple feat as dressing.

He was waiting in a small anteroom, his back against the door leading outside, his eyes studying the entrance I finally came through. They flashed with pleasure when they saw me. I thought I should surely fly to him, but he came to me as I stood there in the doorway, frozen, a smile ridiculously slapped on my face, my hand held out to him. He took my hand and supported me with one arm around my shoulders and the other under my arm. "There's a car waiting," he said.

"Oh, could we walk, please? Just for a short way." Somehow I wanted to feel the sun upon us. I longed for us to walk together down an unfamiliar street in a strange city. He nodded his head, and we went out into the bright morning. Nothing had ever seemed so new to me before. Clear and in focus, real. Hans was walking with me, our bodies touching and our hands entwined, beneath a merciful winter sun.

"You've had a rather bad time of it. Are you sure you know what is good for you?" he asked, as we paused just outside the Bahnhof.

"For the first time in years," I replied sincerely.

He led me across the wide Bahnhofstrasse and onto the bridge that spanned the lake surrounding the clean, proud streets of Zurich like a castle moat. It was a beautiful city! Never had I seen such clear, true light. The air was fresh and crisp and the people walked with a purpose. The lake curved around a shore that was banded with boardwalks and boat moorings and yet was bright and neat and freshly painted and carefully kept. We stopped mid-way along the wide bridge. I placed my arms upon the railing and rested my body against it; Hans's arm was still around my shoulders. The morning wind was on the rise and brought the smell of fresh water with it. It stirred my hair and brought an exquisite tremble in my breast. It was a singular moment in my life. I was aware of it and guarded it jealously, silently—while it lasted.

"Warm enough?" he asked, a short time later, noticing the wind was sweeping my hair across my face and whipping the skirt of my coat in front of me.

"Oh, yes!"

"Would you like to talk about it?" I nodded my head. "What happened?" he asked softly.

"It was the buzzards. Well, of course not truly real buzzards. I imagine they were overcoat flaps but they seemed to me like—buzzards." I felt a chill then and he turned up the collar of my coat for me and turned me to him at the same time and looked straight into my eyes. "I found out you had come to Zurich. I left the tour and had gone back to Klosters —to be closer to wherever you were. I waited by the tracks hoping you would take the train back. I guess I thought I would at least be able to spend the extra time on the train with you. But I was so frightened, Hans—frightened you really wouldn't come back at all."

He let go of the collar of my coat and brushed the back of his hand along my cheek. Then we turned back and stood looking across the water to the small boats and the backs of the houses, each rear balcony gay with its tiny potted plants and winter blooms. We stood silently, both knowing this was a beginning, both fearing it and yet, both anxious to begin.

"I have taken a room for you at the Gotthard," he finally said. "We will rest there today and tonight. Either way you turn—Klosters or London, it means going back—and at the same time going forward. I didn't think you could face either at this time. And I think we need to talk about many things," he said seriously. "Do you think you will be able to do that later?"

"Yes, I do," I answered, knowing I wanted to more than I could say, so sure was I that he would help me lift the weight that held me back from freedom.

"Good girl." He smiled.

"You think I should return to London with you?" I asked.

He held my hand tighter in his. "With me," he said. "But you have to know what you are going back to and what you are running from."

We dropped the subject then and chatted of all the unimportant things people in love usually speak together—comments on the people who passed, imaginings about the inhabitants in the distant houses, and exchanges about the weather, and the city. We stood there waiting for a small boat to pass under the bridge where we stood and shouted our hallo's as it approached and waved our frantic good-bys to the one man on its polished deck as it appeared on the other side. We kept on waving until it was only a speck in the distance and the man could no longer be seen.

The Gotthard was directly off the Bahnhofstrasse. It was an old hotel which had been recently rejuvenated but somehow had managed to retain the charm and warmth and stability of its age and combine it with the efficiency and gaiety of its youth. It had been a very good choice. My room was large and high-ceilinged (so unlike my little room at the Weisshaus or the white-curtained room of the night before). French doors led to a balcony which overlooked the tree-lined Bahnhofstrasse and the outside tables of the street cafés I had noticed when we arrived. I could look down and see the shoppers pausing for a coffee or a beer, their backs to the buildings, their eyes front —watching girls being pulled ahead by dogs, and children held back by their nannies. Trees shaded the room so that the sun fell across the carpet in delicate fernlike designs. I threw open the French doors as soon as the bellboy had left us.

"You're sure you want to stay in Zurich?" Hans asked.

"Sure," I replied. I was on the balcony breathing in the smell of the bitter coffee and the acrid beer which rose from the tables below. Hans stood framed at the French doors watching me. "Come on out here," I said. He crossed to where I stood. "Are you staying here with me?" I inquired, attempting to be casual, not glancing at him but leaning over the balcony and watching the scene on the street instead.

"Not far down the hall." He smiled when he saw me straightening, knowing I had been concerned. "Now," he began in a voice that a doctor might use, "we are going to relax today. I have hired a car. We will drive to some of the small neighboring villages. Return in time for dinner. Our baggage will be sent in by train from Klosters and should be here by the time we return." He took my chin in his hands. "You still look tired. Would you rather rest?" he asked. I shook my head in immediate dissent. He was close to me now.

"Luanne, you are to wash everything out of your mind for the day. I promise you that from now on you will be like that small boat we saw making its own way down the center of the wide, deep water. But even so—I won't leave you again, except for a matter of moments. And I will always return. You must remember that. You are not alone anymore though you will be able to make your way alone—like that boat if you have to, but I shall always be with you. No farther apart than our thoughts." He waited a moment. His voice grew quieter. "I will never lie to you again, Luanne, and I promise you it won't be long before you will be able to take the truth and be thankful to receive it." He straightened and released my face from between his hands. More lightly, he continued, "I am going to see to the arrangements for our day. I will ring for the maid for you in the meantime, if you like, in case you might enjoy a warm bath. Sorry I couldn't get you a room with one, but it was short notice. There is a lovely Bath Room directly across the corridor so you don't have to go far." He turned to go, then paused smiling easier now. "Don't enjoy that bath too much. One hour and I expect you to be ready for our day's outing." He gave me a small salute, turned on his heel, and was gone.

The Bath Room was large and bright with a comfortable chair and a wide dressing table. A bath blanket was folded neatly on the chair. A pair of paper slippers were lined up on the floor beneath it. The water was deep and warm and slightly scented. I stepped out of my clothes, sat down and leaned back, my head resting on the rim of the old tub (thankfully not replaced by a smaller more modern convenience), and let the water rise to just below my chin. I glanced with regret at the only clothes I had with me and then occupied myself with the female luxury of planning what I would wear that night for dinner when my cases arrived. I was struck with how funny it was that at thirty-one I was acting like a sixteen-year-old girl on her first date. I felt foolish and yet wonderful at the same time. I began to laugh out of sheer happiness.

The laughter remained with me for the day, riding alongside me in the front seat of the open car Hans had hired. The wind carried my laughter so that it trailed behind, attached to me like the gay-colored ribbons on a child's mandolin. I had left behind all doubts, all fears. I was young again, younger than I had ever been. We drove along the lake for a time, the blue surface rippling gently. The water clear enough to reflect the sun and the trees and the small boats. Then we began to climb a small mountain, the car charging up and forward until it could climb no more. Hans pulled the car onto the siding at the summit and we both got out and looked below to the valley and the blue-ribbon lake. The houses were like toys, each with their little puffs of chimney smoke. Then Hans left me for a short moment and reappeared with a basket in one hand and a car blanket in the other.

We found a large flat rock, smoothed from years of rain, and set our picnic there. Tiny, tenacious winter flowers sprang up from the crevices in the surrounding rock. They were purple and gold and smelled uncommonly like laurel. I picked some and their stems resisted so much that my hand was strapped with red lines where they had fought me. I folded my serviette carefully around them and tucked the small parcel gently in the loose belt of my coat so it would not be crushed. The air was colder up this high though the sun was still in the sky. We sat—I was wrapped in the red plaid car robe, Hans had his collar up around his ears—and looked down to the miniature village below, and warmed ourselves on the cups of hot, thick soup from the thermos. Before long, the afternoon began to take shape and before we had finished our fruit and cheese the sun began its journey behind the far mountain.

I stretched out to try to reach the sun and pull it back so that we could stay up here forever, but I knew this day must also end. I packed the picnic basket and hurried Hans back to the car with a game a child might play of I-will-get-there-first! We reached the car breathless and laughing. Not another car had passed us while we ate but now a queue of them appeared around the turning and tooting us to one side disappeared for a moment, then reappeared, on the rise to the summit of the next mountain. I was filled with the most incredible desire to reach that next summit before anyone else and I urged

Hans to race them to the top. He protested for a moment, and then he gave me a long, understanding look as if he knew exactly how I felt, perhaps had the same feeling himself. The car shot forward and sped down the small slope, across the pass and onto the next mountain. The horn cut through the sound of the wind that the speed of the car created, and we passed the other cars. The wind swept my hair back and stopped my breath as we moved ahead toward a mountain top that had its summit somewhere above the clouds.

As the maître d' led us to our dinner table that evening I thought about how Hans and I must look together. He so commanding—with a face many recognized from his books, a face that held a radiant look of confidence. He was somehow one of the beautiful people. And I? When I had left my room I had felt so glowing, rather specially turned out. Now I was not sure of myself. I could not help holding onto Hans's arm tighter than necessary as we walked across the restaurant. The room was divided by a narrow, simulated stream, the tables were placed on either side of the narrow waterway. As I passed I glanced at the women sitting assuredly opposite their dinner partners, each with hair stiffened and sleeked into a shimmering coiffure which proved they had spent hours preparing for their companion, nails varnished, surrounded by individual and expensive clouds of scent.

My face was still flushed from the day's ride but for the first time I realized I wore no make up (I owned none and had never used make-up on my face in my entire life). I closely observed the lines of pencil which arched those shiny ladies' brows and circled their eyes to give them a doe-eyed look, the tinge of color on their lids, the blush of color on their cheeks, their carefully outlined mouths and the soft dewy hues of pink and red upon their lips. I must have looked like a servant girl Hans was being kind to. I felt eyes glance sideways at us, words whispered so that we could not hear. My ears burned at what they must be saying!

I had taken the laurel flowers and tucked them into the soft silk belt of my green dress. It was the color of bud leaves and fresh young grass. I had been excited over its choice after trying on all the dresses I possessed when I had returned to my room after our ride and found my cases waiting. I was not even ready when Hans came to my door though I had had time enough to dress. I had swung open the door as I slipped the narrow green velvet ribbon in my hair and stood there grinning like—I should imagine—a complete idiot! I was so sure I would make him proud to be with me. So foolishly and childishly self-deluded!

We were seated at the table and thankfully a menu was placed before me. I lowered my head and turned aside so that no one could see me and so they would think I was studying the menu. Hans gently pulled it away from my face.

"You look lovely," he said quietly. "The most beautiful woman in the room!"

"I look so . . . so plain," I whispered, glancing away and staring into the narrow man-made rivulet of water by my side.

He reached for my hand across the table. "Hestia, Aphrodite —Artemis. A flashing goddess from the Moon-World. Every woman in the room envies you. Every man envies me."

I pulled my hand nervously away and tucked it in my lap as the maître d' approached our table. Hans was smiling encouragingly at me and I forced a smile onto my face. I was thankful for the unspoken words which now passed between us. It was such a beautiful, incredible fact that he loved me, and that he did not see the unfashionable, unsophisticated woman everyone else in the room saw.

"They are famous for their lobster here," Hans was saying. "Fly it in from Canada." I was terrified to tell him I had never had lobster before and was petrified I would not know how to eat it. "I should really let you have your own choice," he continued.

"No, I would very much like the lobster," I said.

He seemed happy at that and ordered our dinner with the same enthusiasm with which he had ordered at the Weisshaus. The laughter was gone but a warmth encircled us, radiating a gentle glow that set us apart from the others as it bound us inexorably together. I obliterated all thought of the fashionable women, who had just so little time before, made me feel like the humblest of back-staircase servant girls. That artless girl was lost forever. Never again would she lower her glance to the floor when she entered a room, nervously grasp her hands, or mumble her words when she spoke. She had been banished and in her place was a woman worthy of the attention and consideration of a man of significance. This woman need only to recall this one moment, when ardent green eyes and fond mellow voice sought answer only in *her* own voice, to dismiss that sad guileless creature from her memory. This was the moment a woman was born in me, fully-formed and eager to take her place in the world.

It was a glorious dinner. We sat until the lights were dimmed and there was a polite cough at our elbows to alert us that we were the only ones who remained in the dining room and that the staff would dearly love to go home.

We could not bear to end the evening so soon, to return to the realities of making plans and facing issues. So we walked back to the bridge and watched the changing reflections on the dark night waters, and then rode on the electric trolley from one end of the city to the other before returning to our rooms.

I had left the doors to the balcony open and the moon shone through the tree-blinds making it seem that we were all light and the rest of the world was in darkness. We stood silent under the moonlight for a long time, leaning together, side touching side so that I felt our bodies must be joined. For a brief moment he breathed deeply from the exquisite beauty of that night view. Then he stepped away and I was silent, waiting for him to speak the thing I knew he had come to my room to finally say, what must be said before another day could pass.

Hans walked away and turned on the lamps in the room. There was nothing to be seen from the doorway now except

123

the thick, dark, tangled branches of the trees and an occasional glare of artificial light that poked through the small spaces on the barer branches. The air had that special fresh fragrance of cool night and expected rain. I opened my mouth and drank of it and closed my eyes so that I could feel its soothing moisture on my lids. Then I closed the doors and turned to him.

He was standing at the foot of the bed. The maid had turned it down and placed my nightgown—in an almost human attitude—across the pillow. He leaned forward toward me, clasping the rail of the footboard. I could see his well-trained muscles beneath the sleeve of his jacket. His face had changed in those short seconds since he left me standing in the balcony doorway. Yet, there was no longer any unknown change that that dear face could make. Hans kept clasping and unclasping the hard wood of the bed rail as he spoke, to emphasize what he was saying, but, otherwise, he did not move during his long retelling of his day away from me. His mouth was set, his square chin firm, his eyes straight and earnest, and his voice steady and sure. He said what he had to say without any compromise, without doubting that I would be able to understand and to accept the words and the truth of them. He told me about his trip to London, his talks with Claudia Mitchell, and Mrs. Pritchett, and Mrs. Devlin. His search in my room for a missing manuscript belonging to Irish. And his observations at Laurel Groves.

"You must want to know why this is so important to me and *has* to be *that* important to you." He let go of the bed rail now, stood straight and crossed to me. He placed his unrelenting hands on my shoulders and applied enough pressure to force me to sit down on the edge of the bed. He was clasping my shoulders, unaware that his strength was such that I ached from his hold. But I knew those bruises would be dear to me for as long as they might remain because they marked the depth of his caring.

"I know none of us believe man can really kill in mass," he

said. "I have seen battalions of young, strong men march on unfamiliar dusty, swampy, rocky roads—shoulder touching shoulder, over a hill, down a gully, through a forest—to their death. They went without believing that they were being sent to their death, though any sensible uninvolved man, any observer could have seen that. Train loads of Jews got into cattle cars, passively, nonresistant, and were driven to their deaths. They were suspecting the worst to be what it eventually was. I have felt guilty that I was alive and they were dead. How many real poets, great thinkers, worthwhile, contributing human beings were dead and I alive? But the fact stands I was—and am, and must make my life worthy of their deaths. Do you understand that, Luanne?" He finally released me, pulling away slowly, straightening painfully as if he could feel even now the agony those others had once felt.

From that great height of his Hans stood, looking down at me with deep-feeling eyes and he spoke in a voice that became even quieter as it accused and acquitted. "In my case I can point a finger. The lousy Nazis. The bastard Fascists. The bloody Generals. The loving Politicians. You can't. Yours has been the unknown enemy. But somehow, damn it, darling, we will bring that enemy into the open—and if—if, it turns out to be Irish you must with all finality—for you—*for us*, accept that and acquit yourself."

He had led me to the point where I must speak the one thought, once and for all, that all these years has been so well-seeded, so toughly-rooted, so entangled, that I had been unable to even make an attempt to tear it from me before. I felt the life drain from my face. "And if it is *me?*" I asked.

"It is not," he replied, the tone of his voice never changing.

"It could be. Why can't I remember? I knew they were all dead and yet I don't recall seeing them dead before that one horrifying moment after I left the linen room. You talk about a manuscript belonging to Irish which you obviously believe was in my possession and which I wanted to keep from falling into anyone else's hands. You think I gave that manuscript to

Mrs. Devlin—but I have no recollection of *any* manuscript whatsoever. In the beginning I remained at Laurel Groves because I was frightened. Of what? Someone other than myself whom I *knew* was the murderer or *myself* whom I feared might kill again? In the end I never left Laurel Groves because I came to feel safe there. Safe from what? Maybe just the passage of time—the ten years—had imbued me with the hope that I was cured and if I killed before would not kill again?"

"Luanne, you may not know who it was. You may never have known. But I know it was never you. You are simply suffering from an overwhelming and unrelenting guilt. You lived. They died. Why? I can't tell you. If you were spared because fate kept you from joining them for tea that day, or sent you to a linen room where the murderer did not know you were, or if someone else's twisted thinking and ill-begotten delusion of omnipotence passed a verdict of murder and suicide because your rights were considered violated, your life privileged—none of that guilt is yours. You simply must cast it aside and understand and accept that as irrevocable."

His face underwent a change again. There was tenderness there now and the small flicker of hope that I had seen in courtrooms when a barrister thought his pleadings well-received. "Before I left London," he said now in a warmer voice, "I made inquiries. The house in Hampstead is vacant. The woman who bought it from you has it up for sale with all its furnishings. They tell me she kept the house as you left it and that they have had a difficult time finding a buyer. It is too large for today's city living, not modern enough, and too dear for the current credit squeeze."

He reached into his pocket and placed something hard and cold in my hand. "They gave me a key," he said. "I hope you will come to London with me, in the morning and go with me back to the house. We will not be looking for anything. Perhaps we can reconstruct that day for you, perhaps we can't. That won't be important. What will be, will be your own effort to bury that house and the people who lived in that house with you for the first time in your life. Because, darling, you saw *them* laid to rest, you saw the dust covers on the furniture, you walked away from *their* graveyard and never returned, and gave the keys to the house to an estate agent and never went back—but you never, not for one moment, Luanne—admitted to yourself that *they* and the house were dead—*gone*. You are still keeping them alive in half-dreams and in all their horror, because you thought it was easier to live with them than to fight and expose this guilty thing you think must have been your blame. Well, that is cowardice and I accept cowardice and fear because man is only flesh after all—but it is self-pity as well and I do not and will not accept that, because no one has the right to think so totally of himself."

He was done now and stood completely still. I could not even discern his breathing. It was as though he had sucked in all the air around him and was holding it within himself. Then, slowly, he began to let the breath out.

"You *will* come with me, won't you?" he asked. I nodded and he closed his eyes and breathed deeply now, relief flooding his face. When he looked at me again it was with the same expression which I had watched at dinner. He took a step closer to me and leaned down and placed his hand under my chin and lifted my face up so that we were looking directly into each other's eyes. "Will you be all right here alone?" he asked. I nodded again. "You are sure? Because if you are frightened—and I told you fear is not a thing to be ashamed of—I will stay here, and you know without my having to say it, that until we can come together just as two people in love —not grasping, but loving—I won't let us come together at all." I assured him I would be quite all right and that I thought I would sleep well because I was so exhausted and so happy and so frightened. I told him I would fight the night myself because that would be my first step in our fight together.

He kissed me and left me sitting on the edge of the bed. I could hear the door to the room directly next to mine opening and shutting, but the old hotel was well-built and I could hear no other sounds once he had closed the door. I prepared for the night, got into bed and forced myself to stay awake while I silently repeated over and over again the pledge that this night, while I slept, I would not travel back in time. This night only sleep, blank and timeless, would share my bed. But when I finally did fall asleep I was powerless against the shifting shadows.

The gray morning cast eerie shadows on the white coverlet of my bed. There was no trace of Irish in the room. Even his scent had been replaced by the acrid fumes of the morning fog. The house was silent. It seemed to me it had never been so quiet before. There were no sounds from the kitchen. I glanced at the small clock on the bedside table, feeling sorely the absence of the smashed Wedgwood vase that had rested just beside it. It was just after nine. If Mary Agate had been in the kitchen earlier to prepare morning tea I had heard nothing. Miss Pansy came at ten, but by then the entire family was always awake.

I rose from the bed and quickly put on my old blue flannel robe, tying the cord tightly about me. The room was damp, the air raw. The fire in the furnace had obviously gone out, for the radiators were cold and lifeless. I flicked on the electric fire, stuffed my feet into my slippers and stood before the fire for a few moments warming my hands before exposing them to the chill I knew the outer hallway would have.

There was no hot water in my basin. I washed, with cold, combed my hair, shuffled out of my room and into the small hallway leading to the rest of the house.

The quiet was awesome. I felt a gust of air from the open kitchen door. Someone must have been up and in the kitchen because I had tightly closed the window before leaving it the night before. Except for the window the room was as I had left it. The tea kettle was cold. There were no dishes in the sink. I hurriedly closed the window and lit the fire for the kettle. The fog outside blocked the day from view. I could not even see our rockbound terrace, nor hear the morning sounds. I wondered if there was a world behind the fog or if I might be the only one left in this cloud of thick gray matter.

The top stair in the great hall creaked. It seemed louder than usual, possibly because I was listening for the sound— any sound. I left the kettle to heat and started up the corridor to the great hall. Something bothered me then and I stopped. There was no window in this end of the passage so that even on bright days we were forced to use the electricity. Yet, I was unable to reach up and turn the light on. I stood there, hands plunged deep in my pockets and felt the sweat now on their palms.

There were footsteps in the great hall. A woman's. The narrow heels chattering on Miss Pansy's hard, polished floors. It *had* to be Althea. Mary Agate never wore such heels—and yet—it was not Althea's step. I started up the dark, cold corridor repeating over and over to myself that I was being a ninny. It *had* to be Althea—yet I did not call out to her because I knew it would not be Althea who would answer.

The footsteps stopped. Whoever it was had stepped from the great hall into the thickly carpeted dining room. The dining room had two entrances: the service door led off the passageway I was in, the other, off the great hall.

The large clock in the front parlor struck and I paused to count the hour. Seven! That was it then! My bedside clock must have stopped the night before. It was only seven. Uncle Stanley would rise in half an hour and Mary Agate would come down to fetch his tea. The boys would be up at eight and Althea, usually the last to rise at nine. Perhaps Miss Pansy had come early. And of course, Miss Pansy had a key!

I continued up the hallway more confidently now until I

reached the turn in the passage from which the great hall and the front door were visible. The door was bolted from the inside and I remembered then that Althea also had chained the rear door the night before. Miss Pansy could not have entered even with her key. Irish had left during the night but he was sure to have gone out my window as he often did.

The service entrance to the dining room was directly on my left and closed. Behind me the kettle began to shriek wildly and I threw open the door to the dining room as if it had commanded me to do so.

Our mother turned to smile at me.

She stood beneath her own portrait, wearing the same dress and hat as she did in the painting behind her. It had been her favorite costume and was still in the large trunk in the basement—the trunk I used to set my canvasses upon. The kettle still screamed as I stepped closer. Yet—it did not seem quite the same face—nor the same smile. Then, I knew.

"Eugene!" I whispered across the room to him so that I would not alert the others. "You gave me a terrible start!" The kettle whistle had come loose and I could hear it pop off. I breathed easier, thankful the sound was gone and that no one seemed to have bothered about it in the other part of the house. Eugene just stood there, the smile fading now, the dress ill-fitting, the rough cheeks too red. A tearful, beautiful child of seventeen dressed in his mother's clothes.

"I didn't kill her," he said. "Althea says I did but I didn't!" There were no tears on his cheeks yet he seemed to be crying.

"Of course you didn't, Eugene." I walked over to him and put my arms around his lace-covered shoulders and walked with him away from the portrait and out of the room into the passageway toward the kitchen. I was startled that Althea could have told him such a cruel thing. Our mother had died at his birth but that was hardly a thing one would say to Eugene. I had never recalled anyone speaking of it before. "You shouldn't have gone out the kitchen window, Eugene," I said as we kept walking. The thought came to me that I should have him take off those ridiculous shoes but I could not do it. I kept on talking as though to a very small child. "It's a long drop on that side of the house to the ground below. You could well have injured yourself."

"Althea put padlocks on the bolts and took the keys. But she didn't remember to lock the basement door from the outside," he said. His steps were short and mincing. I tried to hurry him along the best I could.

I had never realized how much Eugene did resemble our mother. This child whom she had not lived to see looked the most like her. For the short walk from our dining room down the still, dark corridor to the kitchen I felt as though our mother was walking beside me. I could almost smell the jasmine perfume that only she used.

L U A N N E . . .

I was seeing London for the first time, seeing things I had never noticed before. We had arrived on an early morning flight. Now, Hans sat facing me in the taxi from London Airport into town. We were traveling on the M4, cutting past giant factories with curious names like "Wimpeys" and "Cherry Blossom." All the traffic was moving with us, toward London. It was still early and the suburbanites were driving to work or to shop. I had not asked Hans where we were going once we reached the city. I knew he would never suggest I stop at Laurel Groves and I felt I wasn't ready to go back yet myself. I had no idea if he had friends in London with whom he might feel indebted to stay. I hoped if that were so he would not suggest I go with him.

"I have managed a room at the Kensington Gardens," he told me as if reading my thoughts. My face must have instantly recorded a small fear that he might be going elsewhere. His large, warm hand covered mine. "I'll be there, too," he said. His hand remained there the rest of the journey, binding us together in silence. It was an unusually bright, crisp morning for a December in London, an omen of sorts, I thought. There was a merciful and gentle-voiced wind that came through the narrow opening in the taxi window. "It won't be long," Hans said, smiling reassuringly.

He had misunderstood my silence for anxiety. It wasn't that at all. I wanted to hold onto and memorize every moment of this drive—Hans smiling at me, his hand on mine, a winter sun, a morning of yellow and soft breeze, the people bright, happy on this morning that London had shed her leaden skies, her draughts, her rain.

I had awakened in Zurich with a deep feeling of unrest. My dream of the night before haunted me as I rose and dressed in a hurry to meet Hans for breakfast in the dining room before we left for Kloten Airport. I had some overwhelming instinct that somewhere, masqueraded as Eugene had been, there was something in that memory that I should recall.

My weather prediction had not failed. It had been raining by the time I was packed and ready to leave my room in the Gotthard. Hans rang me from downstairs and asked me to hurry along but I could not resist staying alone for a moment to listen to the sounds the rain made—silver-tongued and sweet like an orchestra composed of glass bells and tinseled chimes and fragile wooden flutes. I opened the French doors, standing back, but still I could feel a fine spray upon my face and on my hands.

Hans was standing waiting impatiently in the entrance to the dining room. We hurried breakfast, sent out our cases while we ate and rushed to the airline bus terminal where our coach for the airport departed. We boarded the plane in the same rush and with the same narrow margin of time left to us. We had only been settled in our seats for a few minutes after take-off when the stewardess leaned in toward me (I had the aisle seat which I somehow prefer) and offered me coffee and the English papers. When I turned back to Hans I thought he was glancing out the window. But he had fallen asleep. I sat through the short flight studying his face, noting the exhaustion while he slept, and feeling deep pain in knowing that I had been the cause of it. He had obviously had very little sleep that night or the night before. A muscle on the side of his face quivered. He kept shifting his position, furrowing his forehead, moving his hands. I could imagine that he had been awake during the night, concerned about me, fearful of his decision for us both to return to London and for me to return to the great house in Hampstead.

As I looked at him sitting next to me in the back seat of the taxi I could see that the short sleep on the plane had not been enough for him. He still looked weary and in need of rest and a hot cup of tea. But, I knew it would not help him to go to the hotel and attempt this. His mind would be filled with doubts at my ability to stand up to the strain of returning to Hampstead. He would only rest after that mission was complete.

The sun was following the taxi, its warmth settling on our shoulders like a shawl. "The Heath will be so beautiful this morning," I said. I turned to him and took his hand. "I would like to go straightaway to Hampstead. We could drop our cases at the hotel and just continue on."

"I am not sure you should," he replied, but I could see that a weight had been removed from his mind. He was the sort of man who worried until a decision was turned into action. Then he concentrated on the effort and outcome of it. His eyes looked awake now. He was probably working out in his mind how he might handle any unprecedented reaction I might have.

"First we can go to the Heath," I said, "otherwise it will change. The yellow will go, the gray will return. The Heath has always been dear to my heart. I would like to see it as it was to me in happy moments, when the sun shines through

133

the open boughs and the nannies and the children and the dogs are there." I could almost feel the whole happy experience as I spoke.

He smiled and squeezed my hand. "That sounds wonderful," he assured me. I was sure I saw relief in his face that I was apparently going to treat the morning as a kind of excursion. That obviously settled it. He would do what he could to retain that mood.

"The house is directly alongside the Heath," I explained. "Almost carved out of its side. I always thought of the Heath as mine though I knew no one could really possess that patch of nature's abandon. We can approach the house through the Heath and should be able to return to the hotel in time for lunch." I kept my voice light, an easy smile on my face. It was not altogether untruthful. If I feared my return to the great house, I also was filled with a deep-rooted gratitude which spilled over into a tremendous joy at having Hans with me on my return.

He gave directions to the driver and we paused at the hotel only long enough to leave our cases and then continued on our way through the park, in the direction of Hampstead. I burrowed back into the leather seat. The sun was now higher in the sky and it touched the top of my head lightly as if it were the hand of a man of prayer. I reminded myself that soon it would be Christmas and that the children of London were all on holiday at this moment. This brought back a memory of an excursion with Uncle Stanley, one of the only ones Mary Agate ever accompanied us on. It had been Christmas-time and we had gone shopping and then to tea in the top-floor restaurant, where they had installed a mechanical animal band. There had been a bear that played a drum, and a chimpanzee that played an accordian, and a small dog that blew a horn. Mary Agate looked most uncomfortable and unhappy as we walked through the hallowed halls of Harrod's, and sat beside me surrounded by tables of Knightsbridge and Belgravia holiday mothers with their impeccably mannered and dressed children. But it had been one of my happier memories and one of my happier days. Curiously, I had somewhat the same feeling of happiness as I edged closer to Hans in the back seat of the taxi and felt the sun brushing gently across the side of my face.

We rounded a curve and there it was! The Heath rising before us, the grounds still matted with brown and red leaves, the smell of bark and moss thick in the air. My breath caught and my eyes smarted with a tremendous excitement. The taxi drew to the curb and I was out and had taken off my shoes and was walking through the thick winter leaves which carpeted the earth by the time Hans caught up with me.

"You'll catch your death!" he warned.

I laughed and made my way up a small rise, swinging my shoes loosely from my hand as I walked fast and then ran. I reached the top out of breath but never less tired. I stood there watching Hans following after me, slower, not able to shift the leaves as easily with his heavy, snub-toed shoes. I extended my hand to him and pulled him up and on top of the rise.

"Now put your shoes back on," he commanded in a paternal manner.

I could not hold back the laughter inside me. I stuffed my feet back into my shoes and as I straightened scooped great handfuls of damp leaves (the night still resting upon them— the early morning mist not yet evaporated—yesterday's rain now infused in their veins) and showered them over the two of us. Then I started down the other side of the rise. Running. Kicking up the leaves as I went, brushing past the children, the nannies, the dogs I remembered so well from the years of my own childhood. It never occurred to me what a fool I must have looked, acting like a child of ten at my age. But I felt newly-minted. Just awakened. On the start of a great adventure. I raced down one hill, up another, turning my head only to assure myself that Hans was still behind me.

At first he had treated this outburst of mine much like a

father of a ten-year-old who was intent to share an experience with a daughter he could not fathom, but would do his best to humor. He shuffled up the hills and held back his speed coming down them. Then, suddenly he was right beside me, then ahead of me. I could hear his laughter merge with mine somewhere behind the two of us. I was filled with an overwhelming release, and I could not stop until I felt emptied of everything except well-being.

We finally stopped on the top of a tall rise and rested against a large patient oak. The damp bark smell filled my head, and seemed to make it heavy and I leaned close to Hans and rested on his shoulders. He was still breathing heavily, his body rising and falling in great waves and I felt like that small boat we had seen on the lake in Zurich. Neither of us spoke until his breathing became even again and he had sighed and fallen back against the oak which now supported the two of us. He lifted my face to his. "You look lovely," he said quietly. He brushed his lips against my cool forehead sending a small chill along one side of my body.

"I came here often," I finally began. "Always by myself. But the time before the snow falls is always my favorite. No one else ever loved the Heath as I did. They never did understand. Here it stands, wild and true, withstanding the seasons, the years. The people who come here change, leave, grow old, die—but here it is—and there it *was*. It was my great comforter. I thought of it as my real home. I played such games as a child. I lived in a tree like this oak and I spoke the language of the Heath. The rustle of the leaves were words. The creak of the boughs under the weight of wind or snow were words. I imagined the great house a castle where sometimes I was held bewitched." I turned my head and looked across some far rises.

"It is just over there, you know." I must have been lost for a moment in my own thoughts because he took my hand and slapped it gently as one might do to awaken someone from a faint. I raised myself on my tiptoes and kissed him lightly on his chin. "I'm fine," I told him. Then I fell right back into a happy mood. "When you are a child," I explained, "swings and slides seem pale company compared to a leaf-strewn hill you can climb to another world. But, to some children, I suppose, there is no need for another world." I watched a hurrying cloud move overhead, heard the shifting of the leaves in a fresh gust of wind, smelled the wet-bark-and-leaf-and-moss smell that clung to my hair as the wind whipped it across my face. I pushed it out of my way and straightened. I smiled at him and extended my hand. "I'll show you the house now," I said.

I took his hand and tugged him forward and down the hill, across the familiar clearing, past the two old benches (now bearing weary nannies whose charges had quite exhausted their strength), then through the secret path I had discovered myself when I had been very small and which I now shared for the first time. I had guarded that secret so carefully, so that some day I might lead another bewitched one from the castle to live with me under the protection of my trees.

The path twisted and turned, hidden by the leaves but unchanged through the years. I still knew each tree, each bend. We made our way, the densely entwined branches overhead now turning the path into a patchwork of darks and lights, a ray of sun lighting a late brown autumn leaf, turning it to amber, a shadow changing the deep green moss into black patches on the gnarled trees. The air grew cooler, dampness rested upon my bare skin. I was aware that I had lost my feeling of adventure somewhere back along this twisted path, still—I was not afraid. Hans kept only a step behind me. I never paused, knowing, remembering exactly which way would lead us out. Then I heard the sounds of traffic and saw an archway of light. We stepped out of the Heath and onto the road.

The house was directly across the road, a cul-de-sac came along the wall and side gardens of the house. From where we stood only the dead chimney and the gray slate of the roof could be seen above the wall. Someone had scrawled on the wall in bold black paint, "*Achtung, You Are Entering the Eastern Sector!*"

"The front gate is just around this turning," I said, and made my way across the cul-de-sac and around the turning. The ground at the front of the house was lower than in the rear, but even in the front it was difficult to see more than the chimney and slate roof beyond the front wall. I started toward Althea's stone lions which still guarded the front gates. Hans was now by my side, his shoulder touching mine.

"You're sure?" he asked softly.

"Sure," I replied.

The tall black iron gates were locked. There was a sign hung on them which announced that the property was for sale and gave a real estate company's name and address. The trees that lined the front path reached over to interlace with each other and the path itself turned, dropping down and out of sight. During the terrible days after their deaths I had thought this would protect me, but *they* had managed to scale the wall.

"I still have the keys you gave me," I said, and took them out of my handbag and handed them to him.

The lock was not rusted. It opened easily and we passed beneath the stone lions and then locked the gate behind us. I felt no foreboding. (I was sixteen and Christmas was in the air and I was bringing my first beau home to meet my family.) I made my way down the brick path to the house barely noticing how overgrown it was with moss, how sparse the lawns of grass, how wild the ring of roses, how thorny, how neglected. Still, I was not prepared for the sight of the house itself, its white frame peeling, windows boarded, the brick as overgrown with moss and ivy as the path had been. It was the silence that disturbed me the most—like the silence in the dream I had when I found Eugene in the dining room dressed in our mother's clothes.

I looked back over my shoulder but the gates, the lions,

were lost to my sight. A cloud passed before the sun and the path tangled and darkened. Though the sun broke swiftly through, the chill of that moment remained with me, and when I turned to look at the house again it seemed wrapped in a strange wet mist. There were no boards on the attic windows—*Irish's rooms*—and for a brief, tantalizing moment a shadow moved across them as if someone had been watching, seen us approach, and was now hunched in the corner of his room, seeing but unable to be seen.

I started forward but Hans had hold of my arm and drew me back. "Maybe I was wrong. Perhaps we should wait. I'm not sure you are up to this," he said.

"I am," I said, pleading with his sense of urgency. "We were to face the truth. That means to bring the shadows from all the dark corners."

He relaxed his grip on my arm but supported me as I went up the few steps to the great house. The brass dolphin on the door was tarnished and green. I could not help recalling how proud Miss Pansy had been to keep it shining and bright. Hans was at my elbow and handed me the keys. It was a moment before I could remember which key opened the front door, then I realized I knew all the time. Althea had once painted the top of it with red paint so that none of us would have this confusion. One of the keys was still touched with red, long-worn, but the same color Althea had used. They had not changed the locks or made new keys since the house had been mine.

It was a moment before the door opened. I paused in a last moment of fear of the waiting shadows the darkened house might be hiding, but as soon as the door had fully opened and the light from behind me and the shadow of Hans beside me fell across the entrance—fear left me. The great hall was filled with light from the massive skylight on the ceiling above the stairwell. I had forgotten the extent of that light—or the great sparkle of the crystal chandelier as the sun hit it through the panes of glass.

I pulled away from Hans and rushed into the center of the great hall, an overwhelming happiness filling me. No shadows! Warm, beautiful, golden sun! All my fears were unwarranted. I spun around as if I was doing a strange ceremonial dance.

"It's quite beautiful," Hans said as he stood beside me looking around.

I took his hand and led him up the staircase. The top step had been repaired. Hans left me standing on the landing for a moment and went before me opening the doors to all the bedrooms. The rooms were as Althea, the boys, Mary Agate and Uncle Stanley had left them. The windows on this floor were boarded only in the front of the house. All the rooms had double exposures so that they were in dim light, but enough light to see that special care had been taken to keep them as they once were. Althea's accounts sat open on her desk, her small, neat legible figures still waiting to be balanced. The book Mary Agate had been reading to Uncle Stanley that day rested on his bedside table, the marker where Mary Agate had left off reading. That funny little woman who bought the house from me had kept it as it was that day— the way I had left it from the day they . . . While I was in the house I could not bear to think that they would reappear and be disturbed to see their belongings had been rearranged.

I started up to the attic on my own but Hans quickly followed. These rooms were the only ones so far which had been dismantled. The floors were bare, the books all in boxes, all of Irish's other possessions in packing cases as well. Irish had been boxed or stacked, all personal traces of him removed.

"I'm sorry," Hans whispered.

"It's all right. Better, perhaps."

I turned quickly and we started down again. The sun had passed behind the house, my feelings of happiness departing with it. The great hall was now a spiral of leaden gray. The silence returned. I had an overbearing feeling that somewhere in that great house someone was waiting for me. I began hurrying down the staircase. I heard Hans's anxious voice call my name but I did not stop. I went down the long, dark corridor, past the closed door to the dining room—hurrying past the kitchen (not looking) toward my own room. Whoever was waiting would not be there. Somehow I knew it. The closer I got the safer I felt. Hans was now only a few steps behind me.

The door to my room was ajar and I pushed it slowly in. The room was totally unfamiliar to me. The previous owner, Amanda Nightly, had obviously lived in this room and the furnishings were her own. It was a ghastly room now, dark and heavy and ugly with art nouveau and cheap Victoriana. I turned to leave. Hans was at my side.

He took my hand. "There is nothing to be afraid of, Luanne," he said, as strongly and positively as he could. "It is only an old house with dead memories. That is all. Nothing more."

I had been listening and I thought I heard a voice call to me. The wind was rattling a blind on a window in another part of the house and I supposed that was it, but I could not be sure. I pulled away from Hans. I knew I had to make my way back alone to the parlor. It was not a thing I could explain, especially not at that moment. I pushed past him, back up the dark corridor, his voice echoing around me as he called out my name.

I stood for a long moment before the door to the front room. The brass handles were black with tarnish. Hans stood back, away from me, the light from the skylight directly over him. He sensed my need to walk into that room alone but I knew he wanted me to know he was right by me. I turned the still brass handles and then I pulled with all my strength on the doors, for they were stuck. There was only the light from the hall now, for the front windows had been entirely boarded up. I strained my eyes to see. Finally the room took shape. I felt the terror rise in me, choking back my breath. The parlor was filled with white sheeted figures huddled together in the center of the room like some ghostly, waiting jury. I felt the scream in my throat, tasted the tears, was aware of my violent sobbing as Hans held me in his arms. I knew it was not *them*. I knew it was only the covered furniture, sheeted and hooded, but somehow the silence had been too loud.

HANS...

Hans stood looking at the small, limp figure which he had so recently made a part of his life. It was now familiar to him in all its attitudes. This moment it was the rag doll, abused, carelessly tossed aside. It made the bed seem large as it lay there, legs and arms appearing loosely attached to the body, face buried under a tangle of black hair. She had opened her eyes. He leaned over her and gently touched her shoulder. She made no sound but she shifted her position slightly so that her face was turned aside, eyes glancing at nothing, hair back and on the pillow. He glanced down to her small, firm girlish breasts. She was taking tiny, even breaths. Hans sat down on the bed.

"Can I get you anything?" he asked.

She reached out and took his hand. A brave smile passed briefly over her face. "Poor Hans," she whispered. "I gave you quite a fright." There was confusion in her eyes.

"I don't even know what time it is!" she said.

He glanced at his watch. "Nearly two."

"You must be hungry. I'm sorry."

"I've eaten," he assured her.

She looked around the room for the first time and caught the sight of the tray with a serviette spread over its top to hide the dirty dishes. She turned to look out the window.

He knew she must be thinking this room was not as pleasant as the one in Zurich. The view was not on the side of the gardens but over the main street. The sun had lowered but it was still quite bright for late December in London. He was thankful for that. It threw things into a harsher more realistic light.

"I thought I heard a voice," she said, at first away from him and then looking directly into his eyes. "Like in the dream, it was buried so deeply in another sound that it could have been no voice at all. I had a dream just last night you see." She looked at him rather childishly. "I tried not to. I did try the best that I could." He lifted her hand to his lips and kissed it and then held it close to him as she continued. "I dreamt about my brother Eugene. It was such a strange dream." She managed a carefree smile, slightly crooked. "A non-fiction dream, I guess you could call it." He laughed gently at her attempt to lighten the mood. "This dream was strange, I suppose, because something seemed to be hidden in it. Something I had not been aware of, at least consciously, when the dream had been an actuality. It was as though the dream was, in effect, a puzzle I must complete. There was a voice, you see. Though until that moment in the parlor of the great house this morning, I had not been aware there had been a voice. I had thought, in my dream, that the tea kettle had been shrieking. But suddenly I knew that under that sound there had seemed to be a voice somewhere else in the house. Then, this morning, I thought I heard it again behind the rattle of a loose blind. It seemed to come from the parlor. As you know, there was nothing in the parlor but the furniture bunched together in the center of the room, covered with sheets. But there had not been a loose blind rattling in there either. The windows were shuttered and nailed securely and no light came through any loose shutter. The only light came from behind me. From the skylight in the hall."

"I heard it, too," he assured her. "But it seemed as if it came from above. I think it was only a branch caught in between some loose roof slates. The voice you heard was most probably only the dry leaves brushing the hard surface of the slate. A voice, you only told me moments before, you had learned in the Heath to understand."

She seemed relieved. She sat up now, alert, awake, and he propped the pillows behind her. "Then there was something else. Eugene's costume. It had been in the trunk in the basement. The trunk was always kept locked and I used its top as a sort of work table when I painted. But its contents belonged to me. No one else beside Uncle Stanley knew what was in that trunk. It had been his, you see, and it was his gift to me when he came to live with us. The things in it had belonged to my mother. There were some of her dresses, and her letters, and things that had been hers when she was a girl, before she married Father. I was the only one with a key. Yet, Eugene was wearing a dress from *that* trunk. I don't know why it didn't bother me at the time. Or if it did why I pushed it so far back into my subconscious. Then, this morning . . ." She was talking faster now, her face flushed. She sat erect, away from the pillows.

"Maybe we should talk about this after a while," he interrupted, fearing she was becoming too agitated.

"No. I would rather talk about it now." She leaned back and let her body relax somewhat. "Then I opened the doors to the parlor, and it seemed like one of Uncle Stanley's juries had been exhumed and were all gathered together—judging *me*. And in that moment I knew I had purposely never consciously thought about Eugene and the dress because the keys to the trunk had been in a little Wedgwood vase which had been smashed the night before. The keys had not been in it at the time or they would have spilled onto the floor. I had been so distressed at the damage to the vase and the ugliness that had precipitated its breaking, that I had not made note of that fact. The keys, you see, had been missing and replaced once before, though I had not missed anything in the trunk afterward. But—there were only two people who

144

knew about the keys to the trunk and where I kept them. Uncle Stanley—and Irish, though Irish had never once seemed curious to see our mother's things and never asked me to open the trunk—which I would have done had he asked." She shook her head from side to side and the smoky cloud of her hair moved on the pillow like shifting ashes. "None of it seems very important, and yet—you see something in my heart tells me that it is."

He leaned toward her, kissed her lightly and got up. "We won't discuss it any more," he said. "Not now anyway."

"But it might be important," she insisted.

"The important thing is, it is out in the open. You've said it. I'll think about it myself. See if I can make some sense of it. But right now I want you to relax. Order some lunch if you like. I have some things I must do. If you think you will be the slightest bit nervous being alone, why don't you ring Mrs. Devlin to come over. Or perhaps, I can drop you over there."

"I don't think so. I think . . ." She stretched and looked again out the window. "I think I may do a bit of shopping!"

He smiled. "Splendid." He started toward the door and then turned back. His expression was sheepish. "Oh," he stammered, "when we came in—you were faint. I had the management put us both in this room." His face flushed. "I wasn't sure—well, you seemed in a serious state of shock. I didn't think I should leave you alone—but then there was nowhere else I could think to take you."

"I understand," she said.

"I can see if there will be another room later," he went on.

"If that's what you want to do."

"Well, I just thought you should know before you opened the wardrobe and found my suit hanging there."

"I see." She gave him a tender smile. "Please be back before it grows dark. That might prove a little difficult."

"I'll be sure I'm here by five. You can even order up some tea for yourself and some whisky for me." He opened the door and then glanced back at her. "I do love you very much, you know," he said. And then he was gone.

Hans had done a great deal of thinking sitting in the small room waiting for Luanne to awaken. Over and over the thought returned to him that the only room in the house in an illogical state had been the attic rooms. The lady who bought the house had been a rather odd person who was a well-known mystic and medium. She wanted the house for its morbid history, and had left all the upstairs rooms as the Woodrows had last seen them. One almost expected her to have set up wax figures of the victims. She had obviously disassembled the parlor and refurnished that with her own belongings, as well as the room which had once belonged to Luanne. Luanne had not observed the parlor closely, but the furniture under those sheets could not have belonged to the original parlor. The shapes of the chairs and the tables were bulky and clumsy. All the Woodrow furniture had been delicate, gently curved and finely hewn. It had instantly caught his eye. When he glanced up to the ceiling he saw a Victorian styled chandelier, multi-colored and poor for lighting, which did not seem to fit the room. It had obviously replaced a crystal one, which would have been exactly right.

Amanda Nightly had turned the house into two things: her home on the ground floor, and her spirit "workshop" in the upstairs rooms. But the attic rooms had been completely dismantled. Since these were the rooms which had belonged to the reputed murderer one would think she would have been most likely to keep them intact. Furthermore, there had not been the musty smell from the boxes which they would have, had they been there for ten years. No, the boxes were new and sturdy. Amanda Nightly had left that room always as it was, until someone had managed to talk her into selling the contents of that one room. There was only one person for whom it made any sense at all to have made such an offer—Claudia Mitchell. Aside from the sentimental attachment she might have for anything belong-

146

ing to Irish, there was that manuscript which she may have been looking for and have thought, perhaps correctly, that it was sealed into some private hiding place in his furniture and oddments.

Assuring himself that Luanne could be left without too much danger, Hans went directly to Claudia Mitchell's flat without ringing her first, not wanting to take the chance that she would refuse to see him. It seemed a sign of good luck that the doorman was away from his post and the lift answering a call on the top floors. Hans took the rear steps two at a time. Just past the first floor landing he heard a slow and heavy footstep approaching. He could not account for his instincts and actions as he quietly retreated to the first floor and backed up and under the stairwell. The footsteps were directly overhead now. Hans held in his breath. Someone was negotiating the stairs with slow and tedious steps. They paused on the landing only a yard or so away from Hans, waited a moment, then continued across the landing and started down the remaining flight of steps to the front lobby.

Hans cautiously moved to a position where he could catch a glimpse of whoever it was. A woman clung to the bannisters as she dragged herself down one step at a time, her shoulders hunched. It was Mrs. Devlin. That she and Claudia Mitchell knew one another was surprise enough. (The coincidence of Mrs. Devlin knowing anyone else in the building seemed impossible!) Her desire to keep their acquaintance so secret that while the lift was on the way up Mrs. Devlin was making her "escape" down a back staircase—that was the real surprise!

He glanced through the glass window of the door to the main part of the building. The lift indicator remained at Claudia Mitchell's floor. Hans took the steps slower now. It seemed to make no sense. The return to the great house could well have made him read meanings into things.

The lift doors were just closing and Claudia Mitchell stood poised in her own entrance way as Hans reached her floor. He waited until she closed her door, before leaving the service wing of the building, then he listened for a moment or two at the door. The flat appeared to be quiet. After some time had passed, he rang the doorbell. It was only a moment before she answered. Claudia Mitchell was obviously surprised to see Hans but she managed the moment beautifully. Her hand fell warmly upon his arm.

"Well, do come in, Mister Aldik," she said, and drew him over the threshold and closed the door. "I would like to think I was irresistible." A small smile played at the corners of her unrouged mouth, the words sliding, with only a light trace of her Gallic background, over the tops of her even teeth.

"I hope I haven't taken you away from your work," he replied, with an attempt to appear slightly sheepish.

"If I had been working I would not have been at home to you—or anyone. I never answer doorbells when I am working. Or telephones." Her eyes invited him to follow her as she turned and went before him into the sitting room. She was wearing a trouser suit of the most feminine style. It was a fragile blue velvet and made her green eyes like great, deep rapids. She stood behind a tall armchair and plumped the pillows for him. The chair blocked all of her except her head with its square chin and long wisps of sand yellow hair.

Hans sat in the pull-up chair he had selected the last time he had been there. Claudia Mitchell shrugged her shoulders. "If you choose. Though it cannot be very comfortable for a man of your size." She made a small gesture of exclamation with her hands and then, after circling the armchair, sat down in it, curling her short legs under her and sinking into the deep seat cushion. The same rich musk perfume he remembered filled the room. She studied Hans as a woman who liked what she saw. She was telegraphing him an obvious message. "Before you ask—whatever it is you have come here to ask—let us first get better acquainted." She purred.

"I would think by now you would be quite bored with me," he said, responding to her mood in spite of himself.

148

"You know you are an attractive man and you know you are not a bore. Men always know such things. Shall I offer you some sherry?"

"No, thank you."

She leaned back in the chair, seeming now to be burrowed like a tiny animal in the deep back pillow. "I was lonely. I am glad you are here," she said, quite simply and directly. "Are you concerned about my husband? Don't be. You might come without ringing me first—but Colin never would."

"That seems like an unusual marriage."

"Do you really think so?" she said, with true surprise. "Colin is a very unkind man, but he has always had the deepest respect for my privacy. But you were really thinking—it is not like a happy marriage. It never had much chance to be that. When we married I was a very ordinary, bourgeois French woman with a small talent for writing. My husband was a most unconventional, aristocratic, and well-disciplined Englishman who had never failed at anything in his life. If our marriage was ridiculous he at least turned me into a woman he need not be ashamed to be married to—for he succeeded in making me demand as much of myself as he demanded of me." She smiled. "And there you have the story of my life."

"Hardly."

"Hardly, as you say," she agreed. "My husband never had the usual English prudery about sex. He was, and is, devoted to the subject. I met him in France at a party when I was still a young girl. We exchanged pleasantries and then he suggested I go to bed with him. He was, and is, a magnificent man. Tall, brooding black eyes, thick hair, a lopsided small-boy smile, an interesting scar on the side of his face, and a slightly gruff way of speaking gentilities. One can smell the bull in him right away." She cocked her head, thinking back. "I said 'No.' I will never understand why. Something I sensed. I kept saying 'No' until he asked me to marry him, and then until we were married. But then, oh—I wanted that man more than I have ever wanted any other man. I showed him just how much I wanted him. He was disgusted, for he was looking for a woman he could set above all other women." She was simply repeating a history she had recited many times before. It was her way of clearing the decks. She would say what she wanted to say and the subject of her marriage was to be dismissed. She maintained a set smile and her voice was cool and detached though she was talking about matters so private as to be embarrassing. "We have one son. They have a rather good male relationship, Colin and Jeff. Long ago I accepted the fact that I did not exist for either of them. Both of them hate women—though I must say they do admire success. And I am a success."

Hans recalled a picture of Colin Mitchell that he had seen in news dispatches many times. Curiously, he had not previously put the last two names together as a match. The man's face had disturbed him, almost frightened him. He had thought Mitchell potentially dangerous and had voiced the opinion that he hoped Colin Mitchell was not successful in politics. In his early days, Claudia Mitchell's husband had been a part of the Foreign Office. Then he had become a legend as a fighter pilot during the war. No other pilot had killed as many of the enemy as Colin Mitchell. He had been seriously injured many times but nothing ever stopped him from returning to the skies and adding to his count. After the war he had become a dynamo in the aviation industry and made a fortune. Hans recalled now that that first success had been in France. Then he returned to England where he still flew to conquer and maintain his latest speed records. The last time Hans had seen much about him was when he had announced he would go into politics. It was unlike Colin Mitchell to let a statement like that go at that. Hans was sure the wheels were solidly oiled and in action.

Claudia Mitchell was smiling at him and Hans realized he had not been paying any attention to what she was saying.

"You are embarrassed by all this," she said. "Don't be. I say these things most indiscriminately to the most casual acquaintance." A shadow crossed her face and the corners of her mouth trembled. "To you I will add the truth. Someday he shall look at me without disgust as many other men have done. Then I shall be able to leave him." She shifted her mood and smiled pleasantly at him again.

She stopped talking—it was time for Hans to state his case. "What I came to ask you about . . ." Hans faltered.

"Yes?"

"It is, of course, none of my business. You have every right to tell me that."

"Oh, my! You want to know something about my dark passions! Then ask, Mister Aldik! Please feel free to ask," she said, with the tracings of gentle laughter.

"Were you sleeping with Irish Woodrow during the time he wrote that unfinished book?" he asked.

"From time to time."

"But there never was anyone else in his life, was there?"

"I never inquired." She was reacting coolly, the smile never leaving her face.

"I'm sorry," Hans said. "I thought that if you knew of anyone, I might talk to her."

She shrugged her shoulders. "You have nothing to be sorry for." She sat there waiting for him again.

Hans could feel the sweat in the palm of his hands. There was only one way he knew he would be able to get the information he wanted from a woman like Claudia Mitchell and he was aware that she expected this and had invited the obvious from the first time they had met. He would have to let her think he was going to make love to her. He stood up now and walked over to the bookcases which flanked the fireplace. "Quite a collection," he said, poking at the row of books with her name on them.

"If you are bored you don't have to borrow a book," she

said, from the depths of her chair. He did not pick it up. "Oh, by the way, would you know where I could reach Mrs. Devlin?" he asked, his eyes still on the row of books and away from her.

"Mrs. Devlin?" She inquired in a voice of nonrecognition. Then, "Is that the woman who was in the house with the girl when the police came?"

"Yes."

"The girl would know, I am sure," she said, without a trace of suspicion in her voice. Hans quickly changed the subject.

"What have you written?" he asked.

"Five novels, two biographies, four collections of short stories and three books of essays and articles. Not too much more impressive than your own collection."

Hans took out one of her books from the shelf. "One of my favorites," he commented.

"Not one of mine," she said, and leaped up catlike, her shoes mysteriously left behind on the seat of the chair. She paused, planting her bare toes into the thick pile carpet and stretched her legs and arched her back. She was only a foot or so away from him. "I'll autograph it and give it to you," she said.

Hans replaced the book on the shelf. "That's kind of you, but I try to keep myself mobile—no possessions." He turned back to her. For all the danger that was potential in the woman, the disagreeable characteristics that were so ingrained in her, and the fact that she was no longer young, Claudia Mitchell was enormously appealing. He was close enough to smell her perfume—for she wore just enough so that you were aware of her scent only when she passed close or leaned in to you. It was an unusual heady, musk scent he had never known on any woman before. "Is your husband liable to ring you any time?" he asked.

"Not on the weekend."

152

"Who knows where I'll be by the weekend." He smiled. "Did you have something in mind?"

"Only that I hate hotel rooms."

"I am not fond of hotel rooms myself," she said. "Perhaps not for your reasons. Recognition is the price of fame. And I am married, you are not."

"How about that barge of yours?" he asked.

"All right," she said. "Tomorrow?" she asked.

"What time?"

"Earlier." She glanced at the clock on the mantle. "Say . . . one?"

"How do I get there?"

"I'll drive you."

"I don't think that's so advisable, do you?"

She shrugged her shoulders. "Why not?"

"Leaving London together is no problem. In a city no one notices. But arriving in a small village where the barge is probably docked is another matter," he explained.

She laughed. "Why, Mister Aldik, I am surprised at you!" She poked him playfully in the ribs. "My husband won't shoot you."

He took a deep breath and brought the words up in spite of the fact that they seemed to choke him. "I know a lady who might poison us, though."

Her face went white. "She's back?" she asked. He nodded his head. "And no doubt madly in love with you and no doubt that is your fault. How ghastly."

"Your husband should be forgotten from this moment and so should . . . the girl. But if some camera bug took a picture of us together and sold it to one of the daily or Sunday scandal sheets for a few quid . . . well . . ."

She laughed again, throaty, the flint shining in her eyes. "The nearest village is Dortington and that's over two miles from where I keep 'The Trusty.' Shall I pick you up?" she asked.

"I'm stopping at the Kensington Gardens. It's out of your way. I'll meet you at the front entrance of the Dorchester," he said.

She smiled. "You are rather a coward, Mister Aldik. I shouldn't think you would appeal to me at all."

"I am a bachelor. I am surprised that I am playing games, Mrs. Mitchell, that as an unattached man I have no need to play." He started toward the front door. She remained where she had been standing.

"You can call me Claudia, Mister Aldik." She smiled.

He let himself out, and ran down the steps of her building without even waiting for the lift. She had revealed the name of the town and the barge too easily. Perhaps she didn't suspect him. He doubted that. Maybe there wasn't a barge. Or if there were, perhaps she knew there was nothing he could find on it.

He now began to doubt there was a manuscript that had belonged to Woodrow. But there was something that she had wanted, something she let remain in the house all these years because she knew Amanda Nightly was no threat to it, but which she feared might fall into other hands. He had no idea at all what he was looking for—but if it was on the barge he was determined he would find it.

A low mist hovered over the tops of the trees in Hyde Park ready to settle down for a long, foggy evening. He glanced at his watch. It was nearly three. He had no idea where Dortington was (and the new thought came to him that there might not even be such a place!)—or how far. With the day turning gray like this it would certainly be dark by five and he felt he should be back to Luanne by then. Still, this was his only opportunity and he had to take it. He began to walk up the street toward the Hilton Hotel where he knew there was a car-hire office. Claudia Mitchell's flat occupied a front corner of the third floor of her building. Her sitting room overlooked the park but as he had let himself out he noted that the rest of the rooms were to the other side and would have looked up Park Lane toward Hyde Park Corner, the direction he was now traveling. He waited until there were a group of young people behind him, some of the boys taller than himself, then he glanced back quickly between two of them, up to the exact position of the flat. A curtain immediately drew closed.

He had a talk with the man on the car-hire desk and he showed him the quickest and easiest way to get to Dortington. He was thankful there was such a place, at least. It would take a little under an hour to get there. But then he had no way of knowing if he could find the barge. There were dozens of small inlets around that area. It could be dry-docked as well. He would just have to trust to luck that some-one in Dortington would know where "The Trusty" was kept.

He hired a small Mini and headed on his way. There would be no commuter traffic at this hour, though coming back it would be different—there would be people coming in for theater, dinner, parties, and it looked like there might be a fog by then. Even if he made the best time and found "The Trusty" without fumbling, he could never be back before six. He thought about ringing Luanne and decided to wait until after he was off the barge and set to come home. He rode along the Thames. It was silent and still, only the ducks stirring up circlets of murky gray as they swam toward the shores in search of food. The mist was lowering. The ducks' squawks echoed eerily over the muddy surface of the Thames. He drove fast. The directions he had been given were perfect.

Claudia had been right to laugh. Few in this small village would have been able to recognize either of them. Most of the water-side buildings were shuttered for the winter. Only a few workers' shacks looked lived in. There was only a short road with a few small deserted shops, and a pub which he headed for.

It was before hours and the place was closed. It was called The Dove and the Swan and once must have perched over the Thames in white painted glory, serving ale and bitters to the tourists and enthusiasts at some regatta. Now it was a shabby establishment which resembled the hull of a deserted boat ready for scraping. Hans parked alongside the service entrance where the proprietor was emptying dustbins. "Not open 'til six, mate," he said when he saw Hans.

"Sorry but I seem to have lost my way. A French lady has a barge that is up for sale. I've come all the way down from London to see it. There's supposed to be someone there to show me over it, but I have been riding around in circles for almost an hour." Hans explained to him hopefully.

"Easy done. Figure you mean 'The Trusty.' "

Hans breathed a sigh of relief. "Yes, that's right."

"You wouldn't see it from the road. It's anchored on the backside of a boathouse. Should have 'Anchorview' still painted across it." He leaned through the window of the car and his breath was warm with whisky and his two gold front teeth had food particles clinging to them. "That mass murderer used to write there. Seemed a nice chap. Warmed his bones here most every evening. Minded the cold a lot that chap. He'd set inside rubbin' his hands together. Big hands. Bony chap."

"I know nothing about that," Hans told him. "Now if you could . . ."

But the old chap was glad for someone to talk to and he went on. "Lots of reporters buzzed around after the murders. Askin' questions. Told 'em I thought he seemed a nice enough chap. No odder than any of them other intellectuals who used to stop here in the old days. They never printed nothin' I ever tol' 'em. Fact is, not one paper ever mentioned the barge, or Dortington. Funny that. Oh, yes," he said, finally remembering Hans needed directions. "You follow the road at that next turning. Keep on even though it seems to be gettin' you no place. Not used much and the county counsel don't send no more road men down to see to it." He didn't wait for Hans to thank him, but he withdrew his head and went back to work on the dustbins.

The lettering on the front of the boathouse had been eaten away by the years. Only the first letters remained readable. Hans parked the car in a large space in front that once had been a driveway. Now the weeds choked the gravel aside. There was a split wood fence and behind it a thick mass of unattended and overgrown shrubs which blocked the view of the Thames and—if the old man had been right—"The Trusty." Hans got out of the car and headed for the fence. He could see the barge now through a split in the fence, the lowering tide slapping against its hull. There was a narrow path, overrun with weeds and ivy, that bordered the boathouse, and it seemed to be the only way to reach the barge. He could feel the mist as he walked up the path toward the old boathouse.

Apparently, at the time Claudia Mitchell originally docked here, this area had been lively, with a boating club, a boathouse and a town close enough to drive to for a drink or to watch a regatta. There were no houses on this stretch of the shore. Why she would keep the barge here now was puzzling to Hans. Certainly this was no place for a woman to come to by herself. The puzzle cleared up immediately. She used it as she was planning to tomorrow. It had become a safe place for an affair.

Hans had meant to circle the boathouse and head straightway for the barge but the front door was slightly ajar and he paused there and called out, "Anyone here?"

There were footprints in the heavy dust on the warped floor. They stopped abruptly midway into the bare interior and returned to the door again. Someone had hazarded his way inside hoping to find shelter and had decided not to remain. Hans could hardly blame whoever it was. The place was dark and smelled of dry rot and damp wood. The windows were boarded up. The high beamed ceiling had some open slits where the roofing had decayed and fallen away. Enough light came through these narrow slits to show the disrepair of the huge, naked room. It seemed to Hans the boathouse should be condemned, since the roof looked as if it might collapse at any moment.

The room had been stripped of all its stores. Only a few rusted nails and some frayed rope remained on the shelves. The quiet was oppressive. When Hans listened closely he could hear the hollow sound of the water against the outside moorings, an uneasy, restless sound. He backed out and closed the stiff door and tried, but could not bolt the rusted latch against some child who might endanger his life in search of an irresistible adventure. It seemed an odd thing for him to do, but he searched through the high weeds, found a dry stick and bolted the door with it as well as he could. Then he made his way cautiously up the path and around to the back of the boathouse where the path became a narrow wooden bridge which skirted the river bank. Hans stepped as lightly as he could and kept close to the boathouse which at this point was one side of the bridge, in case the wood beneath him gave way.

It was cold and wet now, and the day had darkened into a thick bank of gray. The bridge spanned a small cove sheltered by an overgrowth of low shrub. This was the same shrub and cove Hans had seen from the front of the boathouse. "The Trusty" was moored in the cove, and the bridge brought Hans alongside it. A duck had strayed from its course and squawked loudly from the far side. There was an answering "Caw!" in the distance and then a hard flutter of damp feathers as the lonely black bird swam through the dark waters and was lost in the heavy mist.

"The Trusty" was a great ugly barge that had never known better days. It did look sturdy, however, and Hans made the short jump from the bridge to her deck, glad to be on firmer ground. The barge bore no traces of any sea or river-faring days. There were not even the usual fittings. The cabin was oversized and had apparently been added since the days of the barge's first appearance. There were tightly drawn curtains on the windows but they were not boarded up. Hans made his way up the deck to a side door. There was a padlock on the latch. Hans moved up front.

The latch on that door was padlocked as well. The air was still but the low tide caused the barge to stir slightly in its moorings bringing with it small wisps of the chilled mist. On the far side of the barge there was the sound of a shutter or a door slapping. Hans followed the sound.

On this side, the growth on the shore hung over the deck and the wet leaves clung to the railings. There was a slight tilt to the deck and Hans had to work to balance himself. The mist was thickening into a fog and it rolled across the deck like some creeping serpent, seeming to have devoured the rest of the barge behind it. A door struck the side of the cabin again. Hans could see it now.

The latch had been broken. Hans stooped to clear the low doorway. He was standing in the main lounge of the cabin. It was large and well-furnished in bright chintzes and came as a happy surprise. There was a comfortable sofa, a long uncluttered desk, bookshelves filled with books and oddments —bottles with small ships inside them, a glass menagerie. There was an odor that was familiar. Grease and sausage. Apparently someone had recently made a meal downstairs. Hans made his way down into the modern galley. It was lighted by a burning candle—a pan of drippings still steaming beside it.

"Hello?" Hans called out.

There was no answer. Hans started toward a closed door, at the end of the galley, with a candle in one hand, picking up a kitchen flatiron from a shelf with the other.

"Hello in there?" he called again.

He turned the knob and pushed the door in quickly. There was no one there. Even in the light of the small candle this could be discerned. The room was totally and completely stripped of any furnishings at all. Hans was aware of a light bulb dangling in the center of the room. There was a switch on the side wall. He turned it and was surprised to see the light go on. Obviously the barge had its own generator. He didn't know why he should have been surprised. Common sense should have told him that the place had been inhabited by some hobo who was passing, who was afraid the electric light might announce his presence. If it had been a caretaker, he would have called out immediately when Hans got on the barge and there would have been evidence of him. Well, she hadn't rung anyone from London then. This had to be the room that had belonged to Irish. She had not been concerned at all about his coming because she knew there was not one thing here to be seen. Hans walked across the room and looked out the window. This room had the best view. If the fog had not been so low you could probably see down the length of the Thames until the next turning. Hans turned back into the room and stared at it. He knew he had thought he would see some of the same boxes that had been up in the attic rooms—or the furniture that had once been there. He had thought there would be chests to go through, wardrobes where things could be hidden. There was nothing like that. There were no drawers at all and no wardrobes, only pegs on the walls. Only the galley had any cupboards at all.

There was the sound of footsteps on the deck and in the main lounge above. Hans turned off the light and came out of the room where he stood holding the iron in his hand. He blew out the candle and the smell of the wax mingled with that of the cooking grease.

The figure that came down the stairway was bowed and old. A man in near tatters stood holding a bundle of wood in his arms.

"I mean naught 'arm!" he cried out, the fear crusting his voice.

Hans moved to the nearest light switch and turned it on.

160

The old man threw his hands over his head, dropped the bundle of wood to the floor, and stood there trembling. "It's all right, old fellow. Don't be frightened," Hans said.

"I mean naught 'arm, guv!" he said again, obviously thinking Hans was the owner of the barge.

"You broke the latch on the door?" Hans asked.

"It come away. I swear it did!" the old man said, as he began to retreat up the stairway.

"I won't hurt you," Hans assured him.

The old man turned on his worn heel and ran across the lounge and out onto the deck. Hans started up after him.

"Hey!" he called, but there was only the sound of the old man's footsteps on the wooden bridge, a crunching of gravel and then nothing more.

"Poor old coot!" Hans thought. The old fellow must have needed a night's lodging and had tried the boathouse first before stumbling onto "The Trusty." He had just gone to gather some wood for the grate to settle down to a cozy evening, probably his first prospect of such domesticity and luxury in a long while, and had not seen Hans's car in the fog when he returned.

Hans went back, switched off the light and then continued up to the lounge.

He closed the door as well as he could and shivered in the late day, the dampness from the cold Thames penetrating his body and settling in his bones. He understood why, if Irish spent time out here, he had had a hard time warming out the chill that would burrow deep down in one's marrow in fog like this. He would see if he could ring Luanne from the main road.

The boathouse rose from the fog and Hans kept carefully close to it as he made his way back to the car. The fog had filled the car through the open driver's window and for one brief moment Hans was uneasy as he turned his back to the rear seat to start the motor. The quick response of the car comforted him and the uneven familiarity of the sound bridged a slight nervousness. He backed the car up and turned it around, the headlights beamed toward the boathouse.

The old man could be seen as a narrow shadow in the entrance. Then the shadow was gone. For a moment Hans considered getting out of the car and telling the old man it was all right. It wasn't his barge. The old coot could do what he wanted. But he decided against it, knowing if the old man would remove the bolt he had put on the boathouse door he would go back to the barge when Hans was gone for certain anyway.

He straightened the wheel and drove slowly through the low fog until he reached the first turning. Then he steered the car away from the Thames and motored toward the highway where the fog would not be so thick.

LUANNE...

The sun had already left the sky and the day had turned gray with the first whisperings of an evening fog. I was filled with a tremendous feeling of well-being as I made a decision to turn off the High Street and walk adventurously on a less frequented side road. All the apprehensions the return to the great house had incurred were dissolved into less than the memory of a dream. I knew now that I could, if need be, return again, and this time the voices, the shadows, the echoes would be gone. I had awakened in the hotel to find Hans beside me, so happy to have him there, and so thankful that while I slept there had been no half-whispers of voices once heard, no mirror images of things once lived. I had slept, freed at last from the double life my sleeping hours had created for more than ten years.

162

The passers-by on this road all seemed very young. They would glance at me disinterestedly in passing, to the sidewalk, or aimlessly into the lowering cloud of fog. I seemed old to them, not worthy of their attention. Only on the telly had I ever seen young people dressed in this manner. My short excursions from Laurel Groves had led me on more provincial paths, or—of course it was possible that they had been there and I, in my own world, had not seen them. They straggled, they loped, they zig-zagged past me, like clowns in a circus parade. No two were alike—and yet, they were alike in their effort to look nonconformed. Long-haired boys with meticulously poor grooming. Girls with close-cropped hair whose make-up made them all eyes, their lips lost in pale mask faces, their bodies grotesque patches of high boots and colored thighs and short skirts. There were others who resembled Yorkshire terriers with faces hidden behind a mass of unruly hair, their figures devoured by bell-bottom trousers and long ill-fitting jackets. There were some boys who dressed like Edwardian dandies with frilled shirts and velvet collars, their hair trimmed in the manner of those times.

I passed a boutique and from inside I could hear the blastings of discordant music. Through the windows I saw racks of clothes all in jarring color and harsh design, and alongside them, pegs holding strings of beads alike in their nugget bulk and garish shades. I stood for a moment watching the young girls prancing like gangling colts, back and forth in their new clothes, as their youthful admirers gave their approval in a glance or a small gesture. This moment I pitied them their youth and their need for games and capers, but as I turned to continue on, I remembered that naïve girl of only two days before who had played the same child's game in a small ski-village boutique. How fast that girl had grown to woman!

There was a small antique shop a short distance up the road with a heavy spiral paperweight in the window showcase which caught my eye. Its center was a deep, cobalt blue swirl ruffling its way to the slender tip. The tiny crystal bubbles which followed its path made the blue look like cornflowers with rain falling from their petals. Mrs. Pritchett had a similarly shaped paperweight on her desk which had the look of fresh blades of grass in the same gentle rain. I thought they would make a lovely pair and went inside to price the object. It was unusually dear but once I held it in my hand and placed it to the light and turned it slowly so that the blue whirled and darted and the crystal droplets glistened from within, I knew I must have it. The clerk wrapped it carefully in tissue paper for me and I tucked it into a deep corner of my handbag and left the shop feeling even happier than when I had entered.

I had not bought a real gift for anyone in years. There had been a rule at Laurel Groves that on holidays we were never to spend more than ten shillings on a present for anyone. I had usually made things I thought the staff and residents might like, because it was impossible to find anything worthwhile for that small amount in the shops. It made me feel especially exhilarated, therefore, to have purchased something as extravagant as the blue glass paperweight for Mrs. Pritchett. It could only mean one thing. I no longer considered myself a resident of Laurel Groves and could therefore disregard all rules.

It was near the hour Mrs. Pritchett would be leaving her office to go to her own room where she would remain, her time her own, for two hours, while she had her tea and attended to her personal needs. The thought in my mind as I hailed a taxi was that I would give Mrs. Pritchett what I considered my going-away present and at the same time, by taking my leave of Laurel Groves on my own, I would be giving Hans a welcome-home present when we met at the hotel at five. I was conscious that the fog was moving in quickly now, but my spirits were high and my sense of independence so great that I had no forebodings whatsoever. In fact, the idea that I was on my way for a visit with a friend pleased me tremendously.

I was shocked to realize that in my entire life I had never gone to visit a friend before, or indeed, beside Mrs. Devlin, had a friend whom I could visit. I mused on that for almost the entire journey. It had never seemed such a serious omission from the normal pattern of living as it did now. I was struck with many other disallowed and curious exclusions. I had never been to a party or had a date. I had never been to the cinema or to the theater. (As a girl they were the only two places I did want to go where Uncle Stanley would not take me.) The pubs we passed reminded me I had not once in my life seen their interiors. I had never taken a tube, received a bouquet, danced with a man, or had an animal I could love. (Though I had often thought of the squirrels on the Heath as mine or the deer in Richmond Park.) Yet, all of these wants filled me with great joy because there would be so many things I could share for the first time in my life with Hans.

I had the taxi leave me off at the top of the road just outside the school. It was in darkness, of course, and the playing fields (on which I had often watched the children at their games from my window), were void of any life. But even a deserted schoolyard is a happy place. One seems to always be able to recall the last time the children's voices called out to one another in play.

I was thirty-one and I had not had a child of my own nor cared for the child of another. I did not know what that feeling would be—to hold a child in my arms. I thought about myself with *our* child. Thought about Hans with *our* children. They were silly, harmless daydreams, these dreams which I was sure most women had and which I had never had before.

The fog was thick now, mushrooming over the wall to Laurel Groves and hiding the building from view from the street. I opened the gate and started up the path. I had been away only a few short days and yet I felt like a stranger to the place and groped my way toward the front door as if I had not recorded the length of the path and number and

165

depth of the steps many times and many years before. Sister Kennedy opened the door before I had a chance to ring. It was, of course, just after four and time for her to go off-shift.

"Miss Woodrow!" She stood looking at me with surprise, not moving to either side of the doorway to let me through.

"Hello, Sister Kennedy." I glanced past her to remind her that I was still standing outside on the top step and that she was blocking my passage. She stepped through the doorway and onto the step near me, holding the door (just far enough so that it would not latch). She took my hand tightly in her free one.

"You are not coming back so soon?" she said, in a whisper. "I was so hoping . . ."

"No, I am here for a visit, but how kind of you, Sister Kennedy." No further words were needed between us. In a curious way it was Sister Kennedy's enthusiasm for this holiday that had been a major factor in my final decision. She was the youngest of the nurses and though we had never become intimates, there had been a rather nice familiarity between us. She would often tell me about her beaux and the places they took her. She was a bright, sensitive girl and I felt I should tell her she had been right, there were so many wonderful things outside Laurel Groves that I had missed! But I said nothing.

A car horn tooted beyond the front gate and she patted my hand. She held the door until I had entered, then she ran down the steps onto the path and was finally enveloped by the fog and lost to my sight. I stood waiting until I heard the gate swing open and a car door close and a motor rev and start up the road. Then I let myself in and closed the door.

I was pleased it was the time when the Sisters on duty would be going off and a new shift coming on. Sister Kennedy always managed to be the first one to leave but the others would be fully occupied completing their reports and discussing the details of the day with the new shift. This way I could go right upstairs, (where I was sure Mrs. Pritchett would be)

166

without stopping to speak with anyone. I hadn't thought about it on the way, but I did not feel ready to visit Laurel Groves. What I intended was only a visit to an old friend. More than that, I suppose, I had a great wish to share the beautiful thing that had happened to me with someone else.

I went directly across the front reception room and up the stairs where Mrs. Prichett and myself both had rooms. There were several other rooms on this floor as well, but none of them were occupied. They constituted the store rooms and equipment rooms and the doctor's surgery. But doctor's hours were always in the mornings. Mrs. Pritchett's door was closed and I rapped lightly upon it.

"Yes," she called.

"Luanne, Mrs. Pritchett."

She opened the door quickly and looked at me as if she were seeing a stranger. Then she recalled that this was her room and she was the hostess. "Come in," she said, and stood to one side as I went past her. She closed the door and leaned back on it for a moment as she studied me. "Nothing the matter is there?" she asked.

"Nothing at all," I assured her.

"I didn't know you had returned to London." She had recovered from her initial surprise and was now facing me just in the entrance to her room. "I was having tea. You will join me, of course."

She led me to the graceful table she had set up near the front window in her room, exactly for that purpose. I could feel the weight of the present I had bought for her pressing against my side from the interior of my handbag. "I would love tea," I said and crossed to the old familiar chair I had so often sat in.

It was a lovely room with its own kitchen. Mrs. Pritchett took down another cup and saucer from a shelf and joined me. The view from the window I sat at was almost identical with the one from my own room, but the fog was so thick that I could see nothing at all. Mrs. Pritchett placed my tea and some cakes in front of me but I could not contain my excitement any longer. I slipped my hand into my pocketbook and drew out the paperweight, still wrapped in its cover of tissue paper, and held it out to her. She took it with hesitation and then sat there holding it in her hands, but not unwrapping it as her eyes remained on my face.

"It's a present, for you," I finally said. "Please open it."

"Are you feeling well, Luanne?" she asked, without changing her position.

"Very. Never better. It's for you. I saw it in the window of a small antique shop and I thought how lovely it would look beside the green one you already have in your office."

"When did you return?" she asked, still not making a move to unwrap the parcel.

"This morning."

"And Mister Aldik?"

"This morning as well. He came with me."

"Is he here now?"

"No."

She placed the unwrapped present on the small tea table and stood up, visibly distressed. "You must be weary. I'll ring Ada to put fresh linen on your bed."

"You don't understand. I haven't returned to Laurel Groves. I have only come to visit *you*." I smiled warmly trying my best to *make* her understand. "I truly am all right," I assured her, noting she was still concerned. "I had a bit of a shock in Switzerland but I am fine now. I see things I did not before. I had no way of setting aside the past you see, because I never had any prospect of the future. Now I do."

"Mister Aldik?" she inquired coolly.

"Yes, Hans," I said, enjoying the sound of his name.

"He's not the right sort of chap for you, Luanne. Too worldly, too mature." She had turned away from me and was looking out the window now. It seemed there were two of her, her reflection was so clear in the glass that it enabled me to see the side of her face which was turned from me. Her

168

eyes had a faraway expression in them and when she spoke now her voice was somewhat distant. "I had not thought it would take this kind of turn," she said. "I blame myself."

"I know about it, Mrs. Pritchett. That you and Hans both planned my trip to Switzerland. That being the case you should be pleased it has worked out as it has. We're in love, you see. It means I can leave Laurel Groves forever."

She faced me, her expression now all sympathy. "I will go to your room with you," she said. She held out her hand.

I backed away. "I'm never going back to that room, Mrs. Pritchett," I said calmly.

"Nonsense." Then she saw the determination in my face. "We can find you another."

"No other, either."

"You think he loves you," she said. "I would want that for you if I believed that were true. But look at the facts yourself." She crossed over and placed her hand on my shoulder. "I don't want to hurt you, but I am sure it is better now, this way, from me."

"You're wrong," was all I could reply.

She sighed deeply. "He is merely after a story. It only came to me after I saw him the last time. He deceived me. He'll deceive you. He's not worthy, Luanne." She placed her hand under my chin and turned my face up to look into her own. "And you could never cope," she said. She let her hand fall loosely to her side, stood looking at me for a long moment and then turned aside.

She stared out the window into the faceless fog. I watched her, saddened, tormented by my loyalty to her and my personal needs. "There are so many others who need your help," I said softly.

"I knew I should make you leave before this, but I could not," she said, without turning to look at me. "I know what it is like out there. I know what *they* are like. Even normal women can't bear the pain *they* can bring into your life."

"Are you saying I am not normal?"

169

She turned. "You are delicate. You know that."

"I think quite the opposite. I was tough enough to survive the murders. Strong enough to face a trial for my own life. Self-protective enough to keep the world away from my doorstep. And now I think I am hardy enough to be a woman."

"Your memory is very short," she said, almost curtly.

"If that were so I could have left Laurel Groves years ago." I answered rather sharply, immediately sorry I had spoken that way.

"I'll pack your things for you." Her expression now concealed anything she might be feeling.

She turned and started out of the room. I wanted to stop her but I could not speak out. I followed her out into the corridor and watched as she opened the door to my room. She entered as one might enter a church. From where I stood everything seemed exactly as I had left it, and yet—(I knew, of course that Hans had been in the room but it was more than that) something seemed different and unfamiliar to me. I crossed the threshold and watched Mrs. Pritchett as she walked slowly around the room, her hand grazing the furniture, brushing the wall, smoothing the bed-linen and then lightly fingering the small objects as she passed them. There was something so private in her actions that I thought I should go and leave her alone. I turned away and started back down the corridor and met Ada.

"Miss Woodrow!" she said, surprised.

"Mrs. Pritchett needs your help, Ada," I told her quietly. Ada craned her neck. "Go on, Ada," I said, almost cross. The woman scurried away toward my old room.

I never looked back as I went down the stairs, across the front reception, and out the door. I was, in fact, half-way up the path to the gate before I paused to glance over my shoulder. The fog was rolling to one side and I could see Mrs. Pritchett and Ada standing in my window straining to see me through the dense fog patches. I saw them both very clearly. Ada with her lamblike eyes and flacid face, and Mrs. Pritchett, an expressionless mask as she looked blindly through the glass pane. I began to run.

I reached the gate and though I knew it was only kept locked after eight at night, I was relieved to find it open. I had planned to ring Radio Taxi from Laurel Groves to come and fetch me. I slackened my pace and headed in the direction of the High Street, realizing a taxi would be hard to come by in this weather. I recalled the underground station was only two streets up and made my way cautiously, but as quickly as I could, toward it. Every step that took me farther away from Laurel Groves would take me closer to Hans. If I could, I would have run, but there was the danger of knocking over some passer-by in the blinding fog if I did so.

I entered the underground station wet with perspiration, my hair astray, and my heart beating so fast that I could hear its pounding in my ears. I did not know what one did to travel via the tube. I stopped and asked directions and started down the deep, long escalator and then, growing dizzy from the height, held on to the rail and let the moving staircase carry me at its own slow pace down to the bottom. I ran then, through the tiled corridors in the direction of the train I had been told to take. I could hear the train pulling in and was determined not to miss it.

It was not until the doors of the train had closed and I was on my way back to Hans and the hotel that I remembered that Mrs. Pritchett had never unwrapped my gift.

LUANNE...

I came out of the underground just a short distance from the hotel. I could not see it even from this close range, but the road where I had purchased the paperweight was to my right which meant I should walk straight ahead no more than a hundred yards. There was an uncanny silence which struck me as I started in that direction. Traffic had stopped. There were few people about. I prayed Hans had already returned and quickened my steps as I cut through the thick gray mist.

I had surely left Laurel Groves for the last time. I knew I would never even send back for my personal possessions. I wanted nothing to remind me. With each step I mourned the days, the months, the years I had let pass in such utter nothingness, and I could not wipe the memory of Mrs. Pritchett from my thoughts.

What disturbed me was my own surprising disengagement from a woman who had been my only friend, (no matter how ill-conceived), when faced with her overwhelming need. I had run from her to save myself. Life had become too sweet to chance its loss. It had been an act of brutality and an act of survival. I found I was unsympathetic to her self-pity, only a disinterested observer to her mental aberration. If her wounds had been physical, I wondered if I would have run from her, leaving her there with only dead memories and no one but Ada to tend her. The answer crowded in on me with sickening clarity. If it had meant endangering my life at this point—I would still have run.

I found my way to the entrance of the hotel. It had a deserted ghostly appearance. There was no one outside. The lobby was nearly empty. All the lights were on, however, and once inside the feeling was warm and reassuring. They were serving tea with sandwiches and pastries directly off the main reception. I crossed to the house telephones to ring the room for I thought if Hans had returned, it would be nice if he came down and we had tea together.

Hans was not in our room. I began to worry then. Not because I was at all frightened of being alone, or of his not returning—I was done with all those emotions of self-commiseration. But, wherever he was, the fog would be dangerous and it would be difficult for him to find his way back except

172

by tube and that might not be convenient or close at hand. From the looks of the wall of fog that could be seen blocking the front entrance, it seemed incredible that it would lift before morning. I convinced myself that if I did not fear for myself any longer that I should not fear for Hans.

I decided to go into the room where they were serving tea and paused at the front reception to tell them where I was if Hans should ring or come in. I felt uneasy as I crossed the lobby, but I smiled to the clerk and made my way into the tea room keeping my pace at a normal speed. The tea room was rather crowded. It was a little late but there was nowhere for people in the room to go so they were sitting over their cold tea, smoking and talking. I chose a table facing the door so that it would be easy to sight Hans if he should pass by. I recognized Claudia Mitchell the moment she entered.

She walked, very business-like, directly to my table and glanced down casually at me. "Miss Woodrow," she said, in a silver-toned voice, "I am Claudia Mitchell."

Her eyes were bright and the smile on her face sincere. I took the hand she offered. "Do join me," I told her.

She sat down immediately. "I shall have some tea, if it is quite all right." She signaled the waiter and he came right away. "Two teas," she told him. She had commandeered the role of hostess. "I seem to like your men," she said as soon as the waiter left. "I suppose that means we should hate each other, but since I am more practiced at hating than you, the advantage would be completely unsportsmanlike. Shall we tolerate each other's company then and simply say what must be said without too many histrionics? I am totally dispassionate to women who cry, and never indulge personally."

"How difficult for you," I said. She looked at me with some surprise. I sat expressionless waiting to see what she had on her mind.

"Better than I expected!" she commented. "You are a fighter. It is, I suppose, the Irish in you." The black humor of that stirred her and she had to work to suppress a laugh.

"I was growing nervous that you might have come to some unfortunate mishap. I have been waiting nearly two hours. Thankfully, you are here and the fog will deter Mister Aldik. I sent him off on—how do you say it?" She grinned rather foolishly. "A wild goose chase."

The waiter had reappeared with our tea and a tray of sandwiches and pastries. He set them before her and she began to pour her tea. She handed me a cup which was dark and well-brewed. "Thank you," I said. She offered me the sugar and cream and then carefully studied and selected a sandwich for herself before continuing.

"You see I felt I must speak with you alone and I was afraid this might be our only opportunity." She ended her words with a neat bite from her smoked salmon sandwich. Her teeth were even and white and her mouth terribly well-drawn. Even in the gesture of eating, Claudia Mitchell had the look of a polished, highly intelligent and alive woman.

"How shameless to send anyone away on a wild goose chase when honesty would have done the trick," I told her.

"Never!" She laughed. It was a deep, well-considered laugh. "Never!" She leaned forward as she popped the remainder of her sandwich into her mouth and quickly devoured it. She let me wait the moment until she could speak, looking directly into my eyes all the time. "He underestimated me—and it seems he has underestimated you as well. It is nice to know such a strong, solid man has his weaknesses." She leaned back again studying me, those eyes never once diverting from my own. "But Irish did not, and that is really the important thing."

"Where exactly did you send Hans?" I asked.

"Dortington. Where I keep a barge. I am sure he hired a car. It is only an hour's drive but the fog will detain him several hours at least. I would not expect him back until much later this evening if I were you," she said brusquely.

I was furious at the woman now and the anger was difficult for me to push down. "That was a stupid and incredibly selfish thing to do," I snapped.

174

She gestured with her hands. "Yes, I suppose." She took a long sip of her tea before she spoke again. "I do know where the unfinished manuscript is, Miss Woodrow, though I only found out after Mister Aldik's first visit. But, I have always known the contents of the manuscript. I don't need it to refresh my memory. I think you and only you should have it, and then if you want to give it to Mister Aldik, that is your affair, or if you want to destroy it, that is another. I searched for it in the beginning so that I could prove that Irish Woodrow knew there would be a murder and that he knew more—who that murderer would be and that he was not that person. I still loved him then and proving his innocence was important to me. Not any longer. Now I know that the survival of what he believed in is more important than that of his good name." She took out a cigarette case and offered me one before taking one herself. She inhaled deeply after hers was lit and then watched my face closely through the swirl of smoke she had blown between us.

"If the manuscript exists, I want to see it and give it to Mister Aldik, and the police, if there is any new evidence in it," I said clearly.

"I don't think so. You see Ira Sean believed you would be the murderer. He set you up, in fact. You were to be his exterminator. And the book is so written that I am sure it would give anyone, Mister Aldik or the police—pause."

I felt the blood leave my face. It seemed impossible that she was saying what I heard. "It is not credible," I said, but my voice lacked assurance.

"Only you can know of course. But, I would think about it very seriously before consulting Mister Aldik." She pressed back in her seat again. "Yours is a new love—not even bound by sex yet." She smiled at my reaction as she said this. "I am a woman who can tell such things," she said dryly. "Without sex, with his principles . . ." She shrugged her shoulders. I thought she might be going to say something in French but she said nothing else. Instead she crammed forward against the table and deliberated for an ungodly length of time on a pastry. Then she lifted it surely to her plate and began to devour it systematically.

My mouth felt dry but I asked the question she knew I would ask. "Where is the manuscript?"

"I think you should consider it first—most carefully. Then ring me. I am in the book. Tomorrow morning, say? I will tell you then where it is." She spoke between mouthfuls. Finally she put down her fork and knife. "I loved your brother very much," she said quietly, her face rearranging itself into a desperate femininity. "I am prepared to help you anyway I can."

"Why now—after all these years?" I asked, the words slipping out before I could stop them.

She merely smiled enigmatically at me. Then she got up, folding her serviette carefully and placing it over her plate. Ring me in the morning and we'll talk then." She glanced out the window. "I shall have to hurry home now before the fog gets much worse." She sighed deeply and let the air out slowly. "Thank you for tea, Miss Woodrow." She smiled. Then she turned on her heel and walked briskly out of the room, across the lobby and was gone.

I had been sitting there nearly a half-hour after her departure, so wrapped up in my thoughts that I had not kept my vigil on the door and seen Hans enter. I was shocked to see him just sitting down in the chair Claudia Mitchell had vacated. He looked pale and exhausted but in good spirits.

"I am thankful you are all right!" I said.

"I am damned glad to find you waiting," he smiled.

"Would you like some tea?"

"I think something a little stronger might be permitted." He called the waiter over and ordered a whisky and soda. "You want to tell me about your day?" he asked.

"I went shopping." I said rather gaily.

"Did you now! Tell me about it."

I proceeded to tell him a gay and much embroidered account of my short shopping excursion, going into details about the young people I had seen and the boutique, taking a

176

glimpse I had had of anything and turning it into a full incident. I was determined to keep the mood light and had made up my mind from the moment he sat down that I would not tell him about either Mrs. Pritchett or Claudia Mitchell.

"What did you buy?" he inquired, once his drink had been served to him and I had given him a moment to put in a word!

"You'll laugh at me—nothing," I lied.

"Out shopping all afternoon and nothing! What an unusual woman I'm in love with!"

"Well, I probably would have done—I had seen something I liked, but then the fog—well, I thought it better to return." I kept the lie up, feeling the heat of it all through me, hoping my eyes and the flush in my cheeks would not betray me.

"And right you were! What a day! I had some business just outside of London. An old publisher friend of mine I had to see," (he was going to veil the truth as well!) "so I hired a car. Drove all the way down there—say . . ." He began to digress and tell me stories about the things he had seen on his way down to Dortington. (He had mentioned the same village so I knew that part of Claudia Mitchell's story was true anyway.) He told me about the poor ducks on the dark, cold Thames and a hobo on the road grilling sausage, he said, in the fog. "Never did get to see my friend. He was stuck someplace else. The fog was so bad, I decided it was too chancy and I parked the car at a train station, took a train in and a tube back to the hotel."

That was how he had returned sooner than she had expected. I wondered what on earth he would have done—any of us would have done—had he returned to find Claudia Mitchell and myself having tea together, and how, indeed, she would have handled such an impossible situation!

"Now," he was saying, "What shall we do tonight? Something special, I think."

"What can we do in this weather?" I smiled.

"Well, I have had a look at the dining room. Desolate! And anyhow, we've had it with hotel dining rooms. But if you sit here, I will fetch a present I bought you." He stood up and I looked at him with surprise. "I came out of the tube station to find myself directly in front of a ladies shop and although it was closed, the owner was stranded there because of the fog and so he let me in." He walked quickly across the restaurant and then reappeared in moments with a large dress box which he had obviously left at the Hall Porter's desk. He placed it on the seat beside me.

"Open it," he said and stood there grinning at me like a small boy. I remembered how anxious I had been to have Mrs. Pritchett open my gift and I pulled the string and undid the parcel as quickly as I could. It was a lovely floor-length gown. I glanced at him with some surprise, not being able to imagine where I could wear such a gown but loving it with all my heart. He was grinning sheepishly and sat down very close to me. He took my hand in his, "We are going to have a very formal dinner right in our own room," he said.

HANS...

She stood in the doorway from the bathroom and the sight of her stunned him. She was more beautiful than he had believed she could be. She had the kind of bearing royalty had. She stood there, with her head high and her shoulders back, making the bathroom threshold seem like the entrance to a grand ballroom. The enamel washbowl, the tiled walls and the sound of adjoining plumbing could not destroy the illusion that a princess stood before him. The dress was exactly right for her. It was a heavy, imported French brocade, beaded brilliantly with emeralds and rhinestones. The neckline rose discreetly to meet the curve in her throat. She was draped in the rich fabric from neck to toe, but her arms were bare.

178

It was the first time he had seen her flesh exposed. The small slope of her shoulder was Rodinesque. Her arms had an incredible vitality to them as if they could be capable of life on their own. The beads on the top of the dress exploded into green and silver reflections beneath her chin, making the white skin seem curiously incandescent. The bodice skimmed smoothly over her high breasts (he noted she wore no restraint) and wrapped itself snugly around her long, lean torso and trim waist. Then the skirt billowed out and fell into the giant waves of white brocade, each wave crested with the same jewels which decorated the neckline of the dress.

He had taken the white pumps from a mannequin in the store window, knowing she would not have a pair of shoes to go with the dress and that it would not be right without them. He had no idea of her size, but now as she stood squarely in them, their rounded tips poking from beneath the deep hem of the dress, the very ease with which she stood in them conveyed their apparent correctness of fit. She had piled all her hair becomingly on top of her head in a bed of thick, black curl. Her ears were exposed and he realized he had never seen them before. They were small and almost without lobes. He made a mental note never to buy her a pair of earrings. She wore no make-up, but it was not needed because there was a special light in her eye and a glow in her cheeks and a moist excitement on her lips that could not have been put there artificially.

She was smiling and holding the gloves he had bought in one hand as if they were her scepter. "These, too?" she asked, a lilt in her voice.

"The effect wouldn't be total without them." He grinned.

As she went to pull them on she was aware for the first time of the table which the waiter had set up while she had been dressing in the other room. It shone with gleaming glass and polished silver and spotless white linen. "Candlelight!" she exclaimed with delight, watching the flames reflect in all the polished surfaces—making the table look almost a living

179

thing. She glanced at him now for the first time. He cleared his throat with small embarrassment. "And you're wearing a dinner jacket!" she added with pleased surprise.

He bowed low and she laughed a deep, throaty well-pleased laugh. Then he took her gloved hand and placed it lightly on his arm and led her to her chair, pulling it aside for her and then helping her slide it back into position before sitting down across from her. The candles were placed so that they framed her face and their flames reflected tiny flashes of red into her shiny black hair and turned the rhinestones on her dress into orange diamonds. She looked very young—not long out of her teens.

"You look positively splendid." She glowed across the table at him.

"You look pretty good yourself," he commented.

Beside them there was a bucket filled with ice and a well-chilled bottle of champagne which he had opened just before she entered the room. He poured them each a glass and she carefully removed her gloves and placed them in her lap and then raised her glass to his as he made the toast. "To Her Royal Highness, may her reign be long and happy and blessed . . ."

"To His Most Serene Majesty," she interrupted rather grandly, and touched her glass to his before sipping the champagne. She breathed deeply as she drank. The bubbles troubled her and made her eyes tear. "I have never had champagne before," she admitted.

He offered her some canapés. "Caviar?" he asked in mock tones of elegance.

She took a canapé gingerly and glanced smilingly at him. "Nor caviar," she confided, making it sound as if she had just shared a state secret with him!

He watched her as she ate, observing every small detail of her face. There was no self-consciousness whatsoever between them. He got up after a short time and crossed to the door which led to the corridor and opened it. A waiter in evening clothes stood just outside. "Her Royal Highness is ready for dinner," he announced. Luanne covered her mouth to hide the smile she could not keep back. The waiter entered the room bowing low. He seemed entranced and honored to be selected to serve this dinner. He kept taking quick side glances at Luanne when he was sure they were not watching him, trying to place her, sure she was really a member of royalty. While he served he thought of all the branches of the different royal families, but never settled in his mind which she might belong to. One thing he was sure of was that she was a true aristocrat. Luanne, enjoying the game, played the game to the hilt. Hans was amused by her. She was a good actress and she had an unrealized sense of humor which now began to expose itself. The room was warm with their pleasure. They chatted effusively. Light banter like rain on a summer's day. They were enacting a charade. He was quite conscious of the change which had come over her. He had sensed it when they were having tea earlier. He was aware that his presence accounted for her new attitude. She was a woman who felt loved now. She was radiant, hopeful, a person of importance. Eventually the mood would have to shift, but he was going to do everything he could to sustain it for her. It wasn't difficult. He felt changed himself.

There was nothing he had not attended to. Although the hotel kitchen was not really first rate, the dinner moved from course to course with such elegance and so many surprises and moments of shared excitement, that the quality of the food seemed of little consequence. He had made sure the menu was properly Continental for the occasion. She had never had most of the dishes before and she clapped her hands with delight and gave the waiter a smiling, "Bravo," as each dish was unveiled. ("I will convey Your Royal Highness's approval to the chef," he would say each time and bob his head, and she would fight back the smile that played at the corners of her mouth and reply, "I will be most grateful.") There was potted shrimp first, then a lobster bisque. Then the waiter entered with a flaming Steak Diane. She drew back in mock surprise when it went up in flames and sighed with deep disappointment when the flames burnt out. For desert there were tiny, pink and white decorated petits fours served with rainbow colored ice. The waiter opened a fresh bottle of champagne as soon as the first was dry and Hans and she took turns creating a new toast.

She grew gently intoxicated as the meal progressed, but Hans watched her carefully, making sure she did not overdo. Both of them had been able to detach themselves from any of the events which had led up to this moment they were presently sharing. Finally, dinner was over and the waiter, with the deepest bow of the evening, thanked Her Royal Highness for the privilege of serving her and then wheeled out the table and left them discreetly alone. Luanne was laughing softly at nothing spoken, nothing gestured. A laugh that came from happiness which was too much for one person to keep inside herself. He thought he loved her more that moment than he had ever thought himself capable. Then, suddenly, tears filled her eyes and her mouth trembled. Hans was up and to her side immediately.

"Luanne," he whispered softly as he wiped the tears from her face with his handkerchief. "Why are you crying?"

"Because I know I could never be this happy again in all my life."

He held her hand to his lips. "I'll see that isn't so," he said.

She sat back now and looked at him, the tears miraculously gone, her face suddenly serious and her voice surprisingly sober. The young girl had left her and in her place was a woman. "Oh, God," she said quietly, "please don't say you want to see me forever like this! Like some princess from an imaginary country. The Land of Cockaigne, or the Kingdom of Mico-mican, or the Isles of the Blest! It has been a most, most beautiful evening, but please, don't make me keep it up. There was a poem. I believe Irish must have written it because I never did see it in any book and he would often recite it to me." She began to recite in a tender, slightly musical voice.

> "There was a dream land
> Dream I, dream I.

A cloud cuckoo land,
Dream I, dream I.

With castles in Spain
And pie in the sky,
With wishes for rain
Dream I, dream I.

Where delusion is seeing
And nothing doth die,
Where fancy is being
...dream I, dream I..."

She sat quietly for a moment, listening to the echo of the words in her own thoughts. Then she smiled obliquely. "I love you, you see. It is the only real thing which has happened to me in so many years that I am afraid I can't count them. What I want, really, deeply—truly, is for you to treat me like any other woman in your life."

"I can't. You're not. You are quite exceptional," he told her honestly.

"Oh, my! It does pain so to be exceptional." She sighed.

"But there is nothing unreal about the way I feel about you," he told her surely. "Nor about the way I intend us to become part of each other's life."

"That means making love, doesn't it?" she asked quickly.

"Yes it does," he answered.

"But you are not sure I am capable of making love, are you?" she asked directly.

He came to her and perched on a table beside her and took her face in his hands and looked very deeply into her eyes. "I am only a man, Luanne. Always remember that. Whatever else I might feel for you I could not conceive marrying you without being damned sure my manhood would be satisfied. Now, I am hoping you will marry me. Quickly if we can. That should put you straight," he said in a very even voice.

"Could we make love now?" she asked. The importance of his answer to her registered in every line in her face.

Hans got up and studied her for a long moment. No words

passed between them. Their eyes conveyed everything they were thinking and feeling. She had to bear out her womanhood right at this moment and he knew it. The candles were still alight, placed now on the top of the bureau, their small lashes of flame reflected in the mirror behind them making it look as if four candles were burning. Hans turned off the overhead light and the flickering flames and their mirror images gave the otherwise darkened room the look of vespers and burnt offerings.

"Would you like me to blow out the candles?" he asked.

"No, I like them," she told him simply.

He walked around the bed and knelt down beside the chair where she remained seated. "Would you like to go inside to undress?" he asked. She shook her head and reached out for his hand. "Have you ever seen a man completely undressed?" he asked gently. She shook her head again. "We'll get into the bed and we'll just lay there for a time and talk. Is that all right?" He waited until she had nodded her head in agreement. Then he got up and walked across the room, turning his back on her as he took off his clothes and hung them carefully inside the wardrobe. He took as much time as possible, listening for her footsteps as she finished shedding her gown and began to cross to the bed. He pretended to be straightening something in the wardrobe until he knew she was safely under the covers. Then, he turned and walked to the side of the bed and got in beside her.

Both of them lay very still for a few moments, their bodies bearing the chill of the cold, clean sheets, not touching, several inches apart, letting their thoughts fly and their bodies relax. The champagne mood of short moments ago was gone and in its place there was the gentle tingling a sweet wine might evoke. Neither of them looked at each other but at the streaks of light on the ceiling which were caused by the reflections of the flames from the candles.

"I'm sorry it's not raining," she said softly.

"Why?" He turned to look at her now. Her glance was still

fixed on the ceiling. The sheet rose and fell with her breaths and her warmth was now reaching out and touching him, but she lay terribly still.

"I like the sound. Especially at night."

"Next time I will have to order it in advance."

"I almost always sleep with the shade up and the window open. I like to see the night sky."

"Next time I'll make sure there is no fog, as well," he said quietly and very seriously.

She turned her face to him. Now they were both accustomed to the dark and could see each other clearly. The candlelight flickered across their faces. Their eyes held.

"I'm not afraid," she told him.

"There is no reason to be."

Later, after she was asleep Hans thought gratefully that he no longer had to live with visions of Irish and herself. *She had been a virgin.*

LUANNE...

Never had morning tasted so sweet! At first I held on to the night, sealing my eyes to the day, stretching beneath the still warm sheets until every muscle, every nerve in my body was awake. I knew I was smiling to myself, unable to forget the feeling of Hans beside me, of his arms around me. I recalled the sound of running water in the bathroom earlier. I opened my eyes as I remembered his voice near me as I lay half-awake on the bed. He had whispered something about being back shortly and leaving a note.

"Hans?" I called out softly—more to hear the sound of his name than expecting him to answer. There were only the voices of the maids chattering in the corridor outside my room.

I lay back on the pillow, grinning idiotically up at the ceiling, closing my eyes again, evoking the vision of rising smoke swirls from last night's candles, and clinging to the forever-after treasured recollection of the fragrance of deep musk meltings. I shut out the forebodings of what might be waiting for us only short hours away and concentrated on bringing back the sound of Hans's voice in a moment of endearment. The smoke dissolved into a drifting shadow of his face, a dream half-remembered, and the musk which had filled my head moments before was now the spice-scent of his after-shave which still lingered.

I came fully awake then. The shades were up and brought the ashen day into the room. The fog was lifting, leaving exposed gray patches of early morning sky interspersed in its layers. The room was on a high floor. Below me the rooms must have looked out on a sky which was leaden and dull, and up to a solid blanket of fog. But through my window there was pattern and form and life in the moving drifts of mist. I watched fascinated for a time, eyes riveted on a space of sky clefted in a deep mass of fog. I was unable to turn away until the last corner of it had been choked from my sight.

I pushed myself up in the bed and ran my hands carefully through my sleep-tangled hair, combing it with the spread of my fingers. Nothing could make the room seem dark or cheerless to me. I saw only the sparkle of my dress resting on a bedside chair, the sun-yellow of the goldenrods in a picture which hung on the far wall, and the clear, cool water in the pitcher on the bureau. I noticed the envelope then, propped up against it with my name written boldly across the front in his handwriting.

186

I started out of bed to fetch it and caught a glimpse of myself in the mirror. The upper half of me was bare. Instinctively I drew the sheet back up around my chin. I was conscious now of the creases in the bottom sheet as they ridged the flesh of my upper thighs, aware of my own warmth as I pushed my legs up and pressed my knees back against my mid-section. I sat there like that for a moment wondering at myself and the great pride of my own body which was now so strong within me. I lowered the sheet and swung my legs over the side of the bed and stood up, never once removing my glance from my own full-length reflection. It was as if I was seeing myself for the very first time. I smiled at the incredible innocence I felt looking at myself that way, understanding that never before had my body seemed anything to be prideful about.

I pushed my feet into my slippers, removed my robe from the wardrobe and slipped into it. I took the envelope and crossed back to the bed with it and plumped the pillows before settling back against them. Then, I opened the envelope.

Darling,
   I will be at the Hampstead police station. Want to check some of their files. Not to worry. I will be back by noon. Love you.

He had not signed the note which gave it an even deeper sense of intimacy. I studied the word, "Darling," feeling it had never belonged to anyone else before. No one had ever called me that—and yet, it seemed the most natural thing for Hans to call me. *Darling.* I savored the two syllables for a long moment, closing my eyes and holding the envelope and the note close to me, saying the word over softly to myself. Then, as if coming out of a trance, I opened my eyes and folded the letter neatly in half and carefully slid it into the pocket of my robe as I began to make my own plans for the morning.

It was now shortly after nine. Too early to ring anyone. I

would take a leisurely bath, dress, go downstairs and have some breakfast in the dining room and ring Claudia Mitchell at ten to ask if she could see me directly. I knew her answer would be "yes." She would put off anything on her schedule for that purpose.

The gown was still resting smoothly over the small chair. I tucked one end of the towel neatly under the other tightly around my chest so it was fashioned into a toga of sorts and crossed over and lifted the dress in my arms. It was quite heavy and yet I recalled when I had worn it it had felt a part of my own skin and no excess weight at all. I hung it very carefully in the wardrobe and then went back and took the shoes and gloves and placed them side by side in one of my cases. I selected the clothes I would wear with utmost care. It was as if I was dressing someone else for the stage. Every detail received my severe scrutiny as I studied the image it created in the mirror. In the end I coiled my hair and secured it close to my head so that it swept off my neck and back from my forehead.

Claudia Mitchell suggested we meet in the coffee shop at the Hilton Hotel. When I arrived she was already seated in a far corner warming her hands on the outside of her coffee cup. There was a flicker of nonrecognition in her glance as I started for her table. Nothing could have pleased me more. I felt a different person than the one who had had tea with her the afternoon before. I knew this morning we met on more than equal terms.

"Breakfast?" she asked.

"I've had mine, thank you. Just coffee."

The waitress in her crisp blue and white cotton dress poured hot coffee from a glass urn into the cup already waiting at my place and left us alone. There was a moment of stiffness between us. Neither of us spoke. I took side glances at some of the American tourists seated at tables around us, listening to snatches of their conversations, but aware always of the presence of the woman across from me. I waited until she spoke first.

"I see you have now slept with Mister Aldik." She smiled.

I tried to cover the embarrassment her words had stirred in me by pretending I had not heard what she had said. I composed my face into an expression of detachment. "You asked me to ring this morning," I said. "Truthfully I only did it out of female curiosity. You interest me, Mrs. Mitchell." I was pleased with the detachment I heard in my voice.

"You are lying badly," she replied.

"Perhaps you have not listened to the truth very often recently," I countered, still feeling in full control.

"Enough to recognize it when I hear it and miss its ring when I don't," she said smartly. She smiled an uneasy smile. "You interest me, too, Luanne," she said with expert charm.

Her use of my Christian name somehow surprised me. I tried desperately to hold on to the discipline which I had just displayed in my expression and voice. "Me or Hans?" I asked.

She took a cigarette from a packet of a thick, French brand resting on the table and struck a match to it with such a strange intensity for so common a gesture that I flinched as if the flame had seared my own flesh. She seemingly forgot me while she inhaled so deeply that her nostrils dilated and her flesh was drawn in against her sharp, square cheekbones. Something frightening was happening in her eyes. They were narrowed with hatred, the corners pinched with bitterness. Yet, at the same time, I could not help thinking she was excited by the extremity of her feeling and reluctant to relinquish its exquisite painfulness. I dared not even lift my coffee cup to my lips for fear any movement might cause her to transfer that terrible violence now within her to me. I sat silently and quietly until this spasm of fury she was experiencing finally passed.

"It is a beautiful feeling to lose one's virginity to a man you love with all your heart, is it not?" she asked to my surprise, her voice once again normal, a smile flickering across her face. She reached across the table and patted my hand. That was all. Then, she became the woman I had met only the afternoon before. "I am thinking about your welfare," she said. "I know you are a delicate girl. I think it is wonderful you are facing life now, but I fear for what your fate might be if your present faith is betrayed." Her voice was filled with sincerity. She looked at me unhappily. "Life has been too sad for you. It has almost passed you by. But here you have been given a second chance. It would be more than one person, particularly such a fragile person as yourself, could be expected to bear— to have your hopes, your trust, dashed against a cement wall of disillusionment and smashed into too many fragments to ever put together again."

She said this in such a way that I had an immediate picture of myself, a pitiful, broken creature, spending the rest of my days in a mental home. It became so vivid—the image of myself dressed in some loose cotton rag, eyes vacant and staring, hair unkempt, a dirty, neglected shell housing the non-living—that I shuddered and felt a strange chill pass over me.

"Are you sitting in a draft?" she asked. "Perhaps we should change places." She half rose from her seat.

"No, thank you."

She sat down again. "I cannot help being concerned about you," she continued. "I loved your brother very much and you are all that is left, isn't that true?" She did not expect an answer. She cast her eyes downward and stirred her coffee thoughtfully with a spoon. "What we had was very pure," she confided. "It was above the common vulgarities of evil tongues and censorious minds." She glanced at me, her head angled but her eyes looking straight at me. "He came to me filled with guilts, suffering for his weakness. He knew how delicate you were. He did not know how to tell you your desires for him were unnatural. How they made him run from his home so that neither of you had to cope with such an overwhelming problem—and yet, how his loyalty to you forced him back. Out of fear. A driving fear that you might destroy yourself."

"It's not true," I said sharply.

"He was just a sensitive, talented man with a terrifying problem when I met him," she continued. " I could not turn away from his great need to unburden himself. He had a talent I considered deserved saving even before I knew he, himself, was too beautiful a man to be lost. Oh, how torn he was! In the beginning I watched his self-torture helplessly. How many times I entered a room to see him pacing up and down, running his hands frantically through his hair—as if trying to tear his thoughts from his head with the gesture."

"I won't listen to any more of this!" I stood up. She took hold of my hand and held it and I was forced to either create a scene or quietly do her bidding. I sat down again.

"So he would go back to you and feed you love as a kindly doctor might spoon an alcoholic spirits so that he might attempt to satisfy and stop his craving at the same time."

I told her, "You had better stop this right away."

Her voice became seductive. "The truth is dangerous. A whip. I know that. But you are all that is left of Ira Sean. Ten years I have considered you dead. The eighth victim. Now—here you are. But I know there is not much time for either of us." She was leaning across the table to me. She still held on to my hand and was drawing me even closer to her. Her perfume choked me. It was a heavy scent. One I was not accustomed to. "To me, you see," she said, "he never died. But while I accepted you as dead, I had to live with your ghost which was ever-present with me. And that ghost has always come between Ira Sean and myself. If you had been buried with them all, it would not have helped. Dead, I could not fight you. Alive, I could and can. As long as you live I can look to you and say, "There she is. She is no ghost." And I can constantly reassure myself with your presence that Ira Sean would turn from you now, turn instead to me—because you see, as an illusion or as a ghost, nothing I am can compete. Ah! But as a woman! I am more woman than you could or ever shall be! I am confident of that. Sure. I could easily drive you from my thoughts then. You will no longer stand between Ira Sean and myself."

She gave up her grasp on my hand then, releasing me with such a convulsive gesture, pushing me away from her so violently as she drew back harshly in the other direction, that for a moment I had the terrifying feeling that in her mind she was pushing me over the side of a cliff willing me to be killed. I experienced almost the same dizzying sensation I might have had had I been falling from a terrible height. I closed my eyes and gripped the edge of the table and the sensation suddenly became a horrifying reality. I could feel the air rush by me, grabbing and tearing at my clothes, could hear its angry howl as it missed me. And when I came close to the end of my fall, I could see the jagged stones beneath me, and an angry sea smashing against them, impatiently waiting to take what might remain of me after I had been dismembered by the sharp rocks, to feed to its hungry water-life. And above it all, that scent—the sweet, overwhelming odor of death. I held onto the table as if it was a branch that had been miraculously held out to me to stop that sickening fall. The feeling was passing. I relaxed my hands and slowly opened my eyes. She was seated easily in her chair. For all the world we were one woman having a casual morning chat with another.

She called over the waitress. "More coffee, please." She spoke with warm politeness. She made some small conversation with the girl about the weather, dismissing my presence completely. When the girl had left our table she did not look up at me. Instead she lit a fresh cigarette, drew on it, rested it in the ashtray, sipped her coffee, and then thoughtfully stirred it, not adding sugar or cream and staring into the small black whirlpool she was creating with great concentration. "You should understand," she finally said, still not looking up

192

at me, "that I have my own selfish reasons for your welfare, and that your present return to actual existence is something which I must do anything in my power to sustain."

She smiled at me now. She was again that attractive and terribly feminine woman displayed on the jackets of her books. "What a terribly perverse world this is," she commented. "Under ordinary circumstances I would not even waste the time to acknowledge a graceless woman like yourself and here I am! Fighting for your life! Perhaps, now, you will believe what I will tell you." The smile disappeared but her face seemed untouched by any anxiety. "I think your Mr. Aldik is a threat to your well-being. He is a man who has lived all his days with murder and death. It lacks reality for him any longer. And for all his success his life has been completely unfulfilled. He is a good, competent writer but not an original thinker. He has garnered financial rewards, but not true critical success. Oh, yes! An early award or two when the critics were hopeful, generous because of his youth. But since then— nothing." She picked up her cigarette carefully flicking the ashes as if removing a delicate growth on a living thing. She looked away from me and impartially glanced around the room. "This book means more to him than it is possible for you to suspect. He believes it will bring him immortality. That means more to any writer than fame or money. He is using you. When the book is done he shall cast you aside."

"If you are quite finished," I said, "I believe I shall leave." I went to push the chair back so that I could rise and found to my surprise that her leg was extended beneath the table so that her foot was behind one leg of the chair and as I tried to pull back she exerted all her strength creating the leverage with that one foot to restrain me. I was locked in close to the table as unable to get up as I had been when her hand held me.

She was smiling at me again. She clucked her tongue as a remonstrating adult might to a disobedient child. "Don't be in such a hurry to run away from the truth," she said. "I am trying to help you and you have to first be aware of the truth. You are a delicate girl. Unworldly. If you aren't aware— totally aware—of Mr. Aldik's ruthlessness you *know* you could break completely. End up some place far worse than Laurel Groves." She smiled seductively. "Don't walk away from the help I offer you," she said.

"I don't want anything from you at all," I replied.

"Of course not. You think you are happy now. You think you are loved. You want nothing to change that." She shrugged her shoulders. "I am a woman. I understand. But nevertheless, you will think about what I have said."

"Nothing you could say could matter to Hans and me," I told her.

"For both of us, I hope that is not so. Oh, yes, I am well aware my feelings for Ira Sean are suspect as well. But I am not mad as you are thinking now, but perhaps I am obsessed. I can see that myself. Admit to it. Maybe the thing I should do is fight that obsession. But then, you see, I will have nothing. It would be suicide for I am a woman now long past fifty. Yes, I am still attractive to men. But, though I amuse myself with the game from time to time, they no longer are truly attractive to me. All I have is your brother. Lose him and as a woman, I am dead." Her face lost all expression for a moment. It seemed only a mask and not a face at all. "So," she continued, "to have the obsession is safer for me than to rid myself of it. Let us agree then that I am a most uncommonly selfish woman, but that it is evident that my intemperance can at this time save your life as well as my own."

A smile returned to her lips. The mask became a living thing. Her voice recaptured the same even pitch, the incredible quiet command which bound me to her and forced attention from me. She had withdrawn her foot from its grasp around the leg of my chair. I took hold of the rim of the table and pushed the chair back and rose as quickly as I could, in one movement. I breathed easier.

I had expected her to anger or perhaps create a new deterrent. I turned my back meaning to walk away from her, intending to dismiss her with that single gesture. "Don't be a foolish woman," she said heavily."

I turned back to her. She now held a manuscript in her hand. It must have been resting under her chair or against it all the time and I had not seen it. I knew it could only be one thing. I could not suppress my surprise. I could feel the jolt of its impact through my entire body. I knew she had to see it. She did not visibly react in any way. Slowly, I held out my trembling hand for a long awkward moment and then took the last work which Irish had done into both my hands and held it against my breast, staring at her as my pulse beat against the leather springback cover. I had immediately recognized it as one I had given to Irish myself as a Christmas present, the cover he always used after that time to bind whatever loose pages he might be working on.

She placed her arms on top of the table. They were unlined and the skin molded smoothly to the fine bones beneath the flesh. She drummed her fingers casually on the tabletop. Her hands were still young and supple and lithe. I could imagine her beauty, her attraction when she was young. I could see the woman Irish must have seen ten years earlier. The room became oppressively close. I found it difficult to turn away, to cross to the door, to take the few steps to the outside street. Finally I stood at the curb, a taxi waiting for me, and I moved to get inside.

It seemed a million years until I leaned back against its comforting leather seat which was still warm from the last occupant, glad to feel traces of the living. I could see Claudia Mitchell through the plate glass window of the coffee shop as she waited while the waitress filled her coffee cup still another time. The taxi pulled away from the curb, and the

195

restaurant was now behind me, but in my arms and still clasped tightly next to my heart—there was the harsh reality of Irish's manuscript.

HANS . . .

Hans had been at the police station ten years before. He was surprised to find the same policeman on the desk and more so that the man recognized him.

"Mister Aldik, isn't it?" the man inquired courteously.

"Yes, it is, but I don't know how on earth you could have remembered my name, Sergeant . . ."

"Calahan. Lost your passport as I recall. Pride myself on things like that. Nothing more important to a man in my job than a good memory." He knitted his thick brows together. "You came in just at the time of the Woodrow murders, if my memory hasn't failed me," he added.

"It hasn't," Hans told him.

"Well—and what can we do for you, Mister Aldik? I do remember that you are a writer. Very quiet in the station lately. Nothing happening to call for international writer-types," he said.

"I'm interested in the Woodrow murders as a matter of fact. Writing a book on them. Reconstructing the crime, really," Hans told him.

'It's been a long while. The file is downstairs," the Sergeant said. "Might take a bit of time to get it up for you."

"I was hoping there might be some men here who were on the case. The personal touch, you understand?" Calahan nodded his head knowingly. "Were you involved in the inquiry in any way, Sergeant?" Hans asked.

"No. I was a rookie then. I only worked the desk. Just

doing one of the young chaps a favor now," he confided, to let Hans know he had risen in the station and now held rank. "Let's see. Well, Inspector Savers was the constable on the beat then. I believe he was the first one at the house after the murders."

"Is he here now?"

"Will be in a few minutes. Just called he was on the way in. Can I be of any assistance in the meantime?" Sergeant Calahan asked.

"Yes. You could tell me what you might remember." Hans leaned across the desk, resting his arms on it. "You were right here on the desk then. You saw everyone who came in and out of the station. And, of course, they had to present themselves to you first. Did anyone or anything strike you as unusual?"

"Everything about the Woodrow murders was unusual," he said with a shake of his head. "In the first place there were never any suspects and in the second place there was not one person who came in offering evidence or claiming he was the murderer though we usually get our share of them. Then there was the young lady, Miss Woodrow. Belonged at Buckingham Palace for a garden party but not in a station house for a murder inquiry. And except for a Mrs. Devlin she was always alone. Never saw anyone else with her. Most unusual. A lady of breeding like that. She was polite and considerate to everyone. Even the reporters, and I must say they were a pretty bad lot! Gave her a very sticky time, poor girl."

The young constable who Sergeant Calahan had been relieving came back to the desk. The two of them entered into a small exchange about calls and messages to be attended to. Hans moved away to one side, lighting a cigarette and drawing deeply on it. He remembered now in almost minute detail the last and only time he had been in this station. It had been the first time they had brought her in for questioning. He had not planned to be there. He had not even intended to become involved with the crime in any way. Yet, from the moment he had seen Woodrow's face on that book jacket he felt directed by some outside force which impelled him to read the book. And when he had heard about the murders and seen her photograph in the newspapers, the same thing had taken hold of him and he simply could not turn away from following it up.

That day, ten years before, he had come to Hampstead to have lunch with a friend of his, an American film writer who was a refugee from the McCarthy inquisitions and who now lived and worked, when he could, in England. He had arrived in Hampstead too early for his appointment and had asked the taxi-driver to ride around for a time. Then it had seemed accidental that they had driven near the great house, mere curiosity which caused him to direct the driver to pass it, coincidence that at that moment she was being escorted to a waiting police car at the front gate. He had had the driver park around the nearest turning (which turned out to be the cul-de-sac near the Heath on the side of the house) and from this point he had caught only a fleeting glimpse of her. She walked with unbowed head, a creature of infinite grace and beauty, a policeman on either side of her, and many others to hold back the crowds that flanked the walk. She was proceeded by a succession of flashes from the cameras of the news photographers. She appeared unaware of them, and of the noisy crowds on either side of her. It was as if she was walking down the aisle of a church toward the altar in a movement of silent prayer. Then, the door of the police car opened for her and in one swift movement she was inside and lost to his sight.

He had the taxi remain there for a moment as he watched the crowds being fought back by the police as they tried to climb over the gates of the house. He knew they had to be taking her to the local station. He asked the driver to proceed there. On that short ride he told himself he could not refrain from reverting to his training as a journalist. She was news. He was basically a reporter and even though this was not his story, he was compelled to at least observe what he could.

When they reached the station he had the taxi park just a short way up the road. They had arrived only a moment after she, and as they drew up she was just getting out of the car, the two policemen immediately to either side of her. A new crowd had gathered in front of the station and another team of officers held them back. The same photographers leaped quickly from their carelessly parked cars and took pictures of her. She held the same expression of divinity on her face and walked with pride. In a moment she entered the station. The crowd did not disperse, obviously set to wait until she would come out again. The newsmen and photographers were blocked from entering and went back to their cars to wait.

Hans paid off his driver and then walked toward the doors of the station. He knew he would never be recognized as a reporter and he knew what he was thinking of doing was very plausible in the face of his being a foreigner. He mounted the steps and approached the constable on duty.

"This is the place I would report the loss of my passport?" he asked innocently.

"You had better see the constable on the desk about that, sir," the man had said, and stepped aside to let Hans enter.

Once inside he carried the thing through. He approached the constable on the desk and told him his story, embellishing it so that it sounded genuine enough. He had done a bit of sightseeing that morning, he told him, and took a taxi from Whitehall to the Palace. No, he had not taken the driver's number. He had not been aware anything was missing at the time, but he had taken his passport folder out in the taxi to check his air tickets and then slipped the folder back into his inside pocket. The passport must have slid to the floor of the taxi at that time. Then when he reached the Palace it had begun to rain but he had already dismissed the taxi. He decided then to visit an old American friend who lived in Hampstead instead of going on with his sight-seeing and had hailed a second taxi and it was not until they were all the way to Hampstead that he discovered (when he took out his folder again—this time to transfer the last of his British currency to his wallet) that the passport was missing and so he had come immediately to the nearest police station.

While the constable was taking down all this information and asking Hans simple questions as to his full name and so forth, Hans had sighted a narrow slit of open doorway at the end of a long corridor off the room he was in. He could hear voices. He had listened closely and was aware of the one feminine voice within. He could not distinguish anything that was being said. But there was a moment in which the door was opened wide and a policeman came out of the room, closing the door tightly behind himself. In that brief moment he had seen her sitting primly on a straight chair, facing a man across a desk, both of them in profile to him. There was a high window over their heads and the light had been slanted by blinds to fall downward. It seemed to outline only her features, throwing the rest of her face into shadow.

The policeman who had come out of the rear room joined the officer at the desk and recognized Hans's name. He told Hans he was an avid reader and enjoyed all Hans's books. Hans thanked him. The man picked up some papers and then went back with them to the room, opening the door (her position had not changed—if anything her head seemed higher, her back straighter) and then quickly shutting it so that she could no longer be seen or heard.

"Could you oblige me with your autograph, sir?" the officer on the desk asked him. "I am not much of a reader myself but my wife is. I am sure she knows who you are and would be very pleased."

"Yes, of course. What is your wife's name?"

"Nora Calahan, sir."

Hans scribbled a few words and his name on a small piece of paper and gave it to the man.

"Thank you very much, sir," Constable Calahan said as he slipped the paper into his pocket. "We'll do what we can about your passport. In the meantime I suggest you report its loss to your embassy straightaway."

"I'll do that. Thank you," Hans assured him. Then it had seemed there was nothing left for him to do but to leave the premises. He turned to go and then changed his mind. "Wasn't that the Woodrow girl they just brought in here?" he inquired.

"Yes, it was, sir."

"I don't suppose . . . no." He started away and then turned back. "Of course I am not a reporter really. Not in the ordinary sense, but a writer—this murder and that girl—well, interesting background material. I might be able to use it sometime."

"They would never let you speak to her," the officer warned Hans.

"I wouldn't want to. But what happens to her now?" he asked.

"Poor lady's being charged. Can't be helped."

"But you think she had nothing to do with the murders?" Hans asked.

"Just strikes me as a real lady, that's all."

"She'll have to stand trial then?"

"I'm afraid so."

"Have you spoken with her?"

"No, sir."

The other policeman now returned and Hans had been so occupied with his own conversation he had taken his eyes off that rear door. "Sergeant Daly here might be able to tell you a little more about the lady," Constable Calahan said to Hans's surprise.

"Purely a writer's curiosity," Hans was quick to assure him.

"Nothing much I can tell you," Sergeant Daly said. "They

were an odd lot and the house an unfriendly place. It was once, a few years ago, on my beat. One full year for that matter. No one ever came in or went out. The housekeeper did all the shopping. There were never any deliveries, not in my time anyway. But I did see *her* from time to time, leaving through the rear door and crossing the cul-de-sac to the Heath. She was always alone and she never looked my way," he finished.

"Is she perfectly all right in there?" Hans asked.

"She's being treated very well. Ladies and gentlemen seem to receive gentle handling even if they may have murdered seven people," Sergeant Daly said with a degree of sarcasm.

"*You* think she is guilty then?" Hans asked.

"I don't know. What I do know is that seven people have been murdered and she is the only suspect we have." With that he had excused himself and there was no longer any alternative but for Hans to leave.

Ten years ago—but it was as vivid to Hans as yesterday. And the memory of her face, in those few glimpses he had had ten years before, were as fresh in his mind as the memory of her face in sleep this very morning, her black hair clouding the pillow they shared. The sounds in the station brought Hans back to the present.

A door opened and shut and an inspector entered. "Oh, Inspector," Sergeant Calahan called out. "This gentleman would like to speak with you, sir." Inspector Savers paused in the center of the room and waited for his sergeant to come around the front desk and cross to him. Hans moved in closer to them. "This gentleman is Hans Aldik, sir, the famous writer," the sergeant said. Inspector Savers took Hans's hand less than enthusiastically, apparently not knowing or caring who Hans was. "We met a number of years ago," Sergeant Calahan continued, his voice now growing softer, more confidential. "He is writing a book about the Woodrow murders and I thought you might be able to give him some of your own personal observations seeing as you were the constable on the beat then and the first one to the scene of the crime."

Hans understood the lowered voice now. The sergeant thought Inspector Savers might not like any references made to his lowly days on the beat. Hans studied Savers' impassive face for only a moment and knew the sergeant had been right. The inspector was an aggressive man with an arrogant attitude, not easily warmed to nor open for casual friendships or exchanges, though obviously a good executive and a good policeman who held the respect—and perhaps the fear—of his men. Hans quickly decided that he would not care to ever be on anything less than equal terms with this man.

"We'll discuss it in my office," Savers said, as if Hans was an underling of his. Hans smiled indulgently and followed the tall, lean man through the narrow corridor to the door of the same room where Luanne had once been charged.

The room was exactly as it had been then. The desk remained at the same angle to the door. The light from the window fell in precisely the same way. Even the day was much like that day, gray—a fog lifting and the light a muted shadowed thing which had then made Luanne appear almost a silhouette.

"Come in. Close the door." Inspector Savers was already seated and shifting papers on the desk. Hans closed the door and crossed to the same chair in which Luanne had braved another police officer's impersonality.

Hans eased his large frame slowly into the chair. The inspector appeared to be busy with some paper work on his desk. Finally he pushed it aside and looked directly at Hans. "There must be something of worth for you chaps to write about beside the world of crime, which you know damned little about," he said dryly.

"I am interested in the Woodrow case," Hans replied slowly, knowing his ability not to be put off by Savers' brusqueness was now to be his weapon, "because there is a book in it that I happen to think might well be 'something of worth.'"

"The case was closed ten years ago. The files are stored away. Inconvenient. I suggest the newspaper morgues. There was little the reporters missed."

"How were you called to the scene of the crime?" Hans asked, purposely throwing Savers a left curve. The inspector shifted uncomfortably in his chair.

"A Mrs. Devlin called the station. The station notified me," he replied coldly.

"Were you there alone with Miss Woodrow and Mrs. Devlin very long?" Hans asked, knowing this questioning was irritating. Hans was letting him know he was aware constables on the beat did not handle important matters like murder inquiries and that he knew the former constable had only been sent along until the big boys got there. Hans was sure Savers was not a man who enjoyed that situation even when he was ten years younger and new on the force. But Hans could not know that what he sensed in this man was the slender string on which Luanne's life had hung all these years.

Roger Savers was a man of flint. Like flint he looked steely cold but could explode into a powerful fire which would devour or which could light up his corner of the world. It was this last hope which had driven Savers all his life. His background made him eligible for the best schools and the right clubs but his family's financial status prohibited them. He bitterly resented his situation, in the belief that he was being cheated out of a future of some distinction in the City or the Foreign Office. If the war had lasted another year or two, he would have been old enough to enlist and work his way up to even minor rank. It would have helped. But the war ended before he had that chance. He was then only one of millions looking for work. His qualifications hardly appeared brilliant on the surface and he had no connections. Now, past forty, he was still unmarried, waiting for that day when he could marry a woman he considered more on his level than the sort who had passed through his life. Nothing was to intrude on his future when he finally had it in hand.

He had joined the force hating the idea of wearing a lowly constable's uniform but believing in his ability to rise quickly and pack it away. All along he had been working for that day when he would make the jump from district to head-quarters. He was convinced the Woodrow case was his passkey. He was convinced Ira Sean Woodrow had not been the murderer. He was certain that the murderer was still at large and that he would finally prove who that person was. Then he would be given a rise and he would be with the men who made the decisions and received the glory—in Savers' opinion, his rightful place.

Hans could not know the danger to Luanne which Inspector Savers' bitter ambition represented. Nor the welcome the man experienced in having Hans come to him. Not liking— but welcome. He had been frustrated at the long time in which he had been unable to complete his planned-for coup. He had even begun to lose spirit and to flounder in other directions. But nothing as spectacular as the Woodrow mass murder had happened again in his district, and he knew that in order to accomplish what he wanted nothing less than the spectacular was called for.

Savers had known immediately who Hans was. He had a complete dossier on the man in connection with the mur- ders. He had gone over and over crowd pictures of the trial. Noting Hans's re-occurring face, he had identified him. Fur- thermore, he had followed his continued contact with the girl and even knew they had met in Klosters.

They were playing a game of cat and mouse completely unbeknown to Hans.

"I was alone with the two women about five minutes," Savers finally replied. He took out a packet of cigarettes and

lit one from it not offering Hans one. Hans smiled and removed a cigarette from his own packet, lit it, and took his
time before speaking.

"I know that was a long time ago," Hans said, "and I am
aware you don't think much about my choice of subjects—
but, for the record, and since I am the only major writer
to ever tackle this story it will stand as the record, I am sure
you are interested in accuracy and I am damned positive
your eye and ear caught more in those five minutes than a
host of reporters could have. You seem that sort of man."
Hans hoped the inspector's ego would rise to the occasion,
and sat back with some relief when he could see he had
hit a proper nerve.

Savers stood up and adjusted the blind so that the light
was thrown up toward the ceiling. "It lacked a sense of
reality. There was no feeling of crime, but rather of sleep.
The house had it. The dead had it. And the two women
who stood in the hallway with me could have just been
awakened to tend to a guest and not the police. The Woodrow girl refused to be seated. She wanted me to be very sure
I understood that she was in complete control of herself. She
was—so much so, it seemed quite odd." He sat down and
leaned toward Hans. There was a slight smile on his face.
"After all, even a lady could be expected to react to the
discovery that her entire family had been murdered while she
was in another part of the house." He sat back now, crushed
out the cigarette butt and took out a pipe. Hans waited
while he filled and lighted it. "I am a compulsive cigarette
smoker," the Inspector said as he drew on the pipe, "but
unfortunately I can't afford the price of cigarettes these days."
He looked at his pipe in disgust and continued. "Almost one
full hour had passed since she had 'feared' they were dead.
When she discovered the bodies she didn't ring the police
but Mrs. Devlin instead. Then she waited for Mrs. Devlin
to arrive and for *her* to finally call the police. Time of course,
to recover from the initial shock, but by then her great loss
should have worried her some."

"What was she wearing?" Hans asked abruptly.

The Inspector seemed surprised but did not hesitate a second before answering. "An orange dress. Silk. It rustled when she walked. She had a mass of black hair but it was immaculately held in place and back from her face with a wide band of velvet in a deep tobacco color. She looked curiously old-fashioned. Like a Victorian painting come to life. The dress rose high on her neck and the sleeves completely covered her arms and came to a point below her wrists. The dress was uncreased. It had no spots and her shoes were freshly brushed suede—all the grain going in one direction."

"You have quite a memory." Hans complimented him.

"It was a *mass* murder," Savers reminded him.

"Did you see the bodies?" Hans asked.

"I was sent to verify homicide. That could hardly be done without seeing the deceased," Inspector Savers answered sharply.

Hans did not let the inspector's edge stop him. "Anything, besides the enormity of the crime, impress you?" he asked.

"The grouping of the bodies. It looked like it was a room in Madam Toussaud's Wax Museum—where, I might add, they do have a very life-like waxen duplication." He thought for a moment. "The older brother. All the others fell as if they did not know what was happening to them. He appeared to have fallen attempting to escape or . . ."

"Yes?"

"Apprehend someone." His pipe had gone out and he went to relight it, then changed his mind and took out a fresh cigarette. He took great care in lighting it and inhaled with a look of deep pleasure.

"Not as if he had known he would die?"

"No."

"Did you testify to that?"

"I was never asked any question relative to it."

"And you left it at that?"

"Legally I had to."

Hans leaned forward. "Otherwise?"

"I wrote a letter to my superior. He chose to dismiss it without further consideration." There was bitterness in his voice.

"And you didn't go over his head?"

"Certainly not!" He sat up straight in his chair. "Any other questions, Mister Aldik? I do have a job to attend to," he said.

"Would you be able to locate the inventories taken of the house and of the possessions of all persons concerned at the time of the crime?" Hans inquired.

"Not easily," Inspector Savers replied.

"I would be very grateful," Hans said. Savers looked unmoved. "You see, in a book like this," Hans continued, "detail is important. Everything must be accurate. I will, of course, use your name with your permission and quote your last opinion about the case if I may," Hans said.

Inspector Savers seemed pleased for the first time. "Yes, of course." He leaned back again in the chair. If he was to be quoted in a book he apparently wanted to earn his full share of the limelight for he now went on talking in a more conversational manner. "When I took over this job, I reopened the case for a time. On my own, of course. Officially it was and remains closed. But I had never been satisfied. I think that girl was as guilty as hell. Seven murders and she went scot-free. I can't try her on that count again, but, mind you, I'll find something I *can* use."

Hans felt a chill go through him. "But the jury," he began.

"Jury hell! That was one aristocratic-looking lady who faced that jury and that jury was comprised of all lower-class people, conditioned through their lifetime to believe the upper classes above such vulgarities as being found guilty of murder!" He got up and opened a nearby file drawer and took out a large folder. "I did a detailed report on every member of that family and the people they knew. Bloody few, I'll tell you! The older brother was the only one who had made a life on his own. He had broken away from them finally. He had less cause to murder them than any of the others."

"There could be extenuating circumstances you know nothing about."

"I doubt it." He looked very directly at Hans, his clear brown eyes bright with his own confidence. "He had made concrete plans to leave that house forever that very next day," he said.

"I don't believe that came out at the trial," Hans commented.

"No. That was the result of my own investigation after— well, long after."

"Where was he going?"

"He had accepted a job in Southern Rhodesia."

"What kind of a job?"

"Magazine. Liberal editorial policy. Fought for the Africans and employed them on an executive basis. That sort. Just the kind of challenge—an anti-apartheid magazine in those parts—that would draw a man like Woodrow."

"How did you find that out? About the job?"

Inspector Savers put the folder on his desk and opened it. "As I said, I investigated everyone, which turned out to be damned few. There was the woman, Claudia Mitchell, whom Woodrow had been friendly with. However, she had been kept almost completely out of the investigation. Only light mention was ever made of her even in the dirtiest press. Her husband, you see, was a very influential man. I left little about him unturned and found he had arranged this job secretly for Woodrow. Without Woodrow's knowledge, that is. Woodrow got the offer direct. Mitchell obviously wanted him out of the way badly enough to allow his name to be used in that manner. It is not a politically sound cause and Mitchell is no left-winger for a start."

"I never liked the look of Colin Mitchell," Hans said.

"Looks mean precious little in murder, Mister Aldik. Motive is the thing. Mitchell had none. His wife's lover was about to be removed from the scene agreeably." He leaned forward across the desk. "But the girl . . . her feelings for her brother bordered . . . well she had a damned good motive."

209

"For the mass murder of her entire family?" Hans asked with shock.

"Six deaths to cover one."

"And how about *those* six? Did you investigate their private lives as well?"

"Impeccable," he said immediately. He straightened in his chair. "The Woodrows lived an insular existence. The older brother was the only one who had a life outside the great house." The inspector's glance turned cold. "At any rate, I have been ordered by headquarters to close my file and put it down in the basement with the old files on the case—an ultimatum as a matter of fact," he said with some sarcasm.

"And you plan on doing that?" Hans asked.

The inspector sat down. "I *am* doing that. Right now, Mister Aldik." He rang a buzzer on his desk. "Now if you don't mind," he turned back to his work ignoring Hans's presence.

The folder was angled between them, a photograph protruding from it. Something about it caught Hans's eye, and he reached over and took it out and studied it. The inspector barely glanced up at him.

"Where was this taken?" Hans asked.

Inspector Savers went back to his work. "Army Prison. First World War," he muttered.

"It had to be a Woodrow. There is a striking resemblance between Ira Sean and the man in the photograph."

"His grandfather." There was a rap on the door and then it opened and the young constable from the other room entered. Inspector Savers extended his hand with the folder in it. "Put this down in the tombs along with the rest of the Woodrow file," he said. The young man took it. Inspector Savers smiled at Hans. "The photograph please." Hans handed it back to him. "With the folder," the inspector said as he gave the photograph to the constable. The man went out again and closed the door.

Hans got up. "You know that makes no difference, inspector. There isn't one scrap of information in any of those Woodrow folders which you have not memorized thoroughly.

Headquarters may have officially closed this case, but you have not. You won't rest until you prove Luanne Woodrow guilty of mass murder and I won't rest until I prove you are wrong. Because you *are* wrong, you know." Hans started across the room and stopped. He knew this was the time to enlist the inspector's unsuspecting aid, or it would be too late. He began to grasp at straws. "Luanne has suspected her Uncle Stanley from the beginning. Certainly he was the one better off dead."

"The old gent was paralyzed," the inspector said coldly.

"I, myself, never gave Uncle Stanley any consideration, but somewhere there was, or still is, his ex-wife," Hans said.

"There is no record of a marriage or a divorce," the inspector snapped.

"Then Mary Agatha was illegitimate. A mistress then."

"We have found no record of the girl's birth, either."

Hans stepped back closer to the inspector, his own interest aroused now. "Maybe you're not looking in the right places."

The inspector held back his anger. "Whoever the mother was, her tracks have been covered well," he said sharply. "The uncle claimed he found Mary Agatha during an air raid. Maybe he did." The inspector was studying Hans. "That's all we know."

"Damned little." Hans turned away.

"Perhaps you know something vital to the case. If so, I need not remind you of your duty, I am sure."

"But the case is officially closed, inspector," Hans flung over his shoulder.

"Let us not play games, Mister Aldik."

Hans faced the inspector. "Right."

"If you do have access to any information that might prove helpful, ring me immediately."

Hans returned to the inspector's desk. "After all these years," Hans said slowly, "it seems that Mrs. Devlin and Claudia Mitchell have been seeing each other. Very secretively, I might add."

The inspector avoided a direct answer. "By secretive I

assume you mean you saw Mrs. Devlin exiting the rear of Mrs. Mitchell's flat. Mrs. Devlin, I will inform you if you don't know, is from a class that normally takes the back staircase." Something seemed to be worrying the inspector though. "They met before—years ago. Mrs. Mitchell is a rather sadly possessive woman. She was apparently driven to excesses in finding out everything she could about Woodrow. She did it while he was living and after he was dead. Couldn't let go, you might say. Woodrow had asked Mrs. Devlin to help clean the barge from time to time. Mrs. Mitchell seemed impelled to quiz her—what she knew about Woodrow's home life. He would pick up and go off for long periods of time. He would say he was going home. Mrs. Mitchell, I would hazard a guess, suspected another woman. But after all these years . . ." his voice trailed off. "As I said," he finally went on, "ring me in case anything vital . . ."

"I'll do that," Hans interrupted and turned quickly and went out of the room. He respected the thoroughness and determination of this gritty man that kept him still on the case though ten years had passed and the court and the man's superiors had decided he was wrong. Hans had not closed the door tightly and when he glanced back over his shoulder, he saw Inspector Savers' sparse figure as he stood looking out the slatted window, a freshly lighted cigarette in his mouth, the high gray light slanted sharply above him.

INSPECTOR
SAVERS...

He sat alone in the tombs, stacks of papers scattered about him. There was not one shred of evidence which had escaped

212

his scrutiny, yet he had not been able to make it all mesh, to form one clear picture. The truth was there, but he could not see it. He had lost good years. Life could have tasted sweeter to a man five or ten years younger. His private dream of advancement, of becoming an integral part of the headquarters he now fought, would never be put down, but the delay in its realization was rankling.

Inspector Savers started the task once more, for perhaps the hundredth time, systematically going through every paper again to see if this time it would not elude him. Woodrow's autopsy had only shown evidence of light traces of strychnine. He had not missed that. Woodrow had been taking a medicine which contained strychnine in minute quantity. There were forbidden photostats from the family doctor's private files. The prescription had originally been given years before. Woodrow had not seen this particular doctor for nearly two years, but Savers had tracked him down, seen the man, and found out that—though the physician had never come forward at the trial, he had been treating Woodrow before his death for heart disease. The meeting had left no question in Savers' mind that Woodrow had died from heart failure brought on by shock and stress.

Now, though, he questioned his original concept that Luanne, who had been the only one with access to this information, had used it to her advantage. It had been she who had filled his prescriptions for him. Easy enough, he had reasoned, for her to give him a substitute and to keep the original medicine until she had accumulated the lethal amount. Woodrow's suicide verdict had been based on the fact that there had been no poison in his cup. This jury apparently made the assumption that Woodrow had waited until they were all dead and then spooned the poison to himself. But the inspector believed Luanne returned to the parlor, thinking them all dead, found Woodrow alive, and that the sight of her and the knowledge of what she had done brought on his seizure. Now Savers realized that he should never have assumed, never supposed. Aldik had obviously seen Mrs. Devlin coming out of Claudia Mitchell's block of flats as recently as this present trip to London. Yet, Savers himself had stopped following Mrs. Devlin years before.

The inspector ripped out the papers that recorded his one meeting with Colin Mitchell. He read the report aloud so that he might recapture the inflection of Mitchell's replies. Then, suddenly, without bothering to return anything to its proper place, he ground his chair back on the stone floor, ran up the staircase, across the front room of the station house and out to his car, without greeting or even noticing any of his men as he passed.

The inspector greatly admired Colin Mitchell for all the things he was—that he had accomplished in his lifetime. A wartime hero. A peacetime success. He had power and wealth and the courage, native cunning, and personal command which made him a good officer, an exceptional executive and a convincing politician. The inspector would have willingly changed places with the man.

Colin Mitchell had a flat he kept separate from his wife. A man-servant met the inspector at the door, and at the humiliating thought that he might be turned away, Savers stepped almost forcibly past the man and into the front hallway where he was left alone for what seemed an unduly long time.

Colin Mitchell was dressed in a navy blue military jacket, the silver buttons polished to a brilliant shine, a silk ascot tied impeccably at his throat. "I thought we had done with all this years ago," Mitchell said, putting distance between them with the tone of his voice.

"I have a few questions to ask you, sir," the inspector said, hating himself for not being able to withhold the last word.

Mitchell walked away and sat down in a stiff leather chair. The room was filled with his memorabilia. There were pictures of the plane in which he had brought down three hundred of the enemy. Medals and plaques were displayed in cases. Photographs of Mitchell with a score of well-known politicians and national leaders stood on the table.

He offered the inspector no form of hospitality and coldly greeted him; "I seldom see people without an appointment. But you are here, aren't you, so let us come to the point as quickly as possible."

"Your wife, Mister Mitchell," the inspector began.

"I don't care to discuss my wife. If you have any direct questions concerning me, we can continue—otherwise, I must ask you to leave."

"I am sure it is not your intention to obstruct justice," the inspector said.

Colin Mitchell regarded him coldly. "This case has been closed by your superiors. I really don't care to be imposed upon further because a man has ambitions larger than his own resources."

Inspector Savers was taken aback. His face reddened.

Mitchell went on, "I will ring headquarters now if you like—while you are here."

"That won't be necessary," the inspector said. He turned to go. The man's attitude was decidedly colder than at their previous meeting, his manner nearly sadistic. Mitchell seemed to be determined to cut down Inspector Savers' stature. Suddenly, this confrontation became the most important in Inspector Savers' life. He turned back.

"You seem terribly concerned about my continued interest in this matter," he said, "unduly so, I would say. Agitated to exaggeration, I might suggest. Perhaps, calling headquarters would not be such a bad idea. There is new evidence I sent over to them earlier which they have probably had time to study by now."

Savers had had no other weapon than this bluff, yet war had been officially declared between them. He waited fearfully for Colin Mitchell to lift the receiver. He did not.

"What is it you want to ask me about my wife?"

"It is about her renewed contact with Mrs. Devlin."

"The name isn't familiar."

"The woman who was with Miss Woodrow when I arrived at the scene of the crime."

"My wife would have no reason to see this person. I am sure you are wrong." Mitchell turned and poured a single glass of sherry.

"I am sure I am not."

It was a shocking moment for both men. Each was committed now to the other's final and full defeat. Colin Mitchell slowly sipped his sherry, looking furiously over the crystal rim at the man so irritatingly and solidly planted in the center of his private retreat. "Why not question my wife?" he finally inquired.

"Because I have reason to believe she would lie to me."

"She most certainly would not!" Colin Mitchell snapped back. The inspector merely shrugged his shoulders. "Question this Mrs. Devlin then."

"I have—endlessly. She would lie as well."

"I am honored that you believe I alone am capable of truth, but I can tell you nothing—truth or untruth. My wife and I are more or less estranged. We live apart, as you see. We remain married as a formality and because we respect each other."

"Do you?" The inspector asked quietly.

"You are pressing too hard," Colin Mitchell said. "I have seen men ruin themselves at the gaming tables in the same way. A man does not have complete control of his mind and his body when he is pressed. He is not fully armed for the unexpected, nor alert to dangers." He walked briskly to the telephone on his desk and lifted the receiver.

As he presumably dialed headquarters, Inspector Savers calmly walked over to the desk and broke the connection. "I am more alert than you suppose, better armed than you suspect," he said, his shoulders squared, his eyes cool and level as he faced his own future. "I have proof your wife had been seeing Mrs. Devlin," he lied smoothly, "which I grant

216

you is not incriminating to either of them. However, I have just had placed into my possession a letter which passed between them before the crime. That letter *is* incriminating, I am afraid, sir."

Colin Mitchell paled. "What are you after, Inspector?" he asked, his voice now soft and touched with concern.

"A mass murderer," the inspector replied sharply.

"The case was solved and closed," Colin Mitchell replied.

"Your political contacts are outdated, Mister Mitchell. Ten years ago you could apply pressure. Not so today. I would say sadly, sir, that you walked away from the career you had because you feared just what is happening now. Both of us lost ten years. Too bad."

Colin Mitchell turned. "This letter," he said quietly. "How much do you want for it?"

"It can't be bought, I'm afraid."

Mitchell sat down wearily. "Have a sherry," he said off-handedly. The inspector poured himself a drink noting the quality of the label, relishing the smooth first taste.

"You have nothing to gain by pressing my wife. She is guilty only of a sexual fixation that is quite harmless to all who are, or were concerned, except myself. He had given her up, you see. Woodrow. She still can't accept it. Claudia is a very possessive woman. She could not accept my physical departure, either. I am sure all she wants, and is probably paying to hear from this Mrs. Devlin, is that Woodrow really loved her. If there is a letter which was written before the crime, I am positive it will confirm this. I keep believing that some-day this will all pass—her fancy for young men and sexual adventures, and that Claudia will become simply a mature lady of letters. Then, I can get on with my career. You see, Inspector, there is a little madness in all of us."

Inspector Savers stood staring at the bent man who was now on the verge of revealing a true emotion. He put down his sherry glass and made his way past his host. Colin Mitchell never glanced up. The inspector paused in the doorway. "There is no letter that I know of, sir," he said. He wiped his brow and wet his lips. "It was rather a nasty trap, which seems to have caught me nothing more than my own tail."

Colin Mitchell still sat quietly, studying the amber liquid in his glass. He did not seem to have heard the inspector's confession. "I will ring my man to see you out," he said finally and in a distant voice.

"I can find the way myself," the inspector replied and turned and hurried down the corridor to the front doorway. The blood rushed to his head. For one mad moment it seemed to him he had seen himself sitting in Colin Mitchell's place. He hurried out into the midday and ran down the steps to his car.

LUANNE...

I returned directly to the hotel and went to my room. Hans had not returned but the maids had already made up the room and it now seemed impersonal and unfamiliar. I stood for a moment looking at the sharply turned corners of the bedspread and the drinking glass in its sealed paper container on the bureau. The shifting fog was gone and the sky was now a solid luminous gray. From the street below I could hear the sounds of late morning traffic. Overhead there was the muffled wheezing of a vacuum cleaner. I loosened the springback binder from my own tight clasp and set it down on the bed. I sat down in the chair near the window.

Claudia Mitchell was forgotten. My mind seemed filled with vivid images of Irish. It was as though my mind was a projection screen and my thoughts fast disappearing frames of film. An image would not even have time to focus before it was replaced by another, giving my mind's eye the dizzying sensation one gets from attempting to concentrate on accelerated film. I could see Irish standing in the basement the day he came down while I was painting. He was smiling at me, but looking so distant, almost too far away—to be in the same room. A lock of his unruly black hair had fallen across his forehead and the high collar of his wool pullover was carelessly and lopsidedly turned down on one side. I wanted to push the hair back, righten his collar, but then that image was gone and instead another one appeared clear and in focus. He was seated beside me at the dining table and I could not see his face because I was unable for some reason to raise my eyes. There was only the sharp contrast of his hands resting lightly on the bright white linen on the table, his long fingers drumming silently on its surface. The rough wool of his jacket sleeve was so close to me it brushed my arm. I wanted to slip my hand under his but I could not move and as his fingers suddenly arched and the outstretched hand began to curl into a tight fist, the image disappeared and instead there was one of his hand as it clutched the edge of the rug in the living room that terrible day.

His hands had been the most vital part of his body. It seemed all else about him could possibly be dead, immobile—but not his most beautiful hands. I could remember them in all their attitudes: as he held a pencil to write, as they rested on the keys of the typewriter while he was thinking. As they held a fork, or carried a book. As they rested on his knees or were entwined around his arms or clasped behind his head even as the rest of him might seem limp on a bed. Or as they helped me pick up the broken pieces of the Wedgwood vase and gently placed them in the apron of my skirt.

I leaned forward and picked up the book and held it again. I ran my own hands over the surface of the binder which had so often felt the moist warmth of his clasp and the unrelenting pressure of his fingers. I could almost feel his touch again—as if their life had been left on that leather surface in some sort of disincarnated form. It was difficult for me to lift the cover. It was as though I was trying to tear his hands from me, pulling away from them. I felt a tremor of pain through my own hands when I finally did so.

Though Irish worked in longhand the manuscript was neatly typed on his old machine. Yet I never doubted it was his work. It had his "stamp"—I was sure Claudia Mitchell had got hold of his old machine, transcribed Irish's work. She must have intended to publish it for him. The print ran together in one blurred swirl for a moment and I had to consciously force my eyes to bring the letters back into focus and shape them into words again. Then, slowly, I continued to read.

It was a violent story. As I read, a chill came over me. The writing was grim and disturbing—unlike the warm, gentle humorous Irish I held so tightly in memory. And yet, it was Irish. The Irish who had sometimes been lost remotely behind a casual smile or beneath an expression of practiced tolerance. Often (whenever I caught such a smile or expression on his face), I had speculated on that other Irish. I sensed his incredible ability to dissociate, withdraw. More than once I had had to force the vision of that other Irish from my mind because in his alienation there had been a cold fierceness which had made him seem capable of hate and cruelty.

The book's characters seemed mad. They lived in a world which appeared as a neurotic fantasy. But I could see beyond this to the people and the world the book symbolized for him. A world which seemed to him a concentration camp. There were only prisoners and guards on one level and rival powers on the other who could reverse the places of prisoners and guards for their own purposes as if they were playing an inconsequential game of childhood checkers.

He had used some of us in all the characters, each of us in one particular character, a thing I suspected all writers did. And there was, of course, a great deal of himself in each character as well. I supposed that was also quite a usual occurrence. But you could not say—this character was myself, or Althea, or Uncle Stanley or Irish. They were what Irish had designed them to be—examples of the best and the worst in people.

It was impossible to say I really liked what I was reading. I found it horrifying and after I had reached page fifty, I had to close the book so that I would not be compulsively forced to continue, for I needed time to consider this side of Irish before I did so. There was no way of being certain of what his final conclusions had been because the book was incomplete, ending on page one hundred and fifty. I would have to draw these for myself but I wanted to do so with great forethought and caution. I had to also give a good deal of thought to why Claudia Mitchell had wanted me to have the manuscript; why she had made such a mystery of its presence; had introduced that presence at all; how she had come by it, and, why it had not been seen by anyone before. I was positive, even with my limited knowledge, that it was an exceptional piece of thoroughly professional writing, and even though unfinished had literary value. Whatever her reason, no matter how long the delay, I knew I had to see that the manuscript was finally placed into print where others could read it. Irish would have smiled with wry amusement at that. It would have pleased him greatly.

The manuscript had probably boon loft with her in the first place and had never actually been missing. I recalled now that Irish never came back from his stays with her carrying anything. Those wonderful hands of his were always loose and free when he would enter and he would always reach out, touch me, place them on my shoulders in greeting. I had not seen that binder for months before that last day we had all been together. The pages held the musty scent of stale salt water. I had been aware of it in the taxi, but had not thought about it then. The manuscript had obviously been kept some-where these last ten years near the shores of the sea or the banks of the Thames.

It came to me then—the only reason Claudia Mitchell would keep the manuscript was to either complete or rewrite it. Something Irish had originally intended for the book to say was a thing Claudia Mitchell had *not* wanted. *How badly?*

I sat up frightened now, alerted to some lurking danger. I could almost feel its presence in the room. I could sense its nearness and drew back from the window as if it might enter that way at any moment. Down below there was an agonized screech of rubber on asphalt. Then the loud squawking of a horn. I forced myself to look out and down the dizzying distance to the street below. There was a traffic tie-up in front of the hotel. I sat back again and waited for my nerves to quiet. The white glare remained in the room, settling now on my hands as they held the envelope in them, turning them into marble, making them appear lifeless. I moved my fingers conscious of how ridiculous it was that I had done so to make sure life did, in fact, still exist beneath the white chalk of my flesh. There was a window cleaner strapped to the sill of the window below and for a brief horrifying moment, he seemed like Hans to me and I could see the straps which held him safely to the building being slashed by someone inside that room. Then he seemed to pitch downward—no way to stop his own fall and no way for anyone to help him. I turned away and then forced myself to glance back. It had all happened in my frightened mind.

A key turned in the door. It was Hans. I rose and went to greet him.

Never had I been happier to see him. I hardly let him close the door before I was in his arms, pressing my cheek against his, kissing his ear and his neck. I wanted him to know just how thankful I was that he existed.

"Rather scandalous behavior for the middle of the day, don't you think?" he said, with a mocking smile as he finally held me away from him.

"Not as scandalous as it could be," I teased.

A most peculiar thing occurred next, for the mood of

gaiety departed the two of us at the same time. One moment my heart was filled with laughter, and the next it had been checkmated by sudden fear. Our glances had met, and as they had, the smile had left his eyes and in its place was apprehension. I sat down upon the bed. He quietly sat beside me.

"Oh, please, dear Lord," I whispered, "don't let anything happen to this beautiful thing we have found." I rested my head on Hans's shoulder as both of us waited for this terrible moment to pass.

When it did we moved away from each other. He stood and crossed to the window, not really interested in looking out of it but doing so to avert my eyes. The light fell across his face. His iron gray hair seemed alive with it. There was strength all about him. It was in his hair, his square chiseled chin, his high rock forehead, his wide boulder shoulders. But, when he did finally turn back to me, there was something soft and vulnerable in his eyes. And when he began to speak I wanted to run to him so that I might press my fingers to his lips and push the words back. I did not move. I remained silent, listening to what he was saying.

"I have been to the Hampstead police station to speak to the inspector there. A man named Savers. He was the constable who first arrived at your house *that* day."

"I remember him," I said while I thought—how could I ever forget that man? "When we let him in, Mrs. Devlin and myself, he stood there already condemning me. It was that first glance at his face which gave me the initial warning that I might soon be on trial for my life. Perhaps I should be thankful to him for that. He prepared me from the very start. I took immediate hold of myself in that instant. He was a most painfully arrogant man," I said, feeling almost the same coldness come over me as I had felt then.

"He believed you were guilty. He still does," Hans said, without sparing me.

"Claudia Mitchell gave me this," I said extending the manuscript to him. He took it, sitting down at the chair by the window, skipping huge sections at a time, skimming over others. He was not even conscious that I was in the room. It was about thirty minutes later when he finally put it down.

"I have a wild hunch," he said, and started for the door. He paused there for a moment. "Now darling," he spoke in a low, earnest voice, "I don't want you to leave this room. You understand that you could be in great danger, don't you?"

I looked up at him. He had the same reaction to the manuscript as I had! "I am more frightened for you," I said.

"Nonsense. There's no reason." He kissed me tenderly. "You are to remain here until I return," he said, as he held me against him. "Don't let anyone in or answer the telephone. If I want you I shall have the operator ring you twice, disconnect, and then ring back again." He held me away from him and turned.

He had his hand on the doorknob when my head finally cleared. "Hans!" I called to him. I wanted to tell him not to leave me, but I knew he had made up his mind to something and that he was not the kind of man who could be distracted or swayed. "I love you very much," I said quietly.

He smiled at me and opened the door. "Lock this after me," he ordered. Then he went out and closed the door and waited until I had turned the latch before he made his way down the corridor to the lift.

LUANNE...

The room was empty without Hans and the light seemed suddenly far too bright. I was sorry I had not asked him to take me with him. I ran to the window but I could not see the sidewalk. Only the street and the moving traffic was visible at this angle. There was no way to stop him. Even had I opened the window and leaned out and shouted his name, no one would have heard me above the loud rumble of the traffic. I was nervous, and furious at myself for being so.

I decided I had better order some lunch to pass the time though I was not hungry at all. I called room service and ordered tea and cold chicken and salad, then let the receiver down reluctantly; the anonymous voice on the other end at least connected me with people. I even thought to ring back and order a sweet, but it seemed too silly to indulge my loneliness this way.

For the first time I really missed the great house. I found I could shut out all unhappy memories of the people who had shared the house with me, and could look back with fond remembrance on the house itself. I had missed the time of the rhododendron. The sturdy shrubs had grown beneath my window and I had tolled the seasons by the tips of bud green and winter brown and the petals which fell from the drooping heads of the blossoms onto the window sill. Irish had always stepped with great care over my precious rhododendron.

The strength, the foreverness, of the great house would still be there. The seasons would come and go. The squirrels would climb over its walls from the Heath and then run back again. The frail summer birds would rest on its roof and its trees, nest there, and the hardy winter birds jab at its earth for food. The wet bark smell would disappear and instead there would be the scent of lilac and crocus and fresh-mown grass. The great house would remain unchanged.

The waiter came with my lunch. He served me with enormous pride, removing the plate covers with a great flourish and holding them in mid-air until I gave him my approval. I locked the door after him. I had not been hungry before. Now I felt ravenous and began to eat with tremendous enthusiasm. I had let the waiter in against Hans's wishes. Now I was sure that Hans had been wrong. I had nothing to fear.

The telephone rang twice and then stopped. I pushed the room service cart away from me and crossed to the bed and stood over the telephone waiting for it to ring again. Only a moment passed when it did. I picked up the receiver eagerly, expecting Hans. To my surprise the voice on the other end belonged to Mrs. Devlin.

"Why, Mrs. Devlin," I answered her greeting, "how on earth did you know I was here?"

"A gentleman give me the number. A Mister Aldik."

"When did you see him, Mrs. Devlin?" I asked, hardly able to keep the surprise out of my voice.

"He just left. He asked me to ring you with a message."

I could not for the life of me figure out why Hans had gone to see Mrs. Devlin but she had used his signal and was evidently speaking the truth. I was ashamed of myself for even doubting her for she had always been terribly loyal. Hans must have had his reasons. "What is the message, Mrs. Devlin?"

"Well, it's an envelope, Miss Woodrow. He just said, 'Ring Miss Woodrow and tell her you have an envelope I want her to have.' Then he left in a hurry he did. Almost forgot to give me the number he was in such a hurry."

"Could you bring it here?"

"He said I couldn't do that. That was the second half of the message."

"Then open the envelope and read what's inside it to me."

"Oh, I can't do that, Miss Woodrow. It was to be delivered right from my hand to your hand! He said no other person but you should see it."

"I don't think that need apply to yourself, Mrs. Devlin," I tried to assure her.

"How could I explain it to him then? He was very explicit, he was!"

"Well, all right Mrs. Devlin. I'll come fetch it."

"We could meet half-way," she suggested. 'That would make it easier on you. The underground at Hyde Park Corner might be good."

"The house in Hampstead," I said. "It will be closer for you anyway."

She seemed to be surprised. "The house in Hampstead, Miss Woodrow? Are you sure?"

226

"Very sure."

"I haven't been back since you left. I'm not frightened, mind you—still . . ." The fear edged her voice.

"It will be perfectly all right, Mrs. Devlin."

"How soon?" she asked after a moment.

"I'll leave now. The taxi will make it in about twenty minutes."

"I'll wait in front," she said.

"No need to wait on the street. They never changed the locks. Do you still have your key?"

"I do."

"Good. Wait inside then."

"But, I don't think . . ." she stuttered nervously.

"I told you, Mrs. Devlin. It will be all right."

I hung up before she could argue any more. I could never explain why I had insisted on the house as a meeting place. Partially, because I had been thinking about it, perhaps. But I knew it was more than that. Somehow it had to do with my thoughts of the house coinciding with Mrs. Devlin's call. It all seemed predetermined. If there was danger I was confident the house would protect me now as it had done once before.

I hurried across the room to the wardrobe and took my coat from it, unlocked the door and made my way swiftly down the corridor to the lifts, putting on my coat as I rushed toward them. The doors of one opened just as I reached them and an Indian gentleman stepped past me and went in the opposite direction from which I had come. I pulled on my coat and tied the scarf in its pocket under my chin.

The temperature had taken a sudden drop. I turned the collar of my coat up, but a bitter wind cut into the backs of my legs. There was no taxi and I waited until the doorman could get one for me. When I finally leaned back in the rear seat of one I knew I had pulled myself together. I was quite able to cope with returning to the great house or anything else for that matter.

It seemed unlike Mrs. Devlin to be so nervous. She had

had such wonderful control that terrible day, and at the funeral as well. But then, she was ten years older now. A woman in her sixties who had lived alone too many years. It was understandable but I was sure she would be her old self by the time we met.

I know it is impossible to go back but as we drew closer to Hampstead and I began to recognize familiar landmarks, it seemed ten years had not intervened between this moment and the last time I had ridden in a taxi by myself, to the great house. It had been, in fact, on that last day. I could feel that same anxiety to reach home. It had been bitter cold that day as well and I had had to stand lashed by biting winds until I managed to hail a taxi.

It had been one of those days. It had begun when I let the bathtub overflow after my meeting with Eugene. Then I had dropped the milk on the kitchen floor. Now I had reached the library before I realized the books I wanted to return were still at home on the table beside my bed. I had been distracted since early morning when I had had that disturbing incident with Eugene, and by noon when Irish returned home I found it difficult to even be civil. The library seemed like a good place to be and as soon as lunch was finished I made my way through the cold wind looking forward to the solitude it offered me.

Lunch had been a particularly somber affair. I could not forget the lost white look on Eugene's face. Somehow his youth had suddenly deserted him. I tried to keep my eyes from meeting his, fearful that any such exchanged glance might bring back the Eugene I had found in the early morning dressed in our mother's clothes.

Althea looked excessively tired and she made no effort to

be her usual animated self. I noted the lines in her face which I had first seen that previous night. She was no longer a girl, of course. Still, I had never thought of her as anything else until our encounter the night before.

She had an unpleasant argument with Liam when we first sat down, over money, a subject we never discussed at mealtime. We seldom discussed it at all, for that matter. We had all been terribly selfish where Althea and the business of our finances was concerned, and we managed to live our lives totally oblivious of the financial burden Althea carried.

Her words with Liam were over some repairs in the house which he had promised to attend to months before and which Althea wanted taken care of before spring arrived. Althea pointed out the saving his doing the work would represent. She repeated her idea of turning the empty garage into the proper music conservatory she had always wanted, and for which she had been saving over the years. Althea refused to let the subject rest until Liam made several promises to start the repairs the following morning. The discussion left Liam sullen and Althea filled with a resentment she could hardly contain.

Uncle Stanley did not join us for lunch, but Mary Agate had prepared the meal and stood by the sideboard helping Miss Pansy serve and watching us closely as we began to eat. Lunch had been particularly tasteless. The fish was dry, the potatoes too heavily watered, and the sprouts not small or new enough. Even the salad had been curiously limp and void of seasoning. No one complained but neither had anyone eaten with any obvious pleasure. Mary Agate finally sat down before her own plate and stared at it all through lunch. I hardly touched my own food and was pleased when Miss Pansy reappeared with plates of fruit and cheese.

Irish was in a world of his own, not communicating with any of us. He had been remote since his return a few minutes before lunch. Something seemed to be weighing heavily on his mind. I spoke to him when dinner began and I tried to divert him during cheese but he replied in an unusual mono-syllabic fashion and I gave up and retreated to my own silence.

The library had been deserted except for the librarian, who did not bother to even glance up from her work when I gave her my new selection to stamp before leaving. I began to walk toward home but became so chilled that I decided to hail a taxi. I stood on the unprotected, windy turning, for several minutes before a taxi stopped.

There had been no one downstairs when I arrived home. There was a stillness in the entrance hall which increased my uneasiness. Then I heard them overhead and told myself firmly that I was acting like a ridiculous child. I did not call out to tell the family I was back, but went straightaway to my own room and closed the door. I put the books down, got out of my outer clothes and warmed my hands by my small electric fire. I heard Miss Pansy return to the kitchen. No one in the house knew I was home and I decided to leave it at that. My nerves were still with me, unaccounted for, a constant spasm of anxiety making my heart beat faster and the blood rush to my head. I crossed and stood by the window. There were no blossoms on the rhododendrons. The shrubs were tall and sparse and brown. I was sorry I had not bought some winter flowers from the florist's shop. The wind was angrier than before. In the distance I could hear the dust-bins behind the basement doors being blown about. I knew the refuse must be scattered over the rear terrace and beyond. On the tree nearest my room the leaves were being torn from its branches and the limbs drawn back, their twigged tips grasp-ing hold of each other like the clinging fingers of a falling man. The sound came right through my closed window. A furious wind, whining branches, and the chatter of falling dustbins. I turned back into the room.

I heard their voices now, but could not make out what anyone was saying. Mary Agate and Althea were in the kitchen with Miss Pansy obviously planning tea and dinner. I took the top book from the small pile I had brought back with me and crossed with it to my favorite chair. I reached down beside it and turned the electric fire to face it. Then I curled up in the chair with the book, telling myself over and over again that whatever I was feeling was not premonition but, more logically, a reaction from events of the night before and of the early morning. Still, my attention kept slipping from the book I was trying to read and I found myself rereading the same page over again and hardly realizing I was doing so.

But something was disturbing me. It had to do with the argument with Althea and the meeting with Eugene. I simply could not make it materialize and so I tried consciously to put the whole matter from my mind. I got up again and stared out the window. The light had gone from the sky. The afternoon would be gray and threatening. My room was dark now. I could not go back and read without turning on the electricity. I decided against it. There were no sounds from the kitchen. It was deserted again. I thought I might be able to paint—yet I knew that was not the reason I went quietly out of my room and, as silently as I could, out the backstairs and down the long flight to the basement.

The room was clouded with shadow. It took a moment before I was able to make out forms and then to make my familiar way over to the part of the room where I usually painted. I did not turn on the overhead light. My canvasses had been placed against the wall, probably by Eugene when he had taken the clothes from the old trunk on which the canvasses had been left. Someone had given him a key. I decided I would never ask him directly. Never remind him of our meeting. For I was certain he had been in a hypnotic state and did not fully recall it, and if it was brought back to him could lead to serious consequence for him. He had been given the key by either Uncle Stanley or Irish. There seemed no other alternative. But, of course there was. One. It came to me now. Mary Agate. She could have found out about the contents of the trunk from Uncle Stanley. I had a moment of revulsion for the only reason Mary Agate could have given Eugene the key was to taunt him with fragments of the mother he never knew. I crossed to the trunk. It had been left carelessly unlatched. I opened it slowly. Eugene had put our mother's clothes, folded neatly, back in place. Overhead there were footsteps again. Someone had returned to the kitchen. I stood in the darkness of the cellar room holding my breath, frightened whoever it was might hear me. I stood there for a long time. The stone walls retained the damp and chill and it went right through me. The tea kettle whistled shrilly in the kitchen above. It stopped in a moment and I knew whoever it had been in the kitchen had only boiled some water and left. Not for tea then. It was too early for tea. The footsteps had been heavy. It had been Mary Agate filling a hot water bottle for Uncle Stanley.

It came to me then with a queer shiver which passed through me. When Eugene and I had started out of the dining room in the morning, the whistle for the kettle had already begun to die out as if the top had been blown off. Then, a sound like the high pitch of the whistle had continued for a moment or two and been muffled as well. Eugene had had no awareness, still in his self-induced trance. And I had been so taken aback at finding him as I had, that I had not really been alert to anything but the sad child who walked beside me. That last sound had been a scream and not the whistle of the tea kettle, and it had been muffled. It was the sound of someone placing a hand over a screaming woman's mouth to silence her. And it had come from the cellar room below the kitchen.

There was no doubt in my mind that the scream had come from Mary Agate. I had heard her scream many times during our younger days, when Liam would frighten and torment her as he always took great pleasure in doing. I wanted to get out of the cellar now, return to the safe quiet of my bedroom. I started back to the stairs and remembered that I had not closed the trunk. I returned to do so. Something ground beneath the sole of my shoe. I paused—puzzled. It was spilled sugar—yet, no supplies had ever been kept in this room. I knelt down and touched it. There was no doubt. It was plain white castor sugar.

I remembered something else. The night before, Althea had bolted every door in the house but this door. You could not have entered the cellar from inside the house, but if anyone had been on the grounds they could have entered from outside and left the same way.

I don't know quite why the impulse was so strong, but I felt I had to clean away the sugar before I left the room. I found an old broom in the coal bin and carefully swept the sugar onto a piece of my art paper. I crumbled the paper with the granules in it, replaced the broom and tossed the refuse directly into the dustbin outside the door as I made my way quietly back to my room. Then I immediately had a good wash and changed into my orange silk dress.

It was almost four o'clock. There were sounds in the kitchen again. Miss Pansy and Mary Agate were preparing tea. I settled back in my chair and picked up my book to see if I could manage to concentrate on it and put all these other seemingly ridiculous speculations out of my mind. I would have until about four thirty to myself. I never joined the others for tea. They would not question my absence from the house for that length of time. But after tea Althea, at least, would come looking for me. She had not yet mentioned the previous night but I knew its occurrence had caused the anxiety, the pale pained whiteness and sharp lines of anger which had been in her face at lunch. She had far from let go of the subject of Irish being asked to leave. After tea, Althea and I usually exchanged confidences. She probably was nervously clicking off the moments until then at this very time, rehearsing in her mind what she was going to say to me.

I heard the rattle of the tea cart as Miss Pansy pushed it

out of the kitchen and propelled it down the corridor to the front parlor where tea was always served. Mary Agate followed her. There was no mistaking that heavy footstep. The tea cart was now being wheeled over the bare floor in the entrance hall. Mary Agate had run past Miss Pansy to open the doors to the parlor. She pulled them back too hard and they banged against the wall behind them. I opened my own door as soon as Mary Agate's footsteps had passed the corridor.

"Mary Agate! Do be careful!" Althea chided. "You are forever digging little ruts into the walls."

I never heard Mary Agate's answer, but I knew she must have become flustered since Althea's taunts always affected her that way. She had most probably entered the room with her head down, nearly tripping over the fringed edge of the carpet in the front room. The doors closed softly after the tea cart made it safely over the threshold.

The house was silent again. The front parlor was virtually sound proof. I decided I did not have the patience to remain in the house. I thought it might help if I took a little walk on the Heath. The wind had died down. It wouldn't be too cold without it, but it looked now like it might rain and my mackintosh was in the cloak room off the entrance hall.

I took off my shoes and held them in my hand as I made my way out of my room, up the corridor toward the entrance hall. I was more careful than usual as I felt I simply could not bear to have Althea hear me and perhaps insist this once that I join them. I was looking straight ahead, in the direction of the cloak room which was directly to the left of the front door, when an uneasiness gripped me. I stopped short. A shadow fell across the floor in front of me, blocking out the skylight. I looked up. Some leaves from the roof were sliding across the thick ceiling glass. Birds had probably knocked them free. I listened but could not hear their squawks. I don't know what made me change my course and head up

234

the staircase instead of continuing on to fetch my mackintosh. As I reached the top step, I froze with fear. A booted foot could distinctly be seen outside on the far corner of the skylight. Then, whoever it belonged to, pulled it up and disappeared. Obviously the person had hoisted himself onto the higher ledge which would lead to the attic rooms which Irish occupied.

I was positive it was a thief. Possibly armed. He would enter the house through the attic rooms and come down the staircase into the hallway directly across from where I stood. He would be in a hurry. I did not have much time. I reasoned that whoever it was had been watching the family from the edge of the skylight and had waited until the parlor doors were shut. He did not know I was in the house. His plan would be to steal downstairs and take the silver in the dining room. I was sure that was all he could be after and I reasoned that he would only use a weapon if interrupted. I would not have time to get downstairs again. I glanced frantically down the upstairs corridor. The linen room was the nearest and the most accessible. I would not even have time to cross the open hallway. I kept close to the wall for the small distance to the linen room door, opened it quickly, darted inside, and closed the door as swiftly and quietly as I could. Then I leaned back against the shelves of linens, scented with my own oranges and cloves, and took a deep breath. I could hear my heart beat like a drum in my ears. I covered my mouth with my hand, frightened that the intruder might be able to hear the sound of my stuttering breath.

I shut my eyes, and prayed and listened. Several minutes passed. I opened my eyes, took my hand from my mouth. The intruder should have come down the stairs into the hallway in that time. I should have heard him, because the door had needed oiling for a long time, but had I not, I should most certainly have heard the terrible groan the top step of the front staircase made as you stepped on it. I placed my hand on the inside door handle, determined to open the door and investigate for myself.

I was shocked to find all the detailed and forgotten moments of that horrifying day now so real and clear. From the moment I had finally left the linen room and gone down to find them all dead, it had been totally blacked out of my mind. At the trial I had not even remembered going to the library that day, although the date inside the library books had attested I had. The librarian herself was unable to make a positive identification.

Now the taxi approached our street. The front of the great house was deserted. Either Mrs. Devlin had gone inside as I had told her to do, or else she had not yet arrived. I paid the driver and stood there until he turned around in the cul-de-sac, passed me, and disappeared around the far turning. The wind seemed calmer now and the cold less penetrating. I braced my shoulders and removed the kerchief from my hair as I crossed to the front gate. It was already unlocked. I opened it, walked beneath Althea's stone white lions and heard the gate shut behind me.

L U A N N E . . .

I walked slowly up the ribbon path, the branches of the overgrown shrubs brushing my legs as I passed. Their winter leaves were dry and brittle and their sharp points pierced and scratched my flesh as I refused to let them bar my way. I knew the great house and my cherished grounds were not as once they had been. And yet, they seemed to be. The

236

dark, the silence—the overgrown and nameless shrubs dissolved behind me as I walked. It seemed the stone walls, gray as I entered, were now white and shining as a late afternoon winter sun bravely pushed its way through the mass of black and threatening cloud. As it had that last day.

It was winter now. It had been winter then. The great house itself spread grandly beneath its lovely curving roof. I paused before the stone steps which led to the front door. It was slightly ajar, left open by Mrs. Devlin no doubt, yet I could not bear to enter. Instead I walked around the side of the house, past the rusty padlock on the side gate, the rutted ditch filled with stale rain water, dead moss along the path.

I could see myself leaning out of my window, much younger, my face framed by the rhododendrons, my hand parting them tenderly as I slid out and over the sill onto the smooth young moss which bordered the path. I watched as I crossed to the gate. The birds were clustered above me and, as I passed through the gate, into the Heath, they lined the stone ledge of the wall, turned away from me.

I shook my head to bring myself back to the present. I told myself again that one could not go back. Yet I could visualize Hans and me living here. I could smell the bacon and coffee from the kitchen, hear the children and the dogs. A dream. The great house would never know my children and their dogs.

The front door was still ajar and I entered without calling out or trying the bell. Mrs. Devlin was perched on a step in the entrance hall. I immediately recognized my misadventure and was furious at myself for being so thoughtless. The poor woman was startled. She bolted upright and clung to the bannister. She seemed smaller and older and more misshapen than she had ever been.

"Oh! Miss Woodrow!" Her small bird eyes widened as much as they could, making her look unfortunately like some poor small animal shot and then stuffed to capture that last moment of terrible terror. "Oh! You did give me a start!" She came down the steps and faced me, her hand clinging, as she reached me, to my arm. "I just don't know why you wanted to come back here after all these years," she whined.

"No need to be frightened, Mrs. Devlin." The house was cold and damp and the opened front door did not help. "It's drafty here," I said, as I started to cross the hallway thinking to go into the dining room where some wood might have been left for us to start a fire. She did not follow me and as I turned to ask her to do so, I noticed she was tossing frightened glances over her shoulder and up the staircase. "Now, Mrs. Devlin." I smiled warmly, wanting to ease her discomfort. "You were never one to act like this. Why, I will never forget that day! You came straight in here, past the parlor, upstairs to where I was. Why, you gave me strength! It was you who called the police, and stood right here in this very spot to face them with me when they came. Certainly *now* you shouldn't be frightened."

She had a curious, almost piteous expression on her face. "I was younger then. Foolish, too, I daresay. I didn't really understand what had happened until long afterwards. I reacted out of habit. You bein' different class, I mean an' me bein' in service all me life. You was the one to be looked after."

I was very touched. I came back to her and took her hand in mine. "We'll make a fire, if we can, in the dining room and rest there for a while. It will be nice to have a chat. We haven't had one for a long, long while."

She drew away from me. "I think I'd rather stay here," she said.

There seemed to be no purpose in pressing the issue. She was apparently determined not to go any further into the house so that she would always be in a line with the front door and her immediate exit. I let go of her hands and pushed my own deep into my coat pockets to keep them warm. "I'm sorry," I said. "I had no idea this would be so difficult for you."

Her purse hung heavily from one of her sharp-boned wrists, making a deep red streak across it, but she seemed unconscious of any pain from it. She opened the purse and took out a sealed envelope. "Here it is," she said, and stepped down onto the level floor and handed it to me, her grotesque body only paused momentarily as she edged toward the opened door.

I took the envelope from her and held it. "I should have kept my taxi waiting for you," I said.

"It's all right. I 'spect I might find one up the high street."

"I hope so." She was already half-way across the room. "Mrs. Devlin?" I called.

She only turned back part way. "Yes, Miss Woodrow?"

"There was no other message you might have forgotten?" I asked.

"No. The envelope and what I told you was all." She started away again.

"If you want to wait just a few moments . . ." I paused as I glanced around. I still had that very strong feeling that I would never again see the great house and that I would like— this time without holding hands with the past—to walk through it, touching things, saying good-by in my own way. "I thought I would like to take a last look around," I finished.

"I'd rather not, Miss Woodrow," she said.

"If you wait outside then, I shall hurry." I tore open the envelope. "I don't understand this," I said, and looked up. She was just going out the door. "Mrs. Devlin!" I called. She came back in only far enough to be over the threshold on the inside. I held up the contents in my hand for her to see. "Money. I don't understand it at all."

"He just said to give the envelope to you. I had no idea what was in it."

"He came to your house and gave you only this?" I asked, not knowing what to make of it.

"Yes he did, Miss Woodrow. Can I go now?" she asked quietly.

I sat down on the steps, holding the envelope (which was blank on the outside, containing no writing) in one hand,

and the money in the other. There seemed to be well over a thousand pounds. "I simply do not know what to make of it."

I was staring down at my hands when I was suddenly aware of her closeness and the sour smell I had forgotten she had about her. She was standing directly in front of me now. She had always been a short woman but now her advanced arthritic condition had bowed her body into near dwarfness. Even though I sat on the first step and she stood on the ground below me, our eyes were level.

"He's a man," she said, with a fixed expression.

Her entire attitude had changed. The fear was gone from her face, the panic lost from her voice. She had the same curious power I recalled her having that last day. A power which I had never discerned before. Her own fear had been conquered, so that she could adequately administer to her lady. Of course, I had not been her lady, but had not questioned that reaction of hers. I assumed Mrs. Devlin had merely carried on in a moment of crisis in her sister's place. It was not unusual in the English way of life.

"It's like that between men and women," she was saying, in the same impassive voice. But I was taken aback by the flicker of something in her eyes that startled me into a new alertness. "You step out of yer class an' there ain't no protection. He's no gentleman, like I never was no lady. He's a bastard for that matter!" She laughed and a hollow echo filled the room. I wondered how she knew that about Hans, but I dared not interrupt her. I likened her present condition to Eugene's that long ago morning. "I must be silent," I thought, "and let this strange seizure pass over her until she is once again the Mrs. Devlin I know."

Her face grew sullen now, her eyes dulled by the cloud of her thinking. "Once he's had you, that's it. If he was in yer own class, he would treat you with respect. Marry you. Otherwise, he just uses you an' discards you like an old glove—not a woman." She laughed again. "At least my man did think of me as a woman, I can tell you! Yers—he only wanted one thing. He was after a story—and there's yer wages!" The laugh became contemptuous. I went to stand up but she clamped her hand tightly on the top of my head. I could feel the pain extend past my neck and down my back.

I was not afraid of her. More honestly at that moment I had pity that this woman had borne such a deep, deep bitterness all these years and I had been too self-involved to notice. "Mrs. Devlin," I said softly, "how terrible. Please forgive me. Some man treated you badly. You have been suffering all these years and I didn't realize it."

She jolted backward and I feared she would lose her balance. I reached out to grab hold of her, to stop her falling, but she misunderstood. She whipped her arm away from my hold and remained standing in an incredibly upright position. "You?" She spat at me. "Me forgive you?" She was laughing again—this time all her bitterness spewing out with it. I managed to stand up and take a cautious step backward, higher up the staircase. I was now looking down at her.

Her mouth twisted ludicrously as she stopped laughing and began to talk again. Her clawlike hands were tearing at her black pocketbook and her head was tilted back, looking up at me as she spoke, making her look like some writhing gargoyle. "Mrs. Devlin! Mrs. Devlin!" she mocked. "I'm not. Never was! He give me the name. He with his evil humor. 'You're bedevlin' me,' he would say. An' when the gel was born he was there an' that was what he had them put on the certificate. Mrs. Violet Devlin! An' the gel? You don't think a gentleman like him would give her his name, do you? Not legal like."

I had taken another backward step. She looked smaller and flatter, as if she might be melting down into nothing but pinched flesh and black cloth. "I never knew you had a daughter," I said. "Miss Pansy never mentioned it."

"Pansy!" She sneered. "She never let me forget. Not for one minute! It was she who did the final bargaining. They both come together. He with his fine hat in his hand, but it

241

was Pansy who done the dirty work. She was always jealous of me. You wouldn't know it now to look at me but then I was a right smart lookin' gel. A man could touch his fingers together when he put his hands round me waist. I had soft, white skin then. They always told me how they liked me soft, white skin. I danced better than any other of the gels I ever knew. Ooo! I made them dance for me, I did! I was happy until he come along. Who asked him for his fancy talk and fancy ways? With all of them he didn't have two haypennies to rub together, he didn't! He hypnotized me, that was what he done! If he had been one of me own he would have married me. Stood there, big an' handsome as all of life when I told them I was in the family way. 'I'll always take care of the child,' he said. The child! But what about me? A lot he cared what happened to me. Or Pansy either! Facin' me like she done—him beside her, 'The gel will be raised as a lady,' she said holier-than-thou! 'No one will ever know.' An' me? I screamed at her. What's to become of me? 'Why nothing at all, Violet dear,' she said in that airy voice she was always takin' on. 'But you will always know the gel has had the best advantages.'"

"You shouldn't excite yourself like this, Mrs. Devlin," I said. I stood above her, fascinated, appalled at the twisted woman I had thought to be so simple and loyal.

"I could have had all the men I wanted then. He knew it and so did Pansy. An' he knew I had no mind for a baby to be about and in me way. 'You'll have to sign a paper, Violet dear,' Pansy said in her la-de-da tones. He put the envelope down on a table between us then. Didn't even hand it to me. 'One hundred pounds,' he said, like he was making a final offer on a piece of land. 'It's all my brother would give me.' 'Who wants yer child?' I told him. 'I don't love you. I never have. Not one moment I was ever with you!' I let him know! An' I signed that paper so fast he didn't know what hit him!"

"I'm sorry, Mrs. Devlin," I said quietly, feeling sincerely so.

"That's right, Miss Woodrow," she said with a sneer. "You

242

never let anything ruffle you. You was born a lady. You walk like one, and talk like one no matter how the world is treating you. But not me Mary Agatha! She never inherited the Woodrow class. More like her mother she was."

I was overcome with closeness. My moist palms slipped down the wood bannister. "Oh, Mrs. Devlin," I said, feeling the great pity which was in my voice, but knowing it was honestly put there. "She was a very good person. Mary Agatha was a very good person, indeed." I pictured Mary Agatha now and understood everything none of us had been able to before. I thought about Uncle Stanley, whom I so dearly loved and this sharp and bitter cripple now ranting madly below me. But she had not been sharp and bitter or crippled then. I stared at her with shock, because I could suddenly see the girl she might have been. Tiny, vivacious, full of the life a young Irishman would have liked.

She had her hand on the bannister. She was in great pain and it rammed across her forehead in deeply sliced trenches and was echoed in her eyes. The spasm had been so severe that it was several moments before she recovered herself. When she finally spoke again it was in a harsh whisper and the words came between shallow gasps. I thought that I myself might keel right over and catapult down the steps between us to her feet.

"I killed them all," she choked. "It was as easy as pie. She didn't have to die with them. It wasn't supposed to be that way. She chose to die with them."

I remembered the cry that morning which I thought had been the whistle on the tea kettle. I remembered my room in the cellar, the sugar spilt on the stone floor. It had been Mrs. Devlin and Mary Agatha! Somehow Mrs. Devlin had forced her to take the poisoned sugar and use it to kill us all. Mary Agatha had argued and some had been spilled. I shut my eyes and fought back the nausea which rose in me.

"She was my daughter, after all," she gasped on. "We could have lived like ladies with all the money rightly ours. She would have got it all. The only heir she would have been. That was the plan. But she did herself in as well, and saved you for his sake—her father's. If she had used it at lunch, like she was told, all of you would have died. I had given her the sugar and told her to serve it on your berries at lunchtime. But not her."

The cheese and fruit at that last lunch now flashed before my eyes. Mary Agatha had never served the berries. I remembered how tasteless everything had been, knowing now that Mary Agatha had been too distracted to care. I recalled how she had sat looking into her plate during the entire meal and I realized now how tortured she must have been. And, suddenly, the truth came to me. I felt like someone was smothering me with an ether-soaked cloth. I could smell it and taste it. I fought to remain conscious.

"Don't think I don't know why she chose tea," she wheezed. "You never joined them then. She knew you were more like a daughter to her father than herself. He wanted to die anyway. He had been begging her to help him do away with himself. She told me that."

Oh . . . Uncle Stanley . . .

"She hated the others. Especially Pansy." She tried to laugh but the effort made her cough. It was a moment before the spasm was over. "Pansy always treated her like a servant, you know? Never could accept one of us really being one of you."

I hadn't known—hadn't noticed, but we had all treated Mary Agatha poorly ourselves, never guessing. It was just some cruel, animal behavior which all of us are guilty of from time to time in our lives. Her voice was beginning to seem farther away. I was only hearing fragments of what she was saying. There was a buzz which filled my ears, crowded my head. There was something I wanted to remember, some*thing* I *had* to recall.

I heard it then. Overhead. That same sound of dry leaves falling down the slanted thick glass of the skylight. Their moving shadow fell between Mrs. Devlin and myself. She had not noticed. She was still talking but I no longer could hear her. I managed to turn my back on her and start up the staircase. She did not follow me. I looked up to the skylight and saw the outline of a boot. I remembered what I had been struggling to bring out of my subconscious.

Irish never had sugar in his tea. He always drank it with lemon. Mary Agatha knew that as well as she knew I never joined them. She had not cared to live, had wanted to see the others dead, but she had saved Irish and myself with full intent. In her own mind, I suppose it seemed highly logical, like giving Eugene our mother's clothes—in a way torturing him for the mother she never knew. Mary Agatha had been on the precipice of madness, handed a weapon, and gone over that precipice. Irish or myself could have stopped her had we guessed. Neither of us had.

I was in the past again, reliving those few terrifying minutes after I had opened the door of the linen room.

The corridor was silent and empty. I still had my shoes in my hand as I stepped out of the linen room and made my way back toward the staircase. I glanced up again, thinking it possible that the intruder had not entered the house after all, and was still crouching there on our roof. I could see nothing but the dry leaves. I decided he had to still be up there and pulling myself together started down the staircase to warn the others and discuss with them what we could do.

The silk of my skirt rustled from a gust of air. I craned my head around the side wall of the staircase. The front door was slightly ajar. My heart began to pound in my ears again. I had locked myself in the linen room, fearful for my own life, and in the meanwhile, the intruder had let himself down from the roof to the ground and entered through the front door, which perhaps I, myself, had left unlatched earlier. The door to the parlor was still closed. The family would not finish tea for five or ten minutes yet. It never crossed my mind that the intruder might have entered the parlor and closed the doors. I would have heard the family had that been the case in the short time that the doors had been swung open. I figured out that he was in the dining room where I had originally thought his forced entry would take him.

I had just made up my mind to return upstairs again and go into Althea's room to call the police. I was occupied with a small prayer that when I lifted the receiver there, the bell on the telephone in the dining room would not echo as it sometimes did, when the parlor doors opened. I started forward to warn whoever it was to stay where they were.

I only saw the back of a booted figure. A long wide mackintosh and low brimmed hat swallowed up the intruder's identity.

"She's not here," I heard Irish say, his voice touched with a strange quality. "She's been away all afternoon." I realized he was talking about me. I looked up the steps terrified, alerted by the warning and fear in his voice. "Thank God, if one of us is to survive, it's her," he said. Then I heard him gasp and fall. The intruder backed out of the doorway. I clung to the inside of the stairway and managed to make my way back to the top, remembering that warped top step, and then dizzy, I stumbled back toward the linen room. I sensed even then with sickening revulsion that they all must be dead. "If one of us is to survive," Irish had said. I thought at that moment that they must have been shot and that the thick parlor doors had held back the sound. I fell back into the linen room, locking the door from the inside. Everything began to fade away. I soon forgot the intruder, Irish, his words. I had lost consciousness.

Now, I was leaning against the bannister and felt my body

go limp. I hung on with all the strength I could muster to keep from falling. My back was to Mrs. Devlin. She was still ranting at me. Her voice was hoarse and the words were wheezing out of her. I felt I could not lift my head. It seemed too heavy for me to do so, too great an effort. I prayed she would stop. I needed silence. A moment or two of quiet to pull my thoughts together.

"I couldn't kill you. Not directly," she rasped at me. "There had to be no connection. But the Woodrows owed me something." She started to laugh but only a dry crackle came out and her voice became even more intense. "Then you did it yourself. Give me the money on yer own. An' they almost hanged you at that!"

I tried to drag myself up to the next step, but I seemed paralyzed there. I could not understand it but, though fear chilled my heart, it was not Mrs. Devlin who frightened me. All I wanted at this moment was to get away from her constant bombardment of words. They were ricocheting through my head, making an excruciating pain. There were moving shadows on the stair carpet below me. Shifting leaves on the outside of the skylight. I had it in my mind to make my way to Althea's room where I had seen a telephone. Though it would be a miracle if it were connected, it seemed a worthwhile chance to take.

"She took her own life. That's what you should do," she kept at me. "What have you got to live for? He paid you off. He was only using you. *News of the World* would have give me ten thousand pounds for me story but it was too dangerous for me to take it. It wasn't fair. But him? He'll get a packet. He'll know what to write, what people wants to read. He's smart. He knows how many likes to read about such things. Needs to read about them to make their own selves easier."

I could hear her heave herself up onto the first step. It was slow and painful for her. It was a moment before she was able to speak. My head was beginning to clear. I was sure now that Hans had never been to see Mrs. Devlin, had never given her all that money to give me. Mrs. Devlin was being used, but not by Hans. She had been used from the very beginning. So had poor Mary Agatha. Both of them were no more than soldiers during a war. Mary Agatha had carried out the murder on command. Mrs. Devlin had passed on the orders. But there had been someone else. The intruder. And I knew that person was on the roof this moment.

He wasn't moving because he was listening, waiting—to see if he had provoked Mrs. Devlin to murder for him. But I was conscious of something he was not. Mrs. Devlin could never kill me. She was too cowed by the system. Mrs. Devlin would never be able to choke the life from me, or shoot a bullet, or plunge a knife into my flesh. She might have done it to one of her own kind. But not me. She had good cause to hate us, to want to see me dead, but Mrs. Devlin was one of the reasons the ghastly system existed. She wanted it that way.

I was able to straighten now. My body lost its tremendous weight. I could move. I removed my hand from the bannister and exercised my fingers for a moment to take the stiffness out of them. I had to be in control of every part, every muscle in my body because I knew, without question, that when the intruder realized Mrs. Devlin could not be relied upon, when I remained still alive in the house, he would do as he had done the last time. He would hoist himself onto the ledge below the attic, lower himself to the garage roof, and then to the ground and enter the house directly through the front door which now stood ajar. This time he knew I was here. This time he planned to murder me.

I stood poised for a long moment. Mrs. Devlin's words were lost to me. I had to either make a dash for Althea's room and barricade myself inside or bolt down the stairs, past Mrs. Devlin. If I went out the side gate there was the proximity of the Heath. But I had noticed the latch was rusty. It could either be stuck fast, or else broken or brittle enough for me to break.

I decided this was my best chance. I might not have enough time if I ran out the front way and there was the outside chance as well, that the intruder was not alone. But it would take a few moments for anyone to reach that side of the house from the front, and a few more for them to realize where I had gone. Once out that door, I was safer in the Heath than in the front of the house and on the street. No one knew their way through the Heath as well as I did and I knew that my old secret path was still there.

I reached slowly down and removed my shoes so that I would not trip over their heels, and then, still in that crouched position, spun around so that I faced Mrs. Devlin. But I began to bolt down the staircase simultaneously. Mrs. Devlin was too startled at my sudden action to fully comprehend what was happening. I swung wide and away from her as I went to pass her, knowing her arthritic condition made it impossible for her to reach me at that distance in such a swift passage of time. I did not even glance over to her, but was aware of her shocked silence. I heard the sudden slide of leaves and branches on the skylight. My head was once again thundering with the tremendous effort I was making. As I turned the corner from the entrance hall to the corridor past the dining room (which led to my room and the window I planned to use as my exit), I heard a shriek, an explosive shattering of glass and another shriek, almost inhuman. Then there was a sickening crash mingled with a cry and then the house seemed to echo with an unbearable silence.

I opened the door to my old room and did not take the time to close it after myself. I was no longer frightened at being followed by anyone inside the house, but aware that whatever had happened behind me (and a wave of nausea rose in me as I was conscious only one thing could have happened— the intruder had slipped, crashed through the glass skylight, bringing himself and those thick, sharp, dagger-like slices of

249

broken glass directly down on Mrs. Devlin), my danger was now in the possibility that the intruder had not been alone. If that was so, I counted on whoever it was being drawn inside by the crash—giving me more time to put a greater distance between myself and the house.

I managed to open the window without trouble. I dropped my shoes so my hands would be free, slid over the sill, and fell easily to the ground. I did not glance around but rushed for the side gate. Thankfully I had reasoned right. The latch was rusty and worn thin by rain and time. I grabbed it with both my hands and pulled with all my might. It gave. I had to work to push the gate open, the ground beneath it was so overgrown with weeds and so thickly lumped with pressed dead leaves.

There was no one in the cul-de-sac. But I heard footsteps now running in my direction on the hard earth behind me. I took a very deep breath and pressed forward even faster, feeling the gravel cut my shoeless feet, not caring, not slowing down, even when I felt the cool, damp leaves on my path in the Heath soothe the wounds which my escape across the gravel-paved road had caused.

LUANNE...

He found me sitting exhausted on a pile of damp leaves quite deep inside the Heath. Never will I forget that moment. There are times now when I walk into a room without his knowing it, the sun resting across his face, and watch him wrestle with his thoughts and I wonder—no matter how often he protests, if the hurt I dealt him that day in the Heath will ever completely leave his heart.

I was terrified as he approached. It had all been such a

frightening dream that at that moment I thought perhaps my love—his love—had only been tricks my mind had played on us. I tried to rise from the earth. I crumpled instead into a sobbing heap on top of the leaves and when he tried to lift me, I beat my arms against his chest and gasped out a call for help. I was convinced he had been with the intruder, had run after me, had followed me to the Heath to finally snuff out the life of the last Woodrow.

Then I found him looking into my eyes. The hurt was too much for me to bear. I fell upon his chest. Begging his forgiveness, clinging to his neck, and he stroked my back and smothered my forehead with small kisses.

"Luanne. Luanne. My poor darling, Luanne," he whispered, in a tortured voice.

"Who was it?" I asked.

"Claudia Mitchell. Dead now."

"And Mrs. Devlin?"

"No one is left who can ever hurt you again," he said, smoothing my hair back from my damp forehead. Then he took my hands and rubbed them. "You're cold. Let's get out of here." He started to help me to my feet and noticed the torn flesh on their bottoms. He lifted me in his arms. "There's a car waiting on the other side of the Heath," he said.

Inspector Savers sat behind the wheel. "You should be the new hero at headquarters," Hans assured him.

"Odd that. It doesn't seem to mean as much as it did," the inspector replied.

"It will," Hans said. He settled me into the back seat of the car and then sat down beside me. "I knew something went wrong when I used our telephone signal and then, when I rang back, the line was busy. When I tried again there was no reply. Then I went to meet Claudia Mitchell. We had made a previous date. She never showed. I went straight back to Inspector Savers," he said.

The motor of the car made a soothing rhythm. The inspector steered the car into the avenue. "Claudia Mitchell was responsible," he said. "She believed it was your brother's family who had really put an end to their affair. Mrs. Devlin had told her about Mary Agatha. She used this information as her own weapon, convincing Mrs. Devlin of the injustice of her position. Mrs. Devlin never hesitated, it seems, in attempting to right this. But she had enough feeling in her to devise a plan that would save Mary Agatha and hopefully make them both rich." Savers was looking at them through his rear view mirror. "Writers shouldn't keep journals when they embark on crime. Claudia Mitchell had recorded all her impressions of her meetings with Mrs. Devlin."

"The manuscript?" I asked softly.

Hans held me closer to him. "She gave it to you out of desperation, but then could only part with half. We found the other half in her flat. She was finishing it herself. Writing what she obviously had wanted Irish to write. But he was too strong for her. She planned to kill you and wanted to set me up to take the rap."

"Will the hotel be all right?" the inspector asked over his shoulder.

I began to cry. "There doesn't seem to be any place else to go," I said.

Hans took my hand. "There will be," he said. We were silent as the inspector drove through the late day traffic. "I still have to write the book," Hans finally said. "Can you face it?"

I was so tired I could only nod my head.

He never inquires at my moments of silence now and I never question the hurt left in his eyes from that one day on the Heath when he knew I doubted him. It disappears when he crosses to the window and watches the children at play. He will turn and look at me at those times as he is looking at me now.

"Shall we walk on the beach?" I will ask.

And he will cross to me and smile and take my hand and we will walk together along the shore with the soft salt mist from the sea blowing gently in our faces.

ABOUT THE AUTHOR

ANNE EDWARDS was born in Port Chester, New York, brought up in Beverly Hills, California, and educated at the University of California and Southern Methodist University in Dallas, Texas. By the time she was twenty-five she was writing for television and films. In 1957, a film assignment took Mrs. Edwards and her two children to London. Since then, she has spent her time in England and Switzerland, and continued writing for films. *The Survivors* is her first novel. Her son, Michael, attends the University of California at Berkeley and her daughter, Cathy, is studying languages in Switzerland.